BRIDE OF GOLD

(CLEAN & WHOLESOME CONTEMPORARY ROMANCE)

MOLLIE MATHEWS

Blue Orchid
PUBLISHING

BRIDE OF GOLD

Mollie Mathews

Blue Orchid Publishing

PRAISE FOR BRIDE OF GOLD

"A great read for anyone, like me, with a passion for art and a love of mysteries embedded in a painting. Bride of Gold is light, fun, suspenseful and full of romantic longings - everything I love in a book. I also enjoyed the New Zealand setting and learning more about this beautiful country. I do love a good Mollie Mathews book!"

~ Lauri

"An engaging and passionate read. Once again Mollie Matthews delivers a story full of passion and makes me keep turning the pages. Mollie's writing is engaging and I didn't want the story to end! I'm looking forward to the next one!"

~ Alli

"An awesome read. Just love Mollie Mathews style. There's a good story as well as the romance, the passion and the pain that goes with deep love. Just had to keep reading - abandoned the chores until I had reached the end. More please Mollie."

~ Rae

"What a wonderful book Bride of Gold was. I just couldn't put it down, but glad to read it in the nights. How wonderful you have written this love story with so much passion and fighting for love and acknowledgement one can give. Thanks once again to have been able to download it and enjoy it with so much eagerness to just keep on reading. Keep up your good work in writing. Such wonderful loved filled clean romantic books. Full of passion, love and tenderness .Words can't describe the real way I found this book. Fantastic."

~Istella

"I loved, loved, loved this book. It had me laughing, crying and gasping following the back and forth between Alexandra and Vitali!! I now want to go to New Zealand even more than I did before."

~ Glenda

"I very much enjoyed reading this book. The author had beautifully descriptive writing. I could easily picture the scenery she described from Gold Ridge Station. Both characters had pasts that held major hurts for them and influenced how they came together. I really enjoyed Alex's spunk and that she was determined to be a partner with Vitali. She was not one to quit no matter what, and I really enjoyed watching her heart open up during the story."

~ Alethia

PROLOGUE

'You should never have responded to that email. I don't understand you, Alexandra.' Bitterness bled from her mother's words.

Alex Spencer pressed her lips together, momentarily fixing her gaze on the desolate New York sky as snow began to fall. 'Okay, so an email arrives out of the blue telling me the man who I thought was my father *isn't*,' she said, shoveling summer clothes into a well-travelled leopard print suitcase. 'And then I find out my real father is dead and he's left me some valuable paintings—and I'm supposed to ignore that?'

'Why do you insist on digging up the past? I've told you no good will come of it.'

Alex knew they would never agree. She wanted to say, "Mom, why are you making everything so difficult? Why won't you talk to me about my father? Why didn't you tell me the truth?" But she'd already tried, and every time her mother evaded answering. Despite what her mother had done, for the sake of their tie of blood, which was the only thing left between them, she had to keep the peace.

'Why do you have to go back to New Zealand? What more do you hope to achieve that wasn't settled six months ago? What point is there?' Elizabeth Spencer pressed, fixing disapproving eyes on her errant daughter.

'You know why I need to go back, Mother,' Alex said quietly, careful to stop exasperation creeping into her voice.

Her mother's brown eyes turned a chilly shade of black. 'After all Charles and I have done for you,' she spat. 'He's been more of a father to you than that man ever was.' Although she would never say it, the accusation whistled through her mother's pursed lips. *Why would you want to do something so selfish?*

Alex forced herself to count to ten. It was as if her mother thought keeping something so important a secret from her own daughter all these years was no big deal. It was as though she thought that replacing a real dad with a surrogate dad gave her a stable identity.

How could Alex possibly explain without severing their relationship for good? Finally, she knew why she had never felt understood, never felt accepted, never felt she belonged. And while everything was such a mystery she knew that she could never find peace until she understood her past.

'Mom, I told you when I came back for Christmas that I'd only be here for a few weeks. Please don't let us spend our last moments arguing.' Alex forced an uncertain smile hoping it would melt her mother's iciness.

Her boutique travel business meant she was never home for long. She was like those dandelions; settling for a spell then drifting away. She was no longer a child. Yet in this matter she longed for her mother's approval.

'Why can't you let go of this thing you've got about your father?' Her mother fired. 'What more do you have to know, for heaven's sake? He was an artist. He left you a few paint-ings. End of story.'

It wasn't the end of the story. Far from it. In fact of the six paintings her biological father had left her in his will she knew with gut-churning clarity that only one would unlock buried secrets. Secrets her mother seemed resolute never to divulge

'I want to know everything. I want to know about the man whose blood courses through my veins. I want to know who I am. Why can't you understand that?'

'There's nothing more to say. I was young. Impulsive. He was a mistake.'

Alex's stomach clenched. *She was a mistake.* Her mother didn't have to say it but her tone made it clear.

She was the girl nobody wanted.

1
———

Alex pressed against a pillar beneath the cavernous ceiling of the Auckland art gallery, suppressing a yawn as she fought a wave of jet lag. Clutching the exhibition catalogue to her chest she swept her gaze over the crowd gathered for the opening of the dazzling retrospective exhibition of her father's lifeworks. Only yesterday she had been in icy New York and now here she was in the heat of the New Zealand summer, surrounded by Veuve Clicquot, popping corks and intoxicating works of art.

At the center of the gallery stood Clive Gacos, the art dealer who had discovered the man she now knew was her father, exchanging air kisses and handshakes. Impeccably armored in a steel-grey designer suit that complemented his trademark helmet of silver hair he looked in his element as he enthusiastically greeted a procession of art collectors and socialites.

Alex crossed her arms protectively over her chest as women flashed him far too-enthusiastic smiles, and fluttered acrylic nails in shallow waves. She hated crowds at the best of times and tonight, surrounded by so much pretense, she felt doubly out of her comfort zone. Nausea crawled through her stomach as she wondered if Clive's insistence that she exhibit the painting had been one giant mistake.

Would tonight flush out someone intimately connected to the powerful, yet haunting image? Someone who would help her unearth the past her mother and step-father were so determined to keep buried?

Her gaze drifted to the vast landscape her father had painted running the length of the far wall. Lost Love. Two words that tore her heart apart. Looking at the painting now she wondered if the name she'd given it still fitted. For some inexplicable reason, unlike all her father's other artworks, he'd left this one unnamed. Why did he leave so few clues to its meaning?

Barely conscious of the crowd pressing around her Alex's heart quickened as she scanned the craggy Southern Ranges, their soaring peaks troughed on the canvas with a hurtle of blue and ochre and gold. Her gaze honed in on the hauntingly beautiful face of a woman, infused within the rocks. Why had her father painted a woman's face into the landscape? And whose was it—so beautiful,

The woman seemed to reach through time and space, lifting agonized eyes, calling Alex's name, drawing her deeper and deeper into the painting's mystery. Instinct told her something deeply personal had happened to inspire the painting, something that could shed light on her past? For twenty-five years her life had been a lie. Months of searching for clues to her past had ended in granite walls of silence.

Yet the way her heart pounded, her eyes pooled with tears, and every hair on her body stood on end each time she looked at the painting, told her that there was a deeper reason her father wanted the painting to remain in her possession. Alex was sure her father was enticing her to discover the painting's secrets. Why else did he leave this particular painting in his will to the daughter he'd never met?

She tore herself away from Lost Love and stood at a distance observing people's reactions in the hope that she would discover someone who found the painting as meaningful as she did. An older woman stared at it the longest, her eyes pooling as she fingered the elaborate gold locket at her throat.

A young man and woman holding hands stopped in front of it, and the woman slipped her palm from her partner's as she stepped closer to study the face of the woman. A middle-aged man's body grew hard and tense as he looked, and he passed quickly by. Another man with a receding hairline flinched as if someone had punched him in the gut. He reached a hand out to the painting, not quite touching the velvet plains of golden tussock and Rātā trees clinging fiercely to craggy rocks.

Dread wormed through her. The strange and enigmatic image evoked powerful reactions in them all, but none of them betrayed the fact they held the missing piece to her painful puzzle. She pressed her lips together, holding her face tight, as tears pricked her eyes. Showing Lost Love was a hair-brained idea, like searching for a needle in a field of grass. What real chance did she have of discovering someone who knew anything truly intimate about her dead father? Yet what else could she do? All her other enquiries had come to nothing.

Alex heaved a sigh of frustration and turned away. From across the gallery Clive Gacos caught her anxious gaze. His fluttering fingers flourished a greeting across the room as he slithered to her side. 'Lost Love. I still think the title's morbid.'

He cocked his head to one side as his gaze darted from the catalogue to the painting before resting on Alex. 'Couldn't you have come up with something more commercial?'

Alex wanted to cry out, "It's how I feel." Instead she said, 'You may be right, Mr Gacos,' painting a mask of detached aloofness on her face. Instinct told her Clive was only interested in his fame and glory—not her own painful story. She took his outstretched hand and felt a shiver snake through her spine as cold, steely fingers shook hers.

'It's a fabulous turnout, my dear.' Bleached white teeth flashed a self-satisfied smile. "I'm absolutely delighted.'

'Are you sure that this is the best way to unearth someone who may know something about this painting, Mr Gacos? You know how firmly my father was against it being exhibited.'

'Field of Dreams or Secret Passion would have been better. The right title can really boost sales,' he said glancing at the painting 'That's interesting', Alex said flatly. 'But Lost Love is not for sale.'

Eerie, pale eyes looked right through her. 'My dear, everything is for sale.'

'No, Mr Gacos. It's not. I'm looking for answers. A sale won't achieve that.' Had she been wrong to trust him? Was he just another person in a long line of people to deceive her? 'Besides you told me yourself, my father made it quite clear that the painting must never leave my possession.'

'My dear, 40 years in the industry has taught me one thing, what an artist says and what an artist means are quite, quite different things. If you gave me ten dollars for every time I've heard, "This is my favorite work, I'll never part with it," or some other nonsense, I'd be a hundred-fold richer.' His reptilian eyes scanned her face as though searching for a weakness in her resolve. 'Of course none of this matters now that your father is dead.'

Dead.

Alex's eyes misted as the finality of the word hit her. It was ridiculous. Eleven months ago she hadn't even known geologist, turned painter, Ted Carr, known in art circles as Jimmie Goldie, was her father and since then she'd had plenty of time to accept the fact that he was gone. But she couldn't help feeling regret.

If only she'd known her father. If only he was by her side now. Although in a strange way he was, she mused, her eyes misting as she gazed at the painting. Infused with his energy, his passion, his spirit, Lost Love was her only link. It was as though the painting was his voice—allowing him to speak through time and space. But only to those with eyes that could see and ears that could hear, and Alex still had no idea what he was saying.

Maybe she was reading too much into it. Maybe it was just a painting. But why did her father demand it never be exhibited in public? And why did he want her to have it?

'I expect this exhibition to arouse even more interest in Jimmies work, and the longer we hold off the more the painting will appreciate in value,' Clive blabbered on, oblivious of her raw grief.

Alex clenched her teeth, shutting back a retort at his thoughtless remark. This wasn't the time to be emotional, nor to incite conflict. She hated disharmony and discord. And although she'd been continually teased because she always chose the peaceful route, putting him in his place would only get him off side.

'Remind me again Mr Gacos, just how well did you know my father?' she said gently.

'I told you—I discovered him. Made him a sell-out success.'

'Yes, but what was he really like?'

'I don't know. We never met.'

'But you were his dealer?'

'I deal in works of art, Miss Spencer. Not people. Besides, your father liked his privacy. I respected that.'

'Didn't you wonder why he hid his true identity?'

'My dear, half the celebrities in the world use fake, made-up names. Careers live and die by people's memorability. It's all part of the game. Do you really think Andy Warhol's paintings would sell for astronomical sums if he went by his real name, Andrew Warhola? Your father was smart. Jimmie Goldie, or Ted Carr—ask yourself, who's the better investment?'

Tension knotted her shoulders. She was getting nowhere.

'Want some advice?'

No.

'Take it from me. There's no mystery—just a finely executed brand strategy. And you are the lucky beneficiary. So what? He left you this painting. Maybe his conscience got the better of him. In my opinion it's an exceptional piece of work, one of his finest, and tantalizingly one that the art world has never seen before. If I were you, I'd sell it. Realize the cash. Return to New York. Go live your life.'

Go live your life. She would—but not before she had her answers. Alex's gaze drifted back to the crowd. Her only hope was that someone would reveal something in their reaction to the painting. Surely if anyone was connected intimately it would hit them with the same power-punch to the gut as it did to her every time she looked at it.

Suddenly she was distracted by a blaze of rustic color as the most ridiculously handsome man Alex had ever seen strode toward her.

2

His six-foot frame wore an immaculately tailored camel jacket, cut from the finest Merino wool and fashionably faded jeans gracing a powerful physique.

His skin was deeply tanned, his hair rich dark chocolate with golden highlights—wavy and slightly tousled. Not a classically handsome pasty metro-sexual like the American suitors her mother continually threw in her path. But a ruggedly handsome man, who looked as though he would be equally at home in a New York boardroom dressed in a sleek Armani suit as he would be rustling cattle in a tough New Zealand Swandri. The man oozed passion, purpose— and danger.

She watched entranced as his gaze swept the room, standing rigidly in the archway with a presence that emanated command. He had a strong, arresting face, coldly handsome with no lines of weakness. A disturbingly primitive tug of attraction quaked through her body. She could imagine this man commanding a Roman Legion, or leading a charge of Templar Knights.

He oozed the power of a leader who made his own rules,

ruthlessly sweeping aside anyone who stood in opposition. A smile fluttered to her lips as she imagined the shock on her mother's face if she married a man so raw and rugged. To her discomfort she found the idea thrilling and quickly sanctioned her recklessness.

Whether the Adonis had read her mind Alex had no idea, but as he carved his way through the crowded gallery he slowed his stride. He paused opposite her and looked at her, a flicker of recognition glancing across his face as though he wondered if he had met her before, perhaps even bedded her.

His gaze narrowed with the level unwavering gaze of a ravenous lion. Whatever he was thinking Alex's heart raced. It was as if he could see right through to the essence of who she really was. It was as thrilling as it was intoxicating and disturbing. Near them people glided around the paintings, the vacuous height of the vaulted gallery ceiling amplifying peoples voices, but she was trapped with him in exploding silence.

Usually she dismissed such attention. But this was more than a fleeting appraisal of desirability, more than an appreciation of the curvaceous femininity of her figure. It was an arrogant assessment projecting the confident knowledge that he could have her if he wanted. The only question appeared to be could he be bothered?

A frisson of danger scuttled down Alex's spine. Under his penetrating gaze she felt like a naked model posing for a ravenous sculptor. She picked at the black sequins of her dress, immediately regretting wearing the figure-hugging cocktail number she'd purchased for the formal opening night.

She never wore dresses ordinarily, and hated wearing black, but she had wanted to blend in with the art-gallery-noir that she knew everyone else would be wearing. It was the only suitable dress she'd found at the second hand store on Queen Street in the few hours she had to spare since arriving in Auckland. As her face flared with humiliating heat Alex tugged the bottom of the clinging dress, cursing the shimmering sequins and the above knee length for attracting his attention.

His piercing green eyes rested for long, uneasy moments on Alex's quivering lips. The perfect lushness of his mouth quirked dangerously as his gaze inched with leisurely thoroughness before dropping to where her dress clung to her chest.

Every whisper of hair on her body stood like sentries armed for defense. Yet to her intense humiliation she found her barriers weakened. Was it pleasure? Longing? Or desire she felt flood her body with warmth? She couldn't be sure. It had been years since she'd been with a man, and never with anyone certainly so virile. For the briefest moment she found herself wondering what it would be like to be taken by him. Every remnant of her rational mind fought the dangerous feeling, but the more she struggled the more her body betrayed her.

Suddenly, with an air of explosive tension the weight of the stranger lurched forward. His face spun away from her. Alex followed the direction of his fixed gaze, piqued that his interest in her had been so totally diverted. She couldn't see his expression but she could sense his undiluted fury.

In the next instant he propelled himself through the crowd, a dozen lithe strides bringing him within a foot of *Lost Love*.

Her pulse rate ricocheted as she watched transfixed as the stranger froze as if in shock, then shook his head in disbelief. After several tense moments he rifled through the catalogue he carried. His shoulders tensed as he read the small caption, then scrutinized the painting again. He thrust his arms out as if to wrench it from the wall. His hand tightened into a closed fist crumpling the catalogue, then thrust it into his pocket.

Alex's heart pounded then took a dive. Her mind raced ahead as she struggled to understand the intensity of his reaction. Could he unravel her mysterious past?

He swung around, his face set in determined purpose, his gaze scanning quickly over the people in the room. They passed over Alex without a flicker of recognition, every muscle of his face taunt with savagery.

'Who is he?'

'I don't know, but he looks important—and *very* wealthy.' Clive said in a low voice. 'Let me handle this.'

Clive was off and moving with the silent speed of a cobra toward the stranger before Alex could object. Tension jackknifed through her chest. What should she do? Run after Clive and risk getting in the way? The stranger had dismissed any interest in her with the aloof detachment of a man who would never cede control. Instinct told Alex where she was concerned he was untamable. Like a wild wolf, the wrong move would send him running. Besides, Clive's reputation for netting the elusive was legendary.

She reached for a glass of champagne from a passing waitress and took tiny gulps as she hovered anxiously. Would Clive find out what had incited such a powerful reaction? Would the stranger reveal why he had responded so strongly?

Perhaps the painting incited something deep within his soul, she wondered. No that was impossible. The brute didn't appear to have a soul or he wouldn't have dismissed her so coolly. Her heart pulsed with the sting of his rejection. He was clearly a collector like many others in the gallery. A numbers man who no doubt prided himself on his many conquests and the number of artworks he possessed.

Alex gripped the stem of the glass as she watched the scene unfold. As Clive tried to beguile him with his charming smile the stranger's shoulders tensed. Fear rumbled through her as cataclysmic as an earthquake. Was Clive failing? She cursed herself for allowing him to take the lead. A woman with a beehive hairdo, her long neck over-saturated with Opium perfume paused in front of her obstructing her view.

'Excuse me,' Alex said, inhaling a heady mix of cinnamon and spice, as she pressed past the woman. The stranger was no longer in front of the painting. Her heart hammered as she stood on her tiptoes and scoured the room. Where had he gone?

A slice of golden caramel moving like a bullet caught her eye as the stranger strode toward the exit. Then, like the sun setting over the ranges in *Lost Love* in a blink he was gone.

3

D espite the fatigue that had seeped into every bone in her body, Alex was still awake, her mind whirring with a kaleidoscope of possible scenarios, when the telephone in her hotel room rang. 'Who could that be?'

She glanced at the digital clock on the bedside table. Ten thirty-five pm. In New York it would be Saturday and her mother and Charles would have just finished a leisurely brunch. Alex propped herself on her pillows and lifted the telephone receiver, bracing herself for the inquisition.

But it wasn't an international call.

'Sorry if I've disturbed you, Alexandra,' Clive Gacos rattled over the line, 'I know it's late but I couldn't wait,' he pressed on, sounding not in the least bit sorry. 'I've received an offer for one of your father's paintings. I've been instructed to close the deal tonight.' He paused, then continued, his tone pinched, 'If you're agreeable, of course.'

An odd feeling of premonition crawled through Alex's chest. 'Which painting, Mr Gacos?'

Clive hesitated then cleared his throat. '*Lost Love*. I've been negotiating on your behalf throughout the evening.'

Her shoulder's tensed. 'Negotiating what on my behalf?'

'You won't believe it. I can hardly believe it myself. It's the stuff of dreams,' he gasped, nearly tripping over his excitement. 'Before you say anything, the client has been informed, as per your instructions, that *Lost Love* is not for sale' Clive rushed on, obviously anxious to defer her refusal. 'However, the offer he is making...it's simply staggering. I didn't feel I could say no. Not without consulting you of course, my dear.'

'You know I can't sell.' Alex said annoyed at the patronizing attitude that snaked through his voice.

'I know. I know,' he repeated, in barely held exasperation. 'But Alex, it wasn't written in his will. There's nothing legally binding.'

'My father was adamant that the painting remain in my possession.'

Clive took a deep breath. 'Alexandra, I don't think you realize how much money is at stake. This is big—'

'No figure would be large enough to make me betray my father's trust, Mr Gacos.' Her throat felt like sandpaper and she reached for the glass of Pellegrino on the bedside table.

'Five million dollars!' he blurted. 'Think how that would change your life.'

The glass slid from her hand. Alex pushed back the blankets and jumped to her feet, her mind spinning. 'What did you say?' Alex kept her voice calm, but the rush pounded through her now, the painting, the adrenaline, five million dollars.

'Five...million...dollars! I think even your father would agree. None of us could have predicted such a meteoric rise in prices for his work. Selling now would catapult your father's name into artistic infamy. Just think what you would be doing for his reputation. 'It's a record sum for a

New Zealand artist. Quite dazzling. But we must move quickly.'

What was the urgency? Clive's pressure addled her brain. Was notoriety what her father wanted? It took a few more stunned moments before she managed to speak again. 'Is this for real?'

'I can assure you the buyer is quite serious.' Clive replied infusing his voice with professional stoicism, but she sensed the zealous excitement he was suppressing. The commission on five million dollars was obviously blinding.

She could well imagine how brokering a deal of this size would clinch Clive's well known ambition to join the elite club of the world's most powerful art dealers. Had the painting been for sale she may have admired his ambitious drive, perhaps even been grateful, but it wasn't for sale, and he was clearly driven by his own self-interest. But what Clive wanted was none of her concern. For once what she wanted would be her dominant priority.

Recovering from the initial shock Alex's mind kicked up a gear. Someone wanted that painting very badly. The question was, who and why?

'Who is the buyer?' she asked, keeping her tone even.

'They have asked to remain anonymous.'

'Of course they have,' she said, wearily.

'I honestly don't know. In this type of situation, the bids always come through a third party. Some people don't wish to be in the spotlight. However, I can assure you the offer is authentic. Just say "yes" and the money will be in your bank account tomorrow.'

Someone wanted the painting desperately. This was what she had hoped for, it was the sole reason she'd agreed the painting be put on exhibition—and the response was beyond her wildest dreams. She had to figure this out carefully. If she couldn't get through all the middlemen she'd blow the opportunity to find out if the person behind the offer knew anything of her father's past.

Alex paced the room, her tension growing. When at last she spoke it was in a flat, detached voice.

'Mr Gacos, tell the intermediaries that unless I deal with the buyer directly there is absolutely no chance of a deal.'

'It's not the done thing,' he spluttered.

'Then I guess it's goodnight,' she bluffed, hoping he didn't detect the squeak in her voice.

'Wait. I'll pass on your instructions. Hold the line.'

Alex's hands trembled as she pressed the cordless phone to her ear and paced the room, her tension growing as the minutes ticked by. She felt desperately tired, but her mind was spinning. Her demand must be meeting with resistance. A great deal of resistance. Hopefully that was a good sign.

'I'm sorry. The buyer is not prepared to discuss the matter in person. It's your decision but I firmly believe if you refuse their terms the bidder will disappear.'

Alex's head pulsed. She had nothing to go on. But if someone was prepared to offer that much, she didn't believe they would walk away. They had to be bluffing to force a quick decision. Bad luck for them that they had seriously underestimated her motivation. No amount of money would ever persuade her to give up *Lost Love*. And now that she knew someone else wanted to possess the painting as badly as she wanted to keep it she was even more determined to follow the trail. She knew now, without a doubt, that *Lost Love* held some special significance to someone else. She took a long, deep breath, needing to slow her pulse-rate before she threw down her last card.

'The answer is no,' she said flatly. 'You can tell them I will never sell to a stranger. They know how to reach me if they change their mind.'

'Alexandra—' She could hear the hiss of Clive's breath as he bit back a protest. 'Very well. As you wish. I'll pass on your reply.' His tone held a note of desperation.

Alex sat on the bed, slid back on the pillows and tried to relax. It was utterly impossible. Her mind kept racing backwards and forwards. Had she played the right hand? She couldn't think how she could have played it differently. Until the buyer made his decision she couldn't plan her next move. But that didn't stop her volleying the possibilities around in her mind.

It was a longer wait this time, but Alex didn't mind. Each minute that passed increased her hope. Obviously they were talking very seriously, and she had no doubt that Clive's tenacity would keep the deal alive.

'Alex—' The note of relief in Clive's voice brought an elated smile to her lips. 'The principal insists that the meeting be kept completely confidential.'

'Absolutely,' she agreed quickly.

'And it has to be tomorrow morning. As early as you can make it.'

The buyer was clearly impatient. While Alex needed as much time with the mysterious person as possible, she just wasn't a morning girl. And since she held the trump card at the moment she would call the shots.

'Lunch near my hotel would suit me better.' She glanced out the window at the Sky Tower dominating the skyline with its commanding presence. 'The Orbit Revolving Restaurant,' she said impulsively. 'Eleven-thirty.'

There was only a short pause before Clive came back with the reply. 'Agreed.'

'How will I recognize them? Don't tell me—red carnation, dark glasses?' she said flippantly.

'I'll be there, Alexandra,' he said quickly. 'To introduce you and to represent your interests.'

'No, Clive. I'm sorry.'

He heaved a reluctant sigh. 'Of course.' A pregnant pause crackled down the line. 'Will you sell, Alexandra?'

'Thank you for negotiating the meeting, Mr Gacos.' She forced her voice to a nonchalant crawl. 'Good night, Mr Gacos. I'll let you know the outcome.'

A Tsunami of exhaustion, anxiety, apprehension and excitement crawled over her as she put the phone down. Maybe the buyer just loved the painting. But it didn't stack up. Five million dollars spelled out a compulsive desire to acquire, and there had to be some reason for it over and above the usual obsession of an art-lover. Her father, while popular in New Zealand, was no Da Vinci. It could hardly be an investment buy at that price. So that left—what?

She stared out the window at the fiery red neon lights of the Sky Tower. Meeting so close to Auckland's casino seemed ironically appropriate. Everything about the meeting was a gamble and she would need to play a skillful hand if she were to win. Would lady luck be her ally or would she shine her benevolent light on the mysterious, but clearly determined opponent?

4
___

Alex pressed against the wall as a Korean tour party posed for the in-house photographer before bustling into the Sky Tower lift.

'I hate having my photo taken even on a good day,' she told him politely as she waited for the second lift to arrive. And today had the potential to be the worst day of her life. As she stepped into the lift her stomach clenched as she thought of what was at stake. This meeting was her best chance. All other attempts had resulted in dead-ends. If she blew today's negotiations she might never unravel the secrets that would help her understand her past.

Alex sighed with relief as the doors began to close. Placing her palm on her belly she lifted her tissue saturated with a confidence-boosting blend of essential oils. Pressing the scent of geranium, lavender and ylang-ylang to her nose she inhaled deeply, hoping to settle her nerves. She looked at her reflection in the glossy wall panels and began to mentally rehearse her strategy out loud. 'Good afternoon, thank you so much for meeting me.' She forced a confident smile 'Before we settle down to business, I'm curious...what draws you to the painting?'

Suddenly a muscled arm forced through the gap in the doors forcing them to crash open.

'What the—' Her tissue flew to the floor as the Adonis who had rattled her equilibrium at the gallery strode into the lift. Heat sparked between them as she saw the flash of recognition. His mouth twisted with cynical amusement at the crimson blush that burned her cheeks. There could be no doubt that he remembered last night's encounter.

A mop of dark wavy hair fell across his face as he raised a quizzical eyebrow. '*Scuse*, was I was interrupting something?' His deep honeyed Italian voice was textured by sexual confidence and power, making her knees go weak.

Oh, crap. He'd obviously heard her rehearsing. She studied her feet, hoping the stain heating her face would disappear—and her with it—as the doors shut, filling the lift with his testosterone-laden presence. The orange blossom and sandalwood scent that oozed from him was reminiscent of the scene of another one of her father's paintings—the beautiful gardens of Isola Bella, one of the Borromean Islands of Lake Maggiore near Milan. Earthy, sensual and thoroughly intoxicating.

A bolt of awareness streaked down Alex's backbone as sexual tension echoed in the silence around them. Excruciatingly aware of his amused stare, she locked her gaze on the elevator panel forcing herself to find it infinitely fascinating, as every fiber of her body orbited in his direction.

No gaping. Didn't the brute know elevator etiquette.

She inhaled sharply and, in an uncharacteristic move of boldness, slowly turned her head and surveyed him with one calm, detached glance.

At least that was what it was meant to be. Maddeningly,

sage green eyes trapped hers, forcing her gaze to sensuous lips curved into a sardonic smile, as he leaned against the wall. Strong arms folded against his powerful chest as he faced her with the arrogant confidence of a non-conformist who found her mortal embarrassment amusing and cared nothing for rules. Clear and confident and incisive, his piercing gaze stirred an instant protective instinct, hammering home her acute vulnerability.

Damn, she thought helplessly. Alex's heartbeat kicked up a gear even as her senses hummed, every cell detonating into life. Up close he was even taller and more warrior like than he'd appeared at the gallery. Long-legged, with shoulders that would be a credit to any Greek god, he was 110% pure man. *1001% pure danger.*

What if he was the mysterious buyer, she thought for a reckless second? No impossible. He looked to be in his early-thirties, not old enough to be a man who had known her father and what had happened over 20 years ago. This man would only have been a child then. And he was far too young and far too casually dressed to be in possession of such a fortune.

Her heart contracting in her chest as she ran a swift glance over his clothes. A rich chocolate hip-length leather jacket covered a V-neck navy cashmere jersey and white shirt hanging informally over ink colored designer jeans. Casual they may appear, but they were tailor made for brute strength, impeccably proportioned for his lean body and long, strong, muscled legs.

Her pulse hammered as the lift began to climb toward the restaurant 192 meters above the city. Don't look down, a voice warned as the lift climbed higher. Alex fixed her gaze on a spot on the horizon, trying to block out the stranger's unrelenting stare.

'*Allora*, is your invisible friend afraid of heights?' His unsmiling, icy calmness was in direct contrast to her uneasy emotions. 'Afraid of heights? Nope,' she lied, hoping he wouldn't detect the fear sucking life from her voice. She hadn't thought about her fear of heights when she'd impulsively picked the meeting venue. She wasn't a planner. She was impetuous, impulsive.

Stupid.

The brute obviously had no empathy. Why the hell hadn't she thought it through? Whether it was a fierce determination to prove him wrong, or the mortification of already having made a fool of herself, she plastered on her most fearless, warrior-woman face and stepped over to the viewing glass inserted in the middle of the floor. Feel the fear and do it anyway, isn't that what the self-help gurus advocated? Heck, it wasn't as if she'd die.

You can do this she told herself, fixing the stranger with a defiant stare. Whether it was fear or the thrill of the crazed energy that sparked between them like wild-fire she didn't know, but her head began to spin as she peered down into the abyss of the lift shaft. Her body tilted as the whole lift seemed to sway, pulling her in one lethal direction.

Gasping, she fought to control her legs. She squealed as she lost her balance. For one stark second she felt the undulating contour of every muscle in his hard torso on her back, and the strength of his arm across her breasts. Sparks like flints on graphite ignited between them as she clung to the man of steel and their bodies momentarily fused.

Although the heat storming her chest robbed her of breath, strength and wits, instinct kicked in. "*Move back!*" it snapped.

'I'm *so* sorry,' she mumbled mortified, her voice barely

audible, as she sprung away from him as though his touch burned her.

'*Che cavolo*! Are you all right?'

'I'm fine,' she said, injecting her voice with her cultivated aloofness. 'It's these heels,' she said, clutching the hand railing with one hand and pointing a blaming finger at the far too high shoes she'd decided to wear to impress the prospective buyer.

Doubly amused at what no doubt he regarded as her foolish antics he smiled with the confidence of a man used to having women throw themselves at his feet. But there had been something about the way his body tensed as his arms had encircled her. Something she couldn't put her finger on. Almost an uneasiness at the chemistry igniting the space between them that belied his smug arrogance.

He laughed, as though sensing her confusion. It was not the easy laugh of a man in full control of his emotions, but a raw, unsteady laugh.

Hurry, she silently prayed wishing the lift were a bullet train speeding to her destination. She drummed her fingers on the steel railing. Thank God she'd decided to get to the restaurant early. She'd need the extra time to regain her composure.

Mercifully, after what seemed like eternity, the lift doors released her. She tumbled out anxious to put as much distance between them. A thrill of exhilaration stopped her in her tracks as she stepped into the foyer and savored the spectacular panoramic views.

Auckland's Hauraki Gulf spread like sapphire silk before her. Sunlight glinted off the serene waters sparkling like a pool of diamonds. All she had to do was stay chilled and maintain her own serenity Alex reminded herself as she gave her name to the waiter.

'I'm expecting a business acquaintance to join me,' she told him quietly, conscious the lift-hunk was behind her. She quickly scanned the restaurant and looked for the best vantage point, then requested a table opposite the lifts. She would size-up the prospective buyer before they identified her and plan her strategy from there.

The waiter quirked his eyebrow and smiled. Alex wondered what he found so amusing as he led her to the table. He offered her sparkling water and, her body still burning from the humiliation of the lift encounter, she accepted it gratefully.

She was relieved, yet a little disappointed, when the lift-hunk's mobile rang and he disappeared around the corner to take the call discretely. Men like him eat women like her for breakfast then throw away the bones, she reminded herself, taking refuge in the magnificent views as she was led to her table.

Besides she wasn't looking for a man. *She was looking for her father.*

She mentally rehearsed what she would say and all the questions she would ask, and visualized how skillfully she would lead the buyer to reveal everything she needed to know. If affirmations and visualizing success could help Olympians win gold they could help her win too. She looked out toward Rangitoto Island, the largest of the fifty or so volcanoes which peppered Auckland's landscape, poking up from sea and land.

'Bloody sky,' she muttered, recalling the passage in her Lonely Planet travel guide summarising the Māori name given to it after a historical bloody battle. Tension held her shoulders rigid. Beguilingly dormant, the island hid latent power, masking the threat that lay beneath the surface and threatening to erupt without provocation.

Taking a slow sip of water, she glanced around the restaurant. Seated at a table to her left she recognized the Korean tour party she had encountered earlier and she smiled politely as they waved at her. The discordant sound of their clipped voices as they resumed their conversations was slightly jarring and she felt her anxiety return.

Go with the flow, she reminded herself gazing down at the cool blue waters. So long as she looked out and not down, she could convince herself she was on *terra firma*. "Go with the flow", that's what her Zen teacher reminded her every time she had paroxysms of anxiety.

Go with the flow. Who was to know? Fake it, 'til you make it. All those other sage words and more. She drank them as thirstily as she downed the glass of Pellegrino. She gazed at the water momentarily to settle her nerves, trying to stay anchored in the present and not give too much energy to what may, or may not happen when the stranger finally arrived.

She smoothed her hand over the cream antique lace of her dress. Even her critical mother would approve of her efforts to look appropriately elegant. It was a good middle of the road option, neither understated nor over the top. Best of all it didn't need ironing and travelled easily. She was no powerhouse negotiator but perhaps if she looked neither too needy, nor too casual, things would go better. Rocking up with a backpack, clad in jeans with her favorite travel camera dangling around her neck wouldn't put her in the power seat. If anything her normal travel attire might cause the buyer to question her integrity.

She felt her heart rate quicken each time someone approached the table. But only a steady stream of tourists emerged from the lift. She glanced at her watch. 11:29. What if the buyer had changed their mind? She scanned the restaurant anxiously. Then she caught sight of the Adonis who had rattled her equilibrium, striding toward her with a cocky grin on his smug face. Like an animal caught in head-lights she stared at him, her stomach fluttering.

Oh, God. Not him!

5

____

He checked his watch then caught her stare as he lifted his head and gave her a faint grin. Mortified at being caught showing interest in him again Alex promptly stared out the window. With any luck she was wrong. He would be seated at the other end of the restaurant and pass right by.

'Miss Spencer?' enquired the familiar honey-textured voice, barely masking mock amusement.

Crap! It had to be him. Other than the waiter, nobody else knew her name. Horror quaked through her body.

Taking a slow, deliberate sip of water to settle her nerves she lifted her gaze coolly toward him. 'I'm sorry, but this isn't a good time,' she said, injecting her voice with as much composure as she could summon. 'I'm waiting for...'

'*I'm* the man you've been waiting for.' His magnetic green eyes shone with captivating intensity, sending her heart rate soaring. A cheeky smile tugging at the corner of his mouth sounded a warning—he thought he could charm his way around her to get what he wanted. Irritation coiled through her chest, awakening parts of her personality that she hadn't been aware existed—like the desire to wipe that superior smile from his annoyingly handsome face. He was teasing her. Flirting with her. Playing with her.

'Waiting for you?' she fired. 'I can assure you I've never waited for any man.'

His strong chiseled jaw, softened into boyish dimples, leaving Alex with the distinct impression he found her indignation refreshing.

'My name is Rossi. Vitaliano Rossi.' A surge of energy sparked between them as his hand reached to shake hers. His fingers tightened around her hand, not too tightly to cause pain, but with calculated firmness designed to send the message that he, not she, would be in control.

Alex took not a small degree of pleasure in reciprocating the firmness of his clasp. Disturbingly, a thrill quaked through her. Contrasting with his immaculately manicured fingers his palm had the powerful texture of a man who could karate chop a thousand Samurai to defend her honor. Against her will she found herself desiring his protection.

His gaze sharpened on hers as though studying every nano movement in her face.

A quivery feeling of traitorous feminine weakness coursed through her veins as he grinned with the easy confidence of a man used to disarming his opponents with his handsome looks and innate power. She slipped her trembling hand from his grasp.

'*Vitaliano Rossi.*' He repeated, his voice lifting as though posing a question he demanded she answer.

What was she missing? Alex patiently waited to be offered further explanation.

'I expect the name means something to you.' He said at last, in a tone richly marinated in cynicism.

'Vitaliano Rossi?' Alex shook her head. 'No. I'm afraid not. Should it?'

His sage eyes turned icy green.

'But then I'm not from New Zealand,' she offered.

She sensed the satisfaction that brought a thin smile to his roguish face.

'So that's the problem.'

Something in his tone led her to believe he felt he had solved a riddle. 'Excuse me?'

'May I?' he swept broad sensual fingers toward the chair opposite her. Not waiting to be invited he sat and regarded her with speculative interest.

'I must confess I was anticipating someone much older.' Alex said, too quickly.

'Me also, but you are a pleasant surprise.'

Alex shifted uncomfortably in her chair. Suddenly she felt incredibly rattled. All her planning, all her preparation was going out the window. Her neck might have turned the color of tamarillos under the intensity of his stare, her mind addled by his movie-star good looks, but the imperative need to ensure the man seated opposite her was in no doubt that he would not flirt his way into her submission, only intensified. She had to disabuse him of the notion fast. What she didn't know yet was how.

He ordered a Peroni beer from the hovering waiter, and returned his attention to her.

'I'm curious, Ms Spender—' His sensual brows quirked as though struggling to maintain the pleasantries.

'Spencer. My name is Alexandra Spencer.'

'*Scuse*. My mistake.' He flashed a charming smile but his eyes remained unmoved. 'How does someone so young come to acquire such an important work?'

Hang on a minute. She was supposed to be asking the

questions, Alex thought as he began mining her for information. It was obviously a tactical move to get the upper hand

'So you are American?' he said, detecting her cultivated accent. He returned to his earlier comment when his interrogation efforts failed. 'Is that the problem with my offer?'

'I'm sorry?'

'Clearly the currency differential concerns you. It makes no difference to me whether I offer five million New Zealand dollars or five million US dollars. Consider it changed.'

Alex bit back a surge of disbelief. His initial offer of five million had just tripled! And he didn't even flinch. Her fingers traced the beveled edges of the gold locket her father had left her, as she forced her face to remain impassive.

'Of course I realize in the current climate of money laundering that transferring large sums of money internationally can be problematic. I have vast assets for this sort of thing. We can work around that.'

'And who is we?' Alex asked.

Something dangerous flickered in his eyes. 'You and I, Miss Spencer, are *we*.'

An uncomfortable silence tugged at the space between them. She burned with the memory of the way he had looked at her last night, and his enigmatic aloofness added fuel to the fire. "What do you want?" her mother had asked when she left New York. For a wild, reckless moment Alex wondered if she would ever want a man like him.

She smiled as her gaze drifted to his sensuous lips. It would certainly be interesting to find out. Alex's imagination carried her momentarily away from the seriousness of her quest, filling her mind with visions of Vitaliano Rossi taking her in his strong arms and lowering his hard, purposeful mouth to her lips. She imagined with not a small amount of pleasure the shock on her mother's face if she returned home with him on her arm—no longer the spinster she always told her she would be. Priceless! Shocking! Scandalous! She forced herself upright in her chair. Totally ridiculous!

'Aren't we here to discuss business?' Vitaliano said, forcing her attention to the only reason their paths had crossed.

'Of course,' she replied drily. His relentless focus on his quest shouldn't have hurt, but irrationally it did. She had always been a magnet for self-obsessed men who were totally consumed about business and cared not a scrap for her. But so long as she was in possession of something he wanted she would enjoy being the center of attention and making him wait.

As much as he was dangerous, he was also fascinating. A chameleon, in equal parts as charming as he was determined to claim what she possessed, and she was beginning to relish the challenge of discovering the truth beneath his enigmatic façade.

She smiled to herself. She would enjoy her time with him, perhaps even play a little, but he was not going to find her an easy conquest. She met his gaze with equal directness. 'I would like to know more about the size of your assets,' Alex forced the urge to laugh at her recklessness. 'Your vast assets—'

She left her unfinished sentence dangling as she took a slow, deliberate sip of water. She slid her finger up and down the smooth stem of the glass, enjoying every scintillating moment as he stared at her with wide, glittering eyes.

'—for working around international currency problems,' she finally added.

The dangerous gleam receded. 'My company has international connections, Miss Spencer,' he said matter-of-factly. 'Now that we have established geography is not a barrier I take it we can conclude this transaction?'

"Not so fast Mr Rossi. Let's savor this moment. Perhaps you have heard of the slow food movement?' she asked as the waiter placed the menus in front of them.

Her question held his attention.

Alex explained the phenomenon and then added, 'You may like to go quickly, but I would prefer it if you could go slowly. I lose interest if it's over too soon.'

His flint-hard gaze didn't shift from her face. 'How refreshing. Something else we have in common,' he said, taking her in with a long sultry stare as the waiter returned to take their order.

'*Prego. Va bene.* We'll have the grilled market fish with the coconut and lemongrass risotto. And Crème Brûlée to follow. *Grazie.*'

Good choice, Alex thought happily as Vitaliano dismissed the waiter.

She steered the conversation back to what she really wanted to know, probing him with questions about his art collection and to her surprise spent the next 30 minutes being thoroughly absorbed by his knowledge of the art world.

The waiter returned and placed their lunch before them. She lifted her knife and fork and cut into the her fish. 'Would you mind telling me first what business you are in, Mr Rossi?'

'I dig things out of the ground,' he said with sardonic amusement.

'That must be profitable,' she said, sweeping her gaze

over his pricey watch caked in bazillions of diamonds.' But what kind of things?'

His eyes mimicked her interest. 'The kind of things that beautiful women like yourself worship. Miss Spencer.'

Flatter, she thought, not buying a word of what he said. She'd never thought herself particularly beautiful and warned herself to be extra vigilant. He was obviously an experienced seducer who thought she was some bimbo fortune hunter who he could charm into submission.

'And just what do I worship, Mr Rossi?'

'Gold.' He studied her and seemed surprised by her still, steady, emotionless gaze. His body had the stillness of a wild animal whose every sense was alert, suspicious and untrusting.

'The Gold Ridge mine yields the finest gold in the world.'

The Gold Ridge mine in Central Otago!

Alex jolted upright. Her grilled Blue Cod nearly hurtled out of her mouth. She clamped her hand over her lips. Her free hand trembled as she reached for her glass of water to wash down the fish lodged in her throat. But she wasn't concentrating and knocked it over, sending a fast-moving puddle toward Vitali's lap.

Suddenly two people clad in electric blue and shocking yellow jumpsuits hurled past the window and plummeted to the ground below. Alex screamed and jumped from her chair.

Vitaliano regarded Alex with intensity as blood drained from her face.

'Has anyone told you you're hyper-sensitive,' Vitaliano said, grabbing his napkin and mopping water from his groin. 'Sky jumpers. Perfectly normal tourist madness.'

People pay hundreds of dollars for the privilege of scaring themselves witless. She knew that. But she was speechless. Refreshingly he hadn't shouted at her for making such a scene. She'd given up counting the number of times she'd been criticized for her sensitivity, yelled at, made to feel ashamed, told to toughen up. But then nothing about him was normal. Everything was hyper-crazy.

Adrenaline lapped through her veins, fueled by the shock of the bodies hurling from the sky, and intensified by what Vitali had revealed. What were the odds? Her father had been a geologist and had spent many years in Central Otago. She had read about The Gold Ridge Mine when she travelled the length and breadth of New Zealand during her first search a year ago.

But it had been established in the nineties, long after her father had moved to Northland's sunny Kerikeri. She had dismissed any connection when she had visited the area last year. The timing seemed off. But maybe she was wrong. How long did it take to establish a mine after gold deposits had been found? And why would her father leave if he'd found gold? It didn't make sense. And what link did Vitaliano Rossi have to her father's past?

Unable to form any words, her gaze froze on his crotch as he dabbed at the puddle of water.

'What precisely do you want, Miss Spencer?' Vitaliano Rossi pushed.'

She fixed her gaze more appropriately on her lunch.

'You wanted to discuss my proposal, non? *Va bene*. Let's discuss it.' He swept his hand before her. 'Ladies before gentlemen.'

Alex hesitated, if she told him precisely what she wanted she might never discover the real reason underlying his obsessive determination to own the painting—and obsession it had to be. Why else would he be prepared to pay such an extraordinarily ridiculous amount of money?

He could easily tell her the first lot of nonsense that came into his head. Finesse was required. And while manipulation was something she despised most in people, what choice did she have? Wasn't he playing the same card? As far as this matter was concerned, she would be just as masterful at playing the winning hand as Vitaliano Rossi.

Even if he had nothing to tell her, Alex wanted her curiosity satisfied about his motives. She had not forgotten his strong reaction to the painting last night. It had completely killed his interest in her. Not that she wanted his interest, she lied to herself, but he certainly had some explaining to do.

She hadn't liked the cynical remark he had just made, either—including her among the most beautiful women who valued gold above all else. How dare he devalue her? He didn't even know her. The arrogance of the man, she fumed, realizing with growing uneasiness that she found him maddingly attractive.

But how dare he attempt to placate her, manipulate her, lie to her? She was no catwalk model. Her mother was the only beauty in the Spencer family. No doubt she had inherited her father's quirky looks. Which was further reason to find out more about the man from whom she had inherited half her genes.

For now, though, it was better not to reveal too much— not even that she was one woman who could not be bought. Not for five million New Zealand dollars, or even five billion euros or whatever other currency he peddled. He would find that out soon enough.

'To tell the truth, Mr Rossi, I'm not sure I want to sell you *Lost Love*,' she said flatly. 'I really don't understand why you want the painting. You're offering me such a ridiculous amount. It just doesn't feel right to take your money.'

His shoulders tensed and she was left with the strong sense that he didn't believe her. There was no longer the slightest spark of amusement or any hint of flirtatious invitation in the green eyes that bored into her. It was as though a steel wall had slammed between them.

'I like it. I want it.' His eyes were hard and purposeful as though he were playing her at her game of detached emotion. He leaned forward, anchoring his elbows to the table, and clasped his large powerful hands. 'At the price I'm offering it will make this the New Zealand art world's "Purchase of The Year." All publicity is good publicity when it comes to appreciating an asset.'

She held his gaze, trying to probe behind the words. Her natural tendency was to trust people but this was no low-stake interaction. The words on their own would have been somewhat convincing but something about the way his voice pitched, the way he never expanded his answers, the way his lips almost unperceptively twitched as he regarded her cooly, warned her he was not telling the truth.

'What can I tell you—I'm obsessive. I buy paintings like Kim Kardashian buys clothes,' he raised a flint-hard gaze.' As a woman, surely you can understand that.'

Alex bit back a retort. She didn't give a toss about clothes. 'Other than your interest in fashion I still don't know why this painting in particular interests you.'

'It may sound absurdly sentimental, but I want *Lost Love* to go to a good home,' she said. 'Somewhere it can be appreciated by someone who truly cares.' This man obviously was either secretive about his passions, or an unfeeling, obsessive collector, impatient to conclude the deal, she decided looking at his impassive face. But she, like any good gambler, needed to play a good hand to seal the deal and lead the conversation towards what she wanted to know.

'For this reason I need to understand why you want to buy the painting so desperately,' she said. 'If I'm honest, my preference is for it to remain on permanent public display so that others, regardless of whether they have money or not, may enjoy *Lost Love*.' It wasn't untrue. Alex felt fiercely protective of the painting, something about it evoked her own deep sense of loneliness and she would rather die than see her father's painting entombed in a billionaire's vault.

'I don't analyze why I like something It either grabs me or it doesn't.' he bit.

'You misunderstand me, Mr Rossi,' she retorted. She matched his penetrating gaze, noticing a hard light flicker in his eyes telling her that something she'd said had rattled his composure. She was not the only one who could see beyond her opponent's aloof façade, slicing beyond well-cultivated masks.

'It's not a question of money. That will not influence my decision. It's a question of motivation. At the risk of repeating myself, unless you tell me why you really want the painting, you have no chance of acquiring *Lost Love*. Let me leave you in no doubt, Mr Rossi, on this matter I will not budge. Take it or leave it.'

His head jerked back almost undetectably. But Alex saw it. She knew she had just played a wild card, made a throw on the gambling table that Vitaliano, with all his wealth, had not betted on. And she had surprised him. She lifted her glass and sipped the fizzling water as he weighed her words, thankful that, unlike her thundering heart, this time her hands were steady.

A faint sardonic smile curved his sensuous lips. 'Perhaps, "Miss Why," you can tell me *why* you're so determined to kill this deal?'

Alex felt her face blanche. 'I'm afraid the information is confidential.'

Vitaliano sat back down, and regarded her with curiosity behind guarded green eyes. He pressed the corners of the napkin to his mouth, then placed it on the table. 'It seems our talks have reached a stale mate.' He pushed back his chair and folded the napkin with methodical precision into a steeple and placed it on the table between them.

'Allow me to apologize.' he said, rubbing his face as though erasing a memory. 'I've rushed you. It seems, Miss Spencer that with more time we may understand each other's motives a little better. Until then, as a sign of good faith, I'd appreciate it if the painting was withdrawn from the exhibition for the next twenty-four hours.'

The request struck Alex as unusual. First the incredible offer that had forced Clive Gacos' hand last night; then, the insistence on meeting with her as early as possible. Now, he was playing for time. Just why, when the painting was not listed for sale, did Vitali Rossi want the painting out of the gallery so badly? The answer shot from Alex's mind.

He wanted it hidden!

He couldn't stand to have it on public exhibition. That was his motivation. It wasn't so much a need to possess, but an urgent need to remove it from public scrutiny. He had revealed his hand without realizing. Yet there was still the all-elusive, "Why?"

'I'm sorry, Mr Rossi,' she said, 'But I can't do that. Not unless you tell me why you want it withdrawn.' Alex kept her voice calm and unemotional, but the rush pounded through her now. Finally, within her grasp—the truth. 'I demand exclusivity.'

'I'm afraid it's not good enough,' Alex insisted.

He shook his head in an exasperated fashion, and then

looked up as the group of Korean's pressed against the table, pushing their camera at Vitaliano expectantly. Throwing Alex a derisive look he rose to his feet. Alex found herself smiling as she watched him tousle the hair of a young boy, then scoop him up against his powerful chest and place the child in his mother's arms. He took the camera and waited patiently while the group assembled for a photo.

'Say "*Kiwi*",' he commanded, pulling silly faces at them to break through their stiff, over-posed facades. If there was a sexier sound than the husky Italian timbre of his voice she'd never heard it.

What a contradiction he was, she mused as the group left the restaurant, and Vitaliano sat back down. One minute, ruthlessly driven, the next charmingly disarming, then adoringly humorous and sentimental. But who was he really? What secrets did he hide? What lengths would he go to conceal the truth?

His brows furrowed. 'I give you my reasons. You won't accept them. What more do you want? Silence swelled between them, then he turned to her and gave her an indulgent smile. 'Perhaps we got off on the wrong foot.' He said, shifting tack. 'I can't help but wonder if I offended you at the gallery last night?'

The unexpected reference threw Alex into confusion. 'Offended me? Absolutely not.' she answered weakly.

His eyes narrowed with a laser-like intensity. 'I realize these sorts of negotiations can be stressful.' He clicked his fingers in the air, and summoned the waiter. 'Champagne with lunch might loosen things up.'

Lubricate her into compliance more like, she thought as he asked for a bottle of the restaurant's most expensive Champagne. When he turned back to Alex, his green eyes glittered with a sea of suggestive possibilities.

'Please, call me Vitiali.' He regarded her with an amusing expression for several moments. 'You really are tantalizingly beautiful. But I dare say you've been told that many times.'

Beautiful? Nope, she could categorically swear it was a term that was never applied to her. Who did he think he was kidding? Did he seriously think she was the sort of woman her could schmooze with champagne and gratuitous charm into compliance? No doubt with his combination of scorching looks and blistering wealth he was used to getting his way. But if he thought she could be won over by a bit of disingenuous seduction, he was wrong.

'The real beauty, Mr Rossi,' she said deciding to keep her distance from him by keeping to the formality of using his surname, 'and the one I can't help but wonder if you find more interesting than me, is the woman in the painting.'

6

His eyes narrowed, but not before she saw a flash of fire blister across them. Anger? Fear? Whatever it was it disappeared behind a shield of feigned nonchalance 'Si. You are very perceptive. I admire that in a woman. I find it quite intriguing the way a random face has been integrated with the background. An artistic tour-de-force.' he said smoothly.

Too smoothly.

'I place a high value on originality,' he said, regarding her with far too hypnotic eyes. 'I've never seen anything like it. That's one of the reasons I wanted to buy it,' he added pointedly. 'So unlike any of Jimmie Gold's many other works.'

Alex knew this was true, but he was still hiding something. And now, more than ever, she knew discovering the woman whose likeness her father has immortalized on canvas held the key to discovering her past.

Effervescent bubbles caught the light as the champagne arrived and was poured into glasses. Vitali Rossi lifted his in a toast. 'To a better understanding between us,' he said with a smile that sent bubbles fizzing in her traitorous heart.

He was do damned, annoyingly and magnetically attractive. Alex struggled to fend off his strongly masculine sex appeal. She could not afford to let him get to her. Nor did she need a waste-of-time fling. Besides, she knew better than anyone the person inside was more important than an attractive exterior.

Determined to keep her mind clear, she took only the smallest sip of champagne. Even so the tiny sparkles glittering from the glass sent her mind spinning. Or was it because the revolving restaurant had just completed its 360-degree spin, bringing them directly in front of Rangitoto Island? Whatever it was she was grateful when their dessert was served immediately afterwards.

She reviewed the situation as she tapped her spoon on her desert and broke through the hard glaze of caramelized custard. Vitali Rossi was not going to be trapped into saying anything he didn't want to say. He was too sharp, too clever, and far too guarded to allow himself to be led beyond where he wanted to go.

But she had discovered something.

He wanted the painting out of the exhibition.

It couldn't be the scene of The Remarkables that concerned him so much. It had to be the woman's face. And that meant it was recognizable. Not only recognizable, but it was of some very real and urgent significance to him that was not be recognized by anyone else.

Why else would he have said the woman was random? Now that she knew who he was, Alex figured it would be easier to find out who the woman was and what link she had to her father. But was the mysterious woman alive and would she be any more forthcoming than Vitaliano Rossi?

'How long have you owned the painting?' he asked.

She glanced up sharply. But there was only a mildly quizzical look on his face. 'Not long.'

'I noticed in the catalogue that the artist died last year. Did you acquire the painting before or after his death?'

'After,' Alex answered softly, her voice catching as she spoke. Was it time now to reveal that the artist was her father? The information was so deeply personal she rarely spoke of it, and sharing it now with a virtual stranger didn't feel natural. No one in her family ever listened to her, so why would he? Besides she wasn't sure if that information would draw more openness from Vitali Rossi, or close him tighter. Somehow it seemed more poignant, more pertinent, more prudent to keep her thoughts private. It made her less vulnerable.

'Then you haven't had it very long,' he commented, and again Alex sensed his satisfaction in her reply. The artist was dead, and his secrets buried with him. That was what Vitali Rossi thought. More importantly, she sensed, it's what he needed, desired, wanted to be true. If she jolted him now with her relationship to Jimmie Goldie, it might thrust him out of his self-satisfaction, but it wouldn't take him long to ascertain her ignorance on the all-important meaning of the painting.

'No, not long,' she prevaricated. 'But I'm not inclined to let it go—if that's what you're getting at. It has...a personal value...to me.' Alex studied him carefully as she added. 'I wondered if perhaps it had a personal significance to you also—over and above collecting.'

He pasted an indulgent smile on his lips. 'I only saw it for the first time last night, Miss Spencer. *I want it.* That's as personal as I ever feel about anything.'

'I see,' she murmured, and went on eating, He wasn't

going to crack. She had to apply more pressure, and there was only one way to do that.

She didn't drink any more champagne. She noticed he didn't touch his glass either. He didn't return to the subject of the painting. He asked her how much she had seen of New Zealand, what she liked and disliked—a pleasantly innocuous conversation peppered by a flattering interest in her. Alex didn't believe in that interest for a moment. She merely played along with it until lunch was over. The whole thing was going nowhere. She needed to cut out now or she would never find out what she wanted. It was a big dead-end. She stood up and offered her hand.

'It's been fascinating meeting you, Mr Rossi. Thank you for your time.'

His nostrils flared as he rose from his chair, a tight, wary look flashing across his face as he took her hand. He held it firmly. 'A pleasure, Miss Spencer. I assume you'll be instructing your agent to go ahead with the deal.'

'I'm sorry.' She pasted a blank expression on her face, masking her fear that he may simply shrug and walk away. 'I've decided not to sell.'

But she needn't have worried. He was hooked all right! His fingers almost crushed hers. A bitter cynicism hardened his eyes. 'I don't like games and I like being played with even less. If it's more money you want, you have only to name your price.'

She held his gaze steadily, without so much of a flicker of movement on her face. 'Mr Rossi, I learnt to live without people and their money a long time ago. Now, if you would please release my hand we can both get on with our lives.'

His fingers locked around her hand like manacles then let go. 'Why did you agree to meet me at all?' he growled. His eyes flashed dangerously and his mouth hardened into a rigid line. He looked like a volcano on the cusp of eruption. Yet she knew he was a man who never ceded control.

Alex didn't flinch. 'To discuss the painting, as we agreed.' she answered with nonchalant, calm, logic. 'I'm afraid, Mr Rossi, you've left me unsatisfied. I'm no closer to learning the real reason you want *Lost Love*. Should you decide to enlighten me—*emphasis on enlightenment*—you know how to contact me. The deadline is close of day today. I do hate to leave matters hanging.'

Her legs trembling and her stomach churning, Alex picked up her bag. 'Thank you for taking the trouble to meet with me personally.'

She marched toward the lift, wanting to avoid the escalating conflict and anxious to end the encounter before he unleashed his full wrath.

Undoubtedly failing to get what he wanted was a totally foreign experience. Alex could not help grinning to herself over that little triumph. It lent a heady exhilaration to every step. He had dismissed her last night. She had well and truly returned the compliment. They were even.

But why didn't she feel even more triumphant?

Her hand trembled as she pushed the button. As the door sprung open she stepped into it quickly, worried he may follow her. The last thing she wanted was to be locked into a confined space with him again. Who knows what tactics he would deploy to try and weaken her resolve. The doors closed sharply, but she had one brief view of Vitaliano Rossi before he was shut out.

Smoldering eyes surveyed her. He hadn't moved. And he didn't look the least bit defeated. In fact, Alex felt a most discomfiting sensation of danger, as if she had aroused a wild warrior that would not rest until he had tasted her defeat. Whether it was the painting he wanted or the woman that possessed it, she didn't know. And she wasn't about to hang around to find out.

She tried to shrug off the feelings of foreboding as the lift descended to street-level, but she was forcefully reminded her first impressions of him last night—a man who let nothing stand in his way.

Her heart pounded as she walked quickly through the foyer and asked the doorman to hail a taxi, anxious to get away fast.

'Where to?' he asked.

The door closed, the doorman already stepping back out of hearing range. 'The waterfront,' she said breathlessly

A ferry ride on Auckland Harbour seemed like a good way to calm her shattered nerves. Any ferry would do. So long as she was safely out of reach. Who knows how he would now react. What she did know is that for the first time in her life she was playing with danger.

And it was intoxicating.

7

———

*T*hink *possible blackmailing gold-digger.* Vitaliano clenched the sides of his iPhone in his left hand and with a firm finger scrolled through the photographs. He lifted his hand from the screen as though the images of Alexandra Spencer burned his fingertips. The shots taken by his private investigator had just been emailed through, and he bent his head to study them more intensely. He caught his breath as he took in the eclectic array of images of her. In all of them she had wild tumbles of irresistible curls, crumpled clothes that had probably never seen an iron. And she frequently had a camera in her hand—all set in a variety of foreign settings. Who was she really? What was her true essence?

In the photos, she'd looked innocent and naïve, albeit slightly disheveled. Whereas in the flesh, the overwhelming impression was of scintillating elegance, sensual refinement and freshness emphasized by provocatively full lips, sculptured cheekbones and wide dazzlingly blue feline eyes.

Had she already played him, feigning her fear of heights, knowing full well who he was, determined to what she wanted? If so she had made her first move with tantalizing skill, managing to look both innocent and seductive, her body fluttering in vulnerability, seeking his protective embrace. But now that he knew that she was the one who possessed the painting there was every possibility that her sensual, innocent vulnerability was a façade. A well-honed lie. Why else would she be so secretive?

Oh, she was good. But she would soon learn that he was better.

Beautiful, sexy and twenty-five-years old, there was every possibility Alexandra Spencer had decided on a career as an extortionist. If he had to throw more money at her to possess the painting and hide it from prying public eyes, he would. Even though it would go against his principles, he would do it to protect his family from scandal.

Ignoring an unwelcome itch of desire, he focused on the photos again with the keen brain and ferocious concentration which had propelled his luxury jewelry emporium into Europe's most exclusive brand. Only with him at the helm had the remote Central Otago gold mine in New Zealand transformed into one of the world's largest and most desirable suppliers of gold.

As he studied the photos again, for a moment he was transfixed by a feral response to the way the sunlight in one of the images, with The Great Sphinx of Egypt in the distance, summoned gold flames from her rippling blonde hair. Although tall like the statuesque models he fleetingly dated, she was built on more voluptuous lines, and her skin gleamed alabaster, rather than horrid sun-bed gold.

Vitaliano liked a girl with curves in all the womanly places, including rounded soft breasts he could cup in his hands, enjoying their sensuous fullness. Oh, she was a beauty all right—even if she didn't seem aware of it, he thought recalling the delectable blush that warmed her face when he'd complimented her. But this artful coyness was no doubt another of her tricks.

His mood darkening, Vitaliano pressed the phone to his ear when the call he'd been waiting for finally arrived, 'Well?' he demanded.

'The American's are very tight-lipped,' the investigator he'd employed said wearily. 'Nobody I talked to was at all forthcoming.'

Vitali's brows shot up. 'I thought they ate gossip with The New York Times and their bagels.'

'Her mother was extremely protective of her. Dare I say...secretive.'

Secretive.

Vitali recalled how she had lifted her glass to her mouth, looking as innocent as a female panther sipping water beside a lake of gazelles. Alarmed by the pagan hunger stirring from its three-year self-imposed hiatus he ruthlessly bent his attention to the investigator.

'So, what you are telling me, Mr. Berclossi is that despite me paying you considerably more than your normal fee, you have come up with nothing. *Niente. Nulla. Zero.*'

'Perhaps with more time...' he protested.

Vitali glanced at his oversized gold Rolex. 'More time, Mr. Berclossi is something you don't have.' Annoyance grated his throat. He'd already paid him three times what the job was worth. It was a bitter confirmation of what he already knew—the deeper your pockets, the more they tried to mine your gold.

Trust no one.

If he wanted a job done expertly he had to do it alone. Fending for himself in boarding school in London where he was dumped as a young boy, had taught him self-sufficiency, and this was his only trust-worthy companion.

Vitali glanced down at the street below, his eyes narrowing with the predatory precision of a falcon as Alex, "the mystery woman", tumbled into a waiting cab at the foot of the Sky Tower, and wondered how best to play his strategy. Whatever happened she must never learn the real reason he wanted the painting destroyed.

Ignoring an unwelcome kick of desire, he focused on her with the keen brain and critical eye that had propelled his gemstone consortium onto the world stage. An involuntary smile tugged at the corners of his lips as Alex wound the window of the cab down and looked directly at him as though scenting his scheme.

Droning in his ear like the distant engine of a helicopter hovering through the skies, the investigator's voice punctured his thoughts.

'I did discover something,' the private-eye said, his voice aching for Vitaliano's approval. 'She's super smart. Her mother did make quite a point about her academic achievements. Although I was left with the distinct impression she regretted that her daughter did not make the most of her opportunities.'

So, that was it. Maybe she hoped to force that opportunity by extracting money from a total stranger, Vitali thought cynically. He bit down on his jaw, summoning the ragged remnants of his self-control. It would take more than a seasoned provocateur to tempt him to empty his pockets of his considerable wealth. Alexandra Spencer would quickly find out that Vitali Rossi wasn't going to be her ticket to a better life.

One way or another he would acquire *Lost Love*.

Outraged and somewhat bewildered by her refusal to

accept the staggering sum he had offered, he took pleasure in knowing she would quickly find herself outplayed. Of all the forms of deceit, blackmail was the most despicable.

Tension jack-knifed through his body as he glanced down at a photo of Alex at a place he immediately recognized as his ancestral home *Isola Bella*, near Milan in Lago Maggiore. Surrounded by the beautiful, world acclaimed garden, like Eve, her face beckoned with beguiling seductiveness. Two could play her game. He would take her to the edge and find out just how far she would go to win her little ruse. And while he was immersing himself in her sensual pleasures he'd find out just how much she already knew about his family.

8

———

Alex strolled along the quay checking ferry destinations and timetables. She glanced at her watch. The ferry to Waiheke Island was leaving in five minutes. Impulsively she made her decision. She purchased her ticket and dashed on board. She would distract herself by taking some photos and think about penning a travel article.

The trip across the harbor was magical. The ferry went at a snail's pace slowing her quaking heart. She sat on the top deck under the azure sky and inhaled the fresh sea air, sighing with relief as the imposing spire of Auckland's sky tower gradually receded into the distance.

Alex managed to push Vitali Rossi out of her mind for a while as her eyes absorbed the gentle blue of the sea. Pretty yachts, their white sails splayed by the warm breeze, glided by like swans. Swans mate for life, she recalled. Would she ever meet a man she trusted enough to love her forever? A man who would accept her for who she was—independent, strong-willed, obsessive. She pushed the silly romantic notion firmly aside. She liked her independence. The last things she needed were the games, the drama, the wondering—the heartbreak.

Vitali Rossi's words rippled into her mind—"*You are tantalizingly beautiful.*" Did he truly believe that? She never thought of herself as beautiful. Her mother often criticized that Alex's skin was flawless now that those "hideous scars had been lasered." Her face was now perfect, but never had she, nor anyone else said she was beautiful. And whenever she looked in a mirror all she saw was the miracle of the skin treatment she had endured.

She swept her eyes along the battle ships as the ferry drew alongside the navy base at Devonport to pick up passengers. The steely grey battle ships instantly reminded her of Vitali Rossi, with his cold, indifferent façade, his heart impenetrable, steeled against attack. Perhaps Auckland Harbour was not such a good way to distract herself from the man she had fled.

Would Vitali be thinking of her? Of course he wouldn't. He was impervious to the hot flushes he incited, and he'd made his interests perfectly clear. The only thing he cared for was possessing the painting. He was not the kind of man who would accept defeat. He would fire all his cannons, launch indefinite rockets, rain his ammunition upon her until she submitted.

Whatever assault he planned Alex was not going to back down until she knew the truth. Vitali Rossi knew something crucial and whatever it was he was determined it remain a secret. It was obviously very, very important. Somehow she would have to extract a confession from him. But what ammunition did she have? She could tell him the truth. That it was her father who had painted *Lost Love*. But somehow she doubted that revealing her hand would prompt Vitali into lowering his defences and telling her what she wanted to know. So, that left what? To do what women in the French resistance also did—seduce him into confessing?

A gentle breeze raked through her hair as the ferry set sail from the Devonport Naval base again. Alex closed her eyes imagining as she did so that Vitali was Zephyrus, the God of Wind in one of her favorite paintings by Botticelli, *Primavera*. Her heart quickened as she surrendered to the fantasy swelling in her mind, feeling his strong, searching fingers comb her hair, lift a curl from her cheeks, and his head bend toward her, as his lips fluttered tiny kisses down her cheeks.

It had been years since a man had held her, and never had a man loved her with the fervent passion her mind now fantasized over. A fervent passion she knew instinctively that her man of steel possessed. A fervent passion locked deep in his heart. Barely detectable on the surface other than the way he had looked at her that first night they'd met at her father's exhibition—his eyes claiming her and marking her as his own.

Ridiculous. Absurd. Laughable. He wasn't her man, any more than she was his woman.

Alex opened her eyes and drew a sobering breath of air. She was being dangerously reckless. Her vivid imagination projecting upon him something that didn't exist. She didn't want to think of Vitali Rossi, or the power of his imagined attraction.

Life had taught her that self-reliance was more valuable than gold. Her heart once broken, would never be possessed. Not by someone so devoid of emotion. He could never love her.

A tiny fishing boat, dwarfed by the vastness of the ocean, bobbed in the middle of the sea. To Vitali she was just as insignificant. A tiny speck on his horizon. A woman he could overthrow and then abandon to his all-important acquisitions. He was an alchemist; capable of inciting emotions she considered buried and dead. Nevertheless, they had to be ignored. Not only ignored, but scrupulously hidden. She had no delusions. If she showed any weakness, he would exploit it mercilessly.

She drew herself upright. She would not allow him to prevent her getting what she so desperately sought. She would take control, ride at the helm and captain her ship. And Vitali Rossi would ride along beside her. No man would have control over her again. She would be his equal or nothing.

But what if...?

What If Vitali Rossi gave her the chance to be his lover?

9

———————

It was late afternoon by the time Alex got back to her hotel. The red light on the phone was flashing. She was disappointed it was only a message from Clive Gacos asking her to call. She decided not to return his call. She didn't want any hassling about the deal. While there was no word from Vitali Rossi yet, Alex felt certain he would make contact before the day was over.

She knew instinctively that the Vitali Rossi's of this world didn't take kindly to losing a deal. And certainly not this one! When his response came, the pressure would be intense, and she had to be ready to cope with it. If nothing else, she intended to earn his respect.

He rang at precisely five-thirty. Her heart fluttered at the sound of his accented testosterone-laden voice.

He commanded wasting no time in getting to the point.

'*Buona Sera* Miss Spencer. Share dinner with me tonight.'

Alex was disconcerted to find her pulse racing. Did she stimulate Vitali Rossi in the same irrational way he stimu-lated her? Two opposingly charged people fusing like chemical compounds? Perhaps this was his subtle intent—his way of disarming her with his European dominance and driven composure.

Perish the thought. This kind of thinking was decidedly dangerous. She had to focus and find out what he knew about the painting before...well, before anything else.

'Fine! There's a champagne-bar beside the restaurant—' Perhaps alcohol would ply the information from his lips.

'You barely tasted a drop this morning,' he said drily. 'Do you think it worthwhile, *mia Tesoro*?'

Mia Tesoro. His treasure. Her traitorous body thrilled to the intimate endearment, but Alex was in no doubt he was referring to the painting he was so determined to possess. 'Neither did you,' she reminded him.

His laugh was a low, throaty purr. 'One should never revisit the places where one has tasted defeat. I shall choose the venue this time. I'll call for you at seven, Miss Spencer. I look forward to meeting you again.'

Vitali hung up before she could ask where he meant to take her, but wherever it was she felt pleased—the battle lines were re-joined.

Alex took a shower and spent a long time washing her hair. She blow-dried it, then flattened her maddening curls with the straightening tongs into shiny smoothness. She looked through her limited travel wardrobe and decided on the beige lace dress. With slimming side panels in contrasting cream silk, it was made of a soft, silky, uncrushable fabric—flattering, uber-comfortable, and dressy enough to cover most social situations.

The dress included a long red sash which could be tied around the waist or hung around the hips. Alex decided it would be unwise to accentuate her feminine curves tonight, and chose to tie back her hair with it and let the ends dangle down her back. She slipped her feet into sensible nude low-heeled shoes, then applied her makeup—a light dusting of mascara and beige-pink lipstick. No jewelry. No perfume. No seduction. Tonight was strictly business. And the deadline she had imposed on Vitaliano ran out at midnight. So something had to be concluded by then.

At precisely seven o'clock a firm knock rattled her door. Alex paused to pick up her cream clutch bag, took a deep, calming breath of lavender oil and placed the scented tissue under her bra-strap and opened the door. She held her breath, catching the whoosh of air in her lungs threatening to expel through her mouth in a noisy gust.

He looked so devastatingly lead-man handsome that Alex felt as though she had been speared by one of cupid's arrows. Vitali Rossi was dressed in an immaculately tailored black dinner suit, and crisp white shirt with an emerald green tie which set off his impossible-to-resist-eyes.

It was just as well she had disciplined herself not to show any obvious reaction to people long ago, because when he smiled his devilishly handsome grin it was extremely hard to keep a straight, unresponsive face. She allowed herself a small, polite smile.

'Beige suits you, *mia cara*' he said. 'Most woman look a washout— but you,'he said, his gaze lingering over her with unabashed directness, 'You look a knock-out.'

'Thank you,' she whispered, her nerves in tangled knots.

He held out his arm, and after a brief hesitation Alex took it and they walked down the corridor to the lifts. Beneath the smooth, silky fibre of his jacket-sleeve his muscled forearm was granite-hard. Alex noticed that the top of her head was level with his mouth. Which put him a couple of inches taller than six feet.

'You didn't say where we were going for dinner,' she

remarked questioningly as they rode down the hotel lifts to street-level.

His mouth quirked teasingly. 'We're not. I decided on somewhere uniquely special. I think you owe me one surprise.'

Owe him one surprise? Once again he was talking in riddles, but Alex decided to play his game of puzzles. His elegant suit suggested a high-class private eating establishment so she decided she had no need to worry about being alone with him. Besides, she had her credit card in her purse for a taxi if she wanted to leave.

She was surprised to see he had not driven a car. Instead a very sleek panther-black limo pulled up to the curb. Instead of stating a destination, Vitali settled back beside her claiming her attention with conversation.

'Did you have a pleasant day?' he asked in the deep velvety voice that caressed every cell of her body.

'Yes. Very relaxing,' she replied, feeling anything but relaxed as his leg grazed hers. She fixed her gaze on the passing cityscape, instead of the powerful expanse of his sprawling legs, noting that the limo was heading down towards the waterfront.

'Didn't you do anything exciting?'

She slanted him a dry look. 'I went for a ferry ride and looked at the battle ships.'

He gave the low, throaty laugh which was somehow very sexy. 'And what did the navy say to you, *tesoro*?'

'Something about keep your opponents close,' she said, then regretted the retort when he did not laugh. He was altogether too coolly confident and self-contained for her peace of mind.

'I don't believe in attacking anything,' he said seriously.

Alex noticed the olive color of his face blanch. 'In fact, I don't believe in killing anything. *Or anyone.*'

Something about the graveness of his tone tore through her. She felt as though she had been both given a warning and reprimanded, but decided that was silly. Besides she would not give him the power to unsettle her.

'How did you spend your day?' she asked, diverting his attention.

'I took your advice and thought about your terms.'

She darted a glance at him and found him smiling at her. 'I hope your thoughts were fruitful,' she said lightly.

'Not exactly. More like seeds in the wind. But we'll see where they blow tonight, *mia cara*'

Something glinted in his eyes and Alex once more felt a frisson of danger run down her spine. She tried to dismiss it, but it didn't help when the limo pulled up outside a majestic glass and steel skyscraper. Vitali Rossi was out and opening her door before Alex had time to ask questions. She'd barely placed her sensible shoes on the sidewalk when he grasped her elbow and steered her towards the huge glass entrance doors.

From inside a security guard moved to unlock them and hold one open. 'Good evening, Mr Rossi,' he greeted politely.

'*Grazie*, Daniel. *Buona sera*,' Vitali returned, leading Alex to a lift which he opened with his voice activated command.

Alex didn't want to step inside when the doors opened, yet she couldn't afford to show hesitation. He would take it as weakness. There was only one button to press, level 33, and at Vitali Rossi's command the lift sped upwards. Either they were going a to a very exclusive night-spot at the top of the building, or she was being hijacked Alex decided, and did her utmost to keep calm.

She had to get her mind steeled to handle this encounter to the best of her ability. But fear was mounting in her. There was no easy smile softening the determined set of his mouth now. She had no idea how Vitali Rossi was going to open the assault, but he obviously had something on his mind.

When she was ushered into a luxurious penthouse apartment with expansive open plan living and floor-to-ceiling windows with panoramic 180 degree views of Auckland Harbour Alex felt exposed.

And stupid.

The wolf had brought her straight to his den, and she, fool that she was, now walked right into his trap.

Of course he wouldn't want other people around. This way he could control the progress of their negotiations. Assuming of course that was his intent. Alex felt a discomforting surge of heat tingle over her skin. Perhaps he intended to seduce her instead. Her response to it was obvious. She had to display complete unconcern.

'What a beautiful place!' she said, moving across the spacious lounge-room to the windows. 'You certainly do yourself proud.' He was a collector, she noted taking in the apartments crisp, clean interior—the hard edge to the stark-white walls softened only by his art collection.

He collects women as he collects paintings. Uses them as he pleases and then moves onto the next acquisition. On that point Alex was certain, yet despite her discomfort, she couldn't help wondering what it would be like to be taken by such a man. To feel the raw power of his body moving over her, surging inside her, touching her in secret, intimate places no one else had discovered. A hot shiver snaked through her.

'You have a formidable collection,' she said, hoping he didn't notice the hot flush crawling up her neck.

'I work very hard for what I have, Miss Spencer,' He said, a sharp edge to his voice. 'It would be extremely wise of you not to overlook that factor in your calculations.'

Alex slanted him a mocking look. 'Work is the arena of life to men like you, Mr Rossi. No, I didn't overlook that,' she added quietly, and turned her gaze back to the view. 'I wonder how often you stop to enjoy what you have?'

He was reflected quite clearly in the window and Alex watched him surreptitiously. He stood his back so rigid she could almost detect the force of his control. What on earth was rattling him?

The muscles along his jawline tightened.

Alex smiled to herself. Body language could be very revealing, particularly when a person thought himself unobserved. She sensed that whatever he said next would be very important, and she concentrated hard on listening to every nuance of meaning in his words.

'The point in question is...what are you after? What do you want?' He bit out the words, still grimly controlling himself.

Alex didn't reply. There was something else on his mind...something he was almost bursting to say...and she wanted him to say it. Yet when it came, what he said was so surprising that she would never have been prepared for it. His mouth curled and he delivered the words with hard, stinging mockery. 'And why the deception?'

'Let's go straight to the heart of the matter, Miss Spencer. Only it's not Miss Spencer, is it? It's Miss Carr. The daughter of Jimmie Goldie—or should I say, Ted Carr.'

10

Alex felt a hot flush of anxiety. It was such a direct hit, it rendered her defenceless. He had taken the surprise element from her and used it himself, accusing her of the thing she detested most—untruthfulness, but that needn't work against her. Not if she kept her wits. She turned slowly keeping her blue eyes clear and steady.

'You have been busy—I'm impressed...to find that out in one day.' She almost added that it had taken her a lifetime to get that critical piece of information, but she held her tongue, hoping to hear what it meant to him.

'It wasn't too difficult to prise the information from Clive Gacos.' His grim expression was mercilessly hard. 'Money is a powerful lubricant. You should have given him clearer instructions to keep your real identity a secret.'

She shrugged. 'There was no point to it. I was going to tell you anyway. I have nothing to hide. Sooner or later.' *I wonder if the same can be said for you?*

'Of course you were,' he said, sardonically, 'now that I have unmasked your deceit. You must have been pleased with yourself last night at the opening when you lured me into your trap. It was a brilliant strategy and perfectly executed. And this morning—oh, that little encounter in the elevator—sheer brilliance. You dragged me right in. But you're not an innocent maiden in need of rescue are you? Tonight...' His eyes gleamed with unrelenting satisfaction. 'Tonight we are going to get this thing settled. One way or another. Once and for all. Until death do we part!'

He was talking in riddles. Although she had hoped the painting would bring something to light about her father's past, Vitali's reaction was impossible to read, and hinted at the complexity of the issues involved. Something highly important. Somehow she had to keep provoking him to do the talking.

'My name *is* Spencer. I was legally adopted by my mother's second husband. But my real father was Ted Carr.' The solemnity of her tone, drew Vitali's eyes to her. She gave him a flat smile. 'I'm not averse to getting everything settled tonight,' she said lightly. It would suit me very well to resolve it for eternity.'

'Then perhaps we're thinking along the same lines.'

'Mmm...perhaps,' she said non-committally, then with cool deliberation she moved her gaze to the paintings on the wall behind him.

'You have a fine taste in art,' she commented, noticing with interest that they all appeared to portray the Central Otago region of New Zealand. But not one of them was a portrait. She felt a little stab of disappointment. Perhaps it was true, the only reason he wanted the portrait was to diversify and add *Lost Love*, with the woman's face embedded in the rocks, to his collection of South Island landscapes.

She knew only too well the compulsive power of passion and obsessiveness. Her own passion to know who she really was, and her obsessive quest to discover the truth had lead her on this mad chase across the world. Alex could think of nothing she wouldn't do to get what she wanted. She sensed Vitali was the same. What he wanted he purchased. He'd said so himself.

'Are they yours? Or do you rent them?' she asked. When he didn't answer she turned her gaze back to him, one eyebrow lifted inquiringly. It wasn't beyond the realms of possibility, but she doubted that he was like her mother's New York friends who cared more about the pretense of claiming to own the works, than the value of the paintings themselves. She wanted to see if her provocation would stir an uncontrolled response.

His green eyes glittered at her in mocking appreciation.

She stirred a response all right, but it wasn't what she had expected. He walked slowly towards her, each step testing her composure. In that heated moment Alex knew with paralyzing awareness what it felt to be an animal pinned by the innate power of another clearly intent on tasting all she had to offer.

She should have stepped back, run even, but she could not tear her eyes from his. Her heart was racing so fast she thought it might explode. He may manipulate her to get what he wanted, but he wouldn't threaten her physically, she reasoned frantically, gripping the stem of the champagne glass. That would be beneath his pride.

He stopped a bare half-pace away from her. His breath fanned her eyelids as he lifted his hand to her face in a gentle movement. He cradled her cheek into the warm hardness of his palm. He seemed inordinately aware of her—even the infinitesimal nod of her head as he spoke softly, his words almost as hypnotic as his actions.

'It's not that I don't appreciate what you've been through.

I do.' His softly spoken words were a million times more disturbing than the dangerous glint in his eyes. 'I even have a certain grudging admiration for the way you've gone about luring me into your web. You're a brilliant strategist, a determined opponent, an intelligent and beautiful woman. For these reasons I'm prepared to reach a compromise. There is always a compromise to be reached with people like you and me, isn't there? Give us what we want and no one gets hurt, am I right?'

What was he talking about? Was he serious, or was he playing with her, intent on piercing her resolve by any means possible? Whatever he was hiding he clearly intended on using every means at his disposal to prevent the truth he held secret from being revealed. But what did it have to do with her? Alex stepped back. And, as if he read the skepticism that dampened the power he was exerting, the glitter in his eyes grew taunting.

'Perhaps the compromise may be in both our interests,' he said in a mocking challenge. There was a touch of steel in his voice now.

It was an act of sheer will-power to strip the passion from her voice and force it into an icy, crisp tone. 'And what interests might these be, Mr. Rossi?'

'To mix business with pleasure.'

'You may wish to kiss me but I have absolutely no intention of kissing you back. I never mix business with pleasure,' she said, swallowing back her nerves. Her mouth was as dry as sandpaper. She gulped down the rest of her champagne.

'Really?' He laughed, even though Alex saw nothing amusing in their situation. 'You're very difficult to read, Alexandra. And your self-restraint is admirable. I thought by now you might have tried to seduce me into some sort of confession, thrown your arms around my neck and tried to kiss me senseless, or perhaps feigned a dizzy spell in the hope that I might carry you to my bed. Clearly I will have to take the lead.'

The gall of the man. While she may have fantasized what it would be like to be taken by him, she would rather die than submit to his arrogant presumption.

He was trying to unsettle her. But as his eyes grew darker, she found the temptation of his sensuous lips inexplicably harder to resist. She fought to restrain a quiver of desire threatening to render her compliant.

'As you've said, I'm a brilliant strategist, and I can honestly say that I'm afraid seducing you or throwing myself into your arms, never entered my mind,' she lied.

The low laugh graveled from his throat as his firm fingertips grazed over her lips to her chin, leaving a trace of shivery sensation in their wake. Again, it took an enormous concentration of will-power for Alexandra to keep absolutely still. At least on the outside. She had no control whatsoever over the adrenaline lapping around her body.

Her stoic effort was rewarded by the admiration that crept into his eyes. She felt almost dizzy with exultation at this unconcealed evidence of respect in such a formidable opponent.

'*Perfecto*,' he said enigmatically as her eyes ran the length of her body as though he was appraising a fine filly he would lead to stud. 'You'll do just fine.'

She sensed she had won a victory, that he conceded something important, but what it was she had no idea. Nevertheless, the more morsels of information he fed her, the more intriguing and tantalizing the mystery became. Alex silently vowed not to give her position away, no matter what temptation he threw. All she had to do was wait, and eventually she would find out just what winning entailed.

'You'll do fine too,' she said, trailing her gaze along the starkly moulded contours of his face. She hoped that matching his move would be met with further revelation.

Something decidedly untamed and dangerous lit his eyes for a fleeting second, sending her pulse soaring. 'Let's conclude the arrangements,' he withdrew a pace and laced his fingers through hers, guiding her over to one of the black leather sofas arranged around a low glass coffee table. She glanced at the tray of hors-d'oeuvres, two very elegant glasses, and an embossed silver ice-bucket which was chilling a bottle of champagne. He said nothing until he had poured the wine and placed a glass in her hand.

'To our relationship.'

'To our relationship,' she said, bringing her flute to meet his. Relieved that she had passed his little flirtation test, she sank into the couch and waited for him to finally tell her all she needed to know about the painting.

He waved an invitation for her to help herself to the *aperitivo*.

'I trust you like oysters. I've had them flown up from Bluff especially. I prefer my food fresh.'

'I love sea food.' Alex murmured. She carefully pieced the oyster with a toothpick and lifted it to her mouth, wondering as she did whether Vitali had chosen them for their renown powers as an aphrodisiac.

He settled on the sofa opposite and sipped his glass of champagne, his eyes boring into her with unwavering intensity. 'You are gambling, you know,' he drawled. 'I don't believe I have any liability in this matter. It may not be worth your while to go on with what you have started.'

Once again Alex didn't know what he was talking about. 'Mmmm...' she murmured as the oyster slid down her throat. 'I realize there are no guarantees, but if you don't gamble you can't be in to win, and I never bet more than I can afford to lose. I think we will find it's worth both our whiles,' she offered, hoping the comment fitted well enough.

'Why not quit while you can—just walk away with a clear five million?' he retorted.

Alex shook her head. 'For one thing, I'm not a quitter. I play to win. Secondly, while for most people five million dollars is a dream, I can't accept your money. There's an issue of trust involved—a trust I mean to keep, however stupid it may appear to anyone else.'

'It's a commendable virtue,' he said, his critical gaze softening. 'The most important thing in life, certainly, is loyalty.'

Was he complimenting her again? It was easier to keep her distance when he was being an arrogant sod. 'My word is important to me,' Alex said, 'and once given I never go back. Family is important to me. You don't sell the jewels.'

'How refreshingly sweet.' His mouth took on a cynical twist. 'Family is important to me also—I will do everything in my power to protect those important to me.' Vitali's distinctly hostile tone suggested swift, merciless retribution from those that trespassed against those close to him. Alex found herself wishing her man of steel was her protector.

Alex nodded her agreement.'Fine,' she said. 'It seems once again we have reached a stalemate. You have something I want, and I have something you need. But I won't propose. Not again. You can be the one to make the first move. I won't leave you dangling in suspense. Propose,' he said, 'And I'll accept. You have my word.'

Alex's mind raced, searching for answers. She didn't know what to propose. She couldn't ask for more money— she'd already told him money wasn't her motivation. What sort of proposition would it take to extract the truth from this man? She picked up her glass of champagne and sipped it as she mulled over the problem. The only solution to the impasse was not to propose anything at all.

Her eyes flicked up to meet his in a bold challenge. 'I'm a feminist. You're the man. You propose. And I'll think about it.'

Her response seemed to take his breath away. 'You're very willful,' he bit out. 'Are you always so singularly determined?'

'In this particular matter, yes!' Alex said confidently, hoping that whatever he intended to propose would be something within her influence to accept. She could raise some cash if she needed—assuming it was money he wanted from her. But why would someone so wealthy as Vitali Rossi possibility need anything from her? Perhaps her father had left debts. Debts Vitali intended to collect? None of it made sense.

The green eyes darkened to jade as he spent several fraught moments fiercely reassessing her. 'You will take no other settlement?'

'None!' She declared, feeling a heady recklessness with this mad game of feeding him cryptic lines.

He stared at her as if he couldn't quite believe her stance. Alex put down her glass and selected a small piece of bruschetta topped with crabmeat from the tray. She ate it with relish. Being with Vitali Rossi sharpen all her senses, heightening her appetite.

'You do realize what you'll be giving up?' he demanded. His dark brows lowered in a heavy frown as though weighted by some terrible sense of foreboding.

She smiled, forcing back her uncertainty. 'I've thought everything through. It's what I want. All I've ever wanted,' she replied, not having any clue about what he was proposing, but feeling deep in her gut that any moment now would he would reveal would fill the huge void of her past with glittering light on her future.

She watched with cautious amusement as he rose to his feet, his powerful body emanating ruthless purpose. What on earth was he going to propose and why was he taking it all so seriously? She watched as he paced the length of the windows. He was worried about something. Alex whimsically decided that ignorance was bliss in this instance.

'*Che cavolo!*' He ran a jerky hand through his hair as though erasing a memory. 'And that's your final decision?'

'It seems that way.' She was getting quite good at this double-talk. It was now sliding right off the top of her head. She took another drink to show how relaxed she was and eased back across the couch. When his proposal came it was sure to be outstanding. Finally, she would have what she wanted.

'*Prego.* That's settled then. It's not ideal, but I had prepared for the worst-case scenario.' He didn't blink as his eyes probed her for some crack in her façade. She gazed back at him without batting one mascaraed eyelash.

'I thought you would have taken the money and run,' he said testily.

Alex shook her head, using silence as a prod for more elaboration.

He compressed his lips into a tight smile. 'It saves on litigation...and does away with any adverse publicity,' he muttered, as though convincing himself. 'And then there's the other matter—'

Alex kept silent, turning his words over in her mind, she wondered what legal action he thought she might have against him. She was quite certain they weren't talking about the painting any more. Maybe her father had once had a legal claim against him. He might also have a moral claim on his gold mine—that would explain Vitali's reaction. Either way, he was foreseeing bad publicity if she fought him in the courts.

In her present state of ignorance Alex knew she didn't have a hope of winning anything, but there was no doubt Vitali was taking the matter very, very seriously. The five million was testament to that.

'Are you fertile?'

Alex nearly spurted the champagne all over herself in a gigantic spray of shock.

'I don't think I could stand it if you were infertile—or frigid,' he said, watching as she brushed droplets of champagne from her chest.

Fertile? Frigid? 'What the heck does my womb or my sexuality have to do with anything?' She was right in her assessment of Italian men. They were uncouth. 'In my limited experience I can testify that were there to be any claims of frigidity it would be the fault of the man who failed to arouse my passions.'

She should have put him in his place but the words slipped out before Alex could catch them back. She had been so preoccupied with trying to figure out the situation that she had made an automatic response without stopping to analyze why Vitali had even asked such a question. She stared incomprehensibly at him.

'You've played Ice Queen all the way to this position,' he said grimly. 'So before we conclude this contract some due diligence and disclosure is required.'

Alex was still struggling to understand as he stepped around the table, took the glass of champagne from her hand, set it down, and pulled her up from the sofa. Whatever he believed she most definitely didn't feel the least bit frigid as he drew her slowly into an embrace that made her overwhelmingly aware of his hard masculinity. Heat raced around her veins. And when he bent his head to claim her lips with his, they quivered with an electric response.

He began a very controlled sensual claim on her mouth which Alex found too intoxicating to resist. As much as mixing business with pleasure might weaken her position—whatever that was —she had been wondering all day what it might feel like to kiss Vitali Rossi and she was not about to pass up the opportunity to find out.

In a limited way, of course. She forced herself not to dwell on what he might be like as a lover. She slid her arms up around his neck, deliberately encouraging a deepening of the kiss. Whether he was surprised by her initiative or not, he took immediate advantage of it. Alex didn't quite know what it was that triggered pleasant excitement into something else, but there was no more testing or conscious deliberation.

Something exploded between them—a voracious desire for more and more sensation...possession...wild erotic intimacy until there could be no separation.

But the separation when it came was brutally swift. Vitali wrenched his mouth from hers and threw back his head, his neck muscles so taunt she thought they'd snap.

She felt hurt, bewildered that he should want to end what had been happening between them. It had been the most sensational experience in her life, and her body craved for it to continue.

Her breasts were pressed so hard against him, they were deeply sensitive to the quick rise and fall of his chest. A fierce elation ran through her as she belatedly registered the unmistakable pressure of male desire against the softness of her stomach.

He was not unaffected by her! He was fighting for control!

The realization gave Alex an exhilarating sense of power. There was no way he could deny his reaction to her, so there was no triumph to be gleaned from her response to him. When he dropped his gaze to hers, she met it with a fearless pride that ceded nothing.

There was a guarded look in his eyes as he assessed the

expression in hers. His mouth quirked in amused appreciation of her challenge. 'Well, your mind might be an ice-trap, but your body is all fiery woman.'

'I'm surprised you doubted it,' she retorted mockingly, summoning more confidence than she felt. 'But it's always reassuring to hear. And I'm delighted to confirm my appreciation of your own manhood has been most whole-heartedly affirmed.'

His low, throaty laugh denied any embarrassment over the proof of his virility. 'Consider the matter settled. We will marry and you will bear my child.'

12

———

Marry?!

Blood drained from Alex's face. Her mind dived through all the conversations they'd had in a frantic grasp for enlightenment.

You...propose...and I'll accept.

When she had demanded that Vitali propose instead, she hadn't meant marriage.

But he obviously thought she had.

Marrying a man she'd known for less than three days was as ridiculous as it was compelling! Life was short. Her father's premature death had taught her that. Besides getting married had never been on her bucket list. But how could she explain that?

And while it was less a proposal and more like a demand, Vitali was waiting for her answer!

She had fantasized about being his lover...but his wife? The idea had an instant and compelling appeal, and after that kiss she wasn't going to say no. Why would she? Saying yes would force them to spend more time together. Time she needed to unlock the secrets of the painting.

Ok, so he didn't love her. But they appeared well matched—equally willful and obstinate. And they shared a passion for art. He was also outstandingly handsome, supremely successful, disarmingly charming—and he wanted her. Well not her—not yet. She was under no illusion on that count. He wanted the painting. But perhaps in time he would come to love her.

'Yes, let's marry. The sooner, the better,' she said, privately acknowledging that she had gone quite mad.

His eyes fastened onto hers, burning with the same reckless fire Alex felt consuming her. He slid his hand sensuously down her back to the base of her spine, deliberately re-igniting the passion that had flared between them. 'Is tomorrow soon enough?'he said.

Excitement fevered her mind and, before the handbrake of reason could prevail, she committed herself recklessly. 'Tomorrow is perfect.' While Alex had no idea how he would organize all the formalities in such a short-time, now that she had settled on the idea the last thing she wanted was to give him time to change his mind.

'I've got nothing else planned,' she said. Nothing else planned for the rest of my life—*until now*, she reasoned. Marrying Vitali would certainly be a change...for better or for worse. No other man had ever made her feel so sharply alive, both mentally and physically. She barely knew Vitali Rossi, but why not give it a chance? To hold a man like Vitali Rossi could be a stimulating challenge—an adventure if nothing else.

'*Bene*, I like a decisive woman. When one decides it is best to move swiftly.'

Alex felt a little quiver of uncertainty as the simmer of desire she'd detected in his eyes retreated into driving purpose.

'I'll make all the necessary arrangements.'

'That suits me,' she said with firm bravado. After all, if she came to her senses in the next 24-hours she could always disappear on the first flight back to New York.

She had come here to find out about her father and been swept into a decision that she could never have anticipated in her wildest dreams. The realization that nothing in life was permanent steadied her nerves. Vitali's proposal only confirmed whatever he was hiding it had something to do with her father and his life.

Something he was determined would not be revealed.

How she was going to find out the actual facts, she didn't know. She didn't even know why he was marrying her. Was it a marriage of convenience—a way to ensure a legitimate heir to the Rossi fortune? Revenge for some past wrong-doing? Some twisted way of resolving a longstanding family feud? Or did he think she was wielding the painting and refusing to sell it to him because she intended to blackmail him?

It was all so confusing. But some things were obvious. *He was complicated. She was complicated. It was complicated.*

Vitali wasn't accepting this marriage with any good will towards her, she was sure of that. He might find her desirable enough to bed for a while. But one way or another he was determined to beat her at the game he thought she was playing. She had a wolf by the tail at the moment. But Vitali would never be tamed.

Their marriage was bound to be a bitter relationship at first with Vitali thinking her a coldly calculating gold-digger who was out to get all she could. On the other hand, he had been doing quite a bit of calculating himself—saving on litigation that he obviously thought would cost him dearly. He couldn't consider her any more mercenary than he was. And he hadn't seemed displeased with the bargain they had struck.

That put them on level terms. And she'd proven she was his sexual equal. The thought gave Alex a surprisingly deep satisfaction. She wouldn't be a mere token female, an ornament in his life. And the painting, for whatever reason, gave her power to blow his hardened veneer apart. And she didn't care if that was fair or not at this stage. On the contrary, it excited her even more.

Vitali forged ahead, settling the practical details that their marriage entailed. Alexandra said 'yes' to everything he suggested, from an unceremonious wedding to a dismissal of any pretense of a honeymoon.

When he dictated that they fly to Gold Ridge Station the morning after their marriage, she didn't even enquire where that was, or what it was, assenting without question, even though she noticed that her agreement brought a wicked glitter to his eyes.

AFTER DINNER he took Alex back to her hotel and saw her up to her room. She had already handed him her passport to facilitate the legalities required to get married. There was nothing she could think of to hold him with her any longer. She opened the door with her swipe-card and paused, half hoping he would kiss her goodnight. His expression was stern and forbidding, which made her wonder if he was having second thoughts.

What had happened to him, she wondered, to make him such a cold, emotionally closed man.? A breach of trust? Some family drama? Or something else traumatic? Whatever it was their mutual wariness made them equals and for some reason she couldn't yet fathom earning his respect and his trust meant everything.

'Goodnight then,' she said quickly.

'One more thing Alexi—' As she stepped inside her room he grasped her arm firmly, not hard enough to hurt, but enough to send a clear message. 'That painting is to be removed from the exhibition first thing in the morning.' His eyes burned with commanding intensity. 'Get Gacos to store it. Replace it with something else. I don't care what arrangements you make, so long as it's never on public view again. Is that understood?'

The painting! Of course, she thought sadly. That was at the heart of everything. The goal that had driven Vitali into the extraordinary moves that would see them married tomorrow.

His fingers dug into her flesh and a flash of ferocity added bite to the command in his eyes. 'You're getting what you want. Now *I* get what I want. From here on in the games are over. Don't doubt that for one second.'

'I'll take care of it first thing in the morning,' she assured him unequivocally, injecting her voice with the same uber coolness expression she plastered on her face.

She had always felt guilty about putting *Lost Love* on exhibition anyhow, and now it had served its purpose. Not that she had all the answers she had been seeking, but she was quite confident that time would bring them to light. Vitali's assumption that she already knew what he was hiding was half the battle. It would all fall into place sooner or later.

Vitali looked at her searchingly as if he wasn't quite sure he could trust her word. Then he nodded and released her arm. 'You're not a fool. I'll say that for you, Alexandra Carr-Spencer.' He shook her hand in a mocking business salute.

He hesitated briefly as though fighting a compulsion. 'Until tomorrow.'

Alexandra released her breath a disappointed sigh as he strode off down the corridor. Obviously Vitali was unwilling to concede anything else to her, although she had sensed he was tempted to kiss her in that moment before turning away. Had the possibility of losing his control made him think twice? Vitali Rossi was a proud, self-contained man, but after tomorrow he would be her husband. He wouldn't turn away then.

A little smile curved Alexandra's mouth as she stepped inside her room and closed the door. Her heart danced a waltz. Tomorrow would come soon enough and she could be so much closer to discovering the truth.

13

———

'You sold it! That's fabulous' Clive Gacos's voice rose in excitement.

'No. I told you I would never sell it, Clive,' Alex said evenly, sipping a cup of green tea as she sat up in bed the following morning. 'I've decided I don't want it shown any more. I'd be grateful if you'd store it for me until further notice.'

'But— ' The tone of his voice suggested deep disappointment. 'How will I explain its absence from the exhibition?'

'The painting my father did of the *Whirinaki* rain-forest is the same size and the title *Lost Love* could apply to it equally well. If you hang that in the gallery it will fill the space and no one will be any the wiser.'

'But...I don't understand. And what of the anonymous buyer?'

Not wanting to alienate him, she injected a light tone in her reply. 'Clive, what you told Vitaliano Rossi was indiscreet.'

There was a short silence. Alex could almost hear the calculating wheels of his mind furiously whirring through all sorts of possible escapes. When he spoke it was with wary circumspection. 'How did you know about yesterday?'

'None of that matters now. But please respect my privacy in future. And to answer your question, no, I didn't sell the painting. I realize losing the commission on five million dollars must hurt, but I believe you did some exceedingly profitable business with Vitali Rossi yesterday,' Alex reminded him. 'Mr. Rossi has a fine art collection and over the years he may very well buy a lot more paintings from you. You've made an excellent contact.'

Despite of his breach of trust Alexandra smiled. Without him she would never have met her future husband and she was confident there would be no more talk about the painting. And the fine arts dealer would be a lot more discreet about her business in future. 'You will remove the painting this morning, won't you? It can't be done soon enough.'

She heard the expulsion of breath on the other end of the line. 'Of course, I'll arrange it straight away.'

'Thank you, I appreciate it. You've been very helpful. I won't forget it.'

Manipulation was such an ugly word, Alex thought as she placed the receiver down and lay back on the bed. She preferred to think of herself as a strategist. Finding the truth about her past was a game of skill. Clive Gacos was well aware he had committed a faux-pas yesterday, and he didn't want to lose her business. And she didn't want to risk alienating the only person in some way connected with her father in case this latest turn came to a dead end.

Alex heaved a sigh. Of all the dead-ends her mother's betrayal and continued stony-silence was the greatest. And while it hurt that she wouldn't tell Alex anything of her past she couldn't forgive herself if she alienated her mother and got married without telling her. It would be bad enough that the wedding wouldn't be a huge society affair in New York. But it would be much worse if somehow the media got wind of it and Alex didn't give her the courtesy of some forewarning.

The extremely short notice would make it impossible for Elizabeth and Charles Spencer to be there. Which was just as well, Alex thought gratefully. They would only come out of duty and if there was one thing Alex would no longer abide, it was pretense.

'You're marrying who?' Elizabeth Spencer stammered. Her shocked disapproval couldn't have been clearer if she had been standing right in front of her wayward daughter. 'This is ridiculous, Alexandra. You've only known him three days.'

Alex felt the muscles in her shoulders knot. 'Vitali is the most handsome-looking man you could ever imagine, Mom,' she said, offering the kind of consolation that might best appease her mother.

'So was your father,' her mother said in terse condemnation.

Her father had been handsome. That was news to Alex. He must have been extremely good looking to pass her mother's exacting standards. It would certainly explain how her mother had come to make "her mistake." And while her father's looks didn't matter to her nearly as much as what he was like as a person, it was the first slither of intimate information her mother had ever shared. Which wasn't such a surprise given that good looks were almost everything to Elizabeth Spencer.

'He's also fabulously wealthy,' she added, loading her voice with incredible excitement as though Vitali's money meant everything, when in fact she didn't judge people on whether they were rich or poor.

'New money or old money? Her mother asked, suddenly interested. 'What from?'

While nothing was ever going to change her mother's innate snobbery, Alex knew she'd scored some mother-pleasing points. 'Gold, Mother. Mountains of gold. As far as eligible bachelors go, I'd say he's probably richer then all the men in Manhattan.'

'Don't be vulgar, Alexandra.' There was a slight pause, then grudgingly, 'I suppose you could do worse. But what about Bradley?'

Alex rolled her eyes. Why did her mother never listen to her? Why did she never care what or who Alex wanted?

'Well, I suppose I should be thanking you for letting me know, Alexandra. It's so very good of you to call.' Her voice was icy with sarcasm. There was a short silence before she spoke again. 'But why the haste? Have you thought how your behavior will disparage this family?

'I'm not pregnant, Mom.' She didn't bother telling her that they hadn't slept together.

'Why aren't you getting married properly? Everyone will ask you know.'

Alex sighed. Her mother's fears were natural enough given her own fast-tracked wedding.

'Please be happy for me. Can you do that for me?'

She could see her mother's immaculately painted lips pursing together as she hissed a heavy sigh. 'I expect Charles' people can put together a dossier on this Viagra Rossi.'

"Vitali, Mom. His name is Vitali.'

'Gold you said?' She continued with frosty resignation. 'Would you be good enough to email me a photo of you both on your wedding day so that we can release the news here? It may make the society pages, but I'm not promising anything.'

'I don't think Vitali will want the publicity anyway.'

'Alexandra, I don't understand you.'

'So you keep saying. One day perhaps I'll understand myself.' Alex knew the last point would completely escape her mother.

'When are we going to meet this Rossi?'

'I'm not sure, Mother. We're flying in his private jet to Gold Ridge Station tomorrow. Once I've settled in—'

'Alexandra!' her mother interrupted. 'Where did you meet this man?' Her voice was no longer the smooth cultivated timbre of a lady of leisure but serrated with rough urgency.

'Mother, please don't worry. I know what I'm doing—'

'Oh, my god. I knew no good would come from going back. It can't be happening,' her mother's voice shuddered. 'Alex,' she said softly, 'Oh Alex I had only known your father for three hours when I...I fell head over toes in love with him. Despite everything we felt, despite the spontaneous urgency of our passions, despite the intense physical attraction—oh, my darling child, please don't make the same dreadful mistake.'

Alex fell back against the bed in shock. Her mother never called her Alex, and she most definitely never called her "my darling." Yet she couldn't recall a time where she had heard such deep, genuine caring and utter concern in her voice.

Pent up emotions pricked the back of Alex's eyes. She wiped her hand as the tears she'd promised herself she would never cry began to flow. All her life she'd never felt cared for. And now, against all odds her mother was showing her concern. And finally she was telling her something of her past. But why? What was it about marrying Vitali now that she knew his connection to Gold Ridge Station that upset her so much?

'I'm not making a mistake. I know it's quick, but perhaps you can understand after all, what it feels like to meet a man and feel he is your past and your future.'

'You won't wait?'

'No.' *I can't.*

'I...' her mother's voice quavered slightly. 'I do love you, you know. I concede I haven't been the best at showing it. But I've always wanted the best for you. You do believe that don't you?'

The lump in Alex's throat made it difficult to speak. 'Yes. Yes, of course I do,' her voice sounded like a whisper.

Maybe getting married would soften the divide and bring them closer. They had different values. Different histories. Different desires. Yet Alex knew better than anyone the importance of accepting people for who they are, not who you wanted them to be.

Her mother had done the best she could. Perhaps when she had her own daughter or son Alex could change the cycle that had nearly destroyed her family. But right now Alex had to be the change she wanted to see. To do that she must forgive.

'I love you too, Mom, and I'm grateful for the way you looked after me when I was ill and for everything you've given me. I know it wasn't easy.'

'Alexandra...' She gave a hard, obvious swallow, 'I do hope you know what you are doing.'

Alex felt her stomach clench. She took a deep breath, then steadied her voice. Her mother was who she was, she reminded herself.

'So do I,' she conceded. 'So do I.'

14

Alex sunk into the bed, relieved to have ended the call. It shouldn't have upset her, but the fluctuating emotions and the intensity of it all was exhausting. Her mother and she had begun to mend some fences but they were still worlds apart. Still, if this was the only time her mother reassured her that she cared for her daughter, beyond parading her in front of her friends, it would be a memory she'd cherish.

Her mother may never understand Alex's real motives, and even though Alex barely understood them herself, what she did know for certain was she was not marrying Vitali Rossi for his looks, nor his squillions.

Nor was she marrying him to mine him for information about her father. It was more primal than that. Something in him drew her irresistibly to meet his challenge. He had thrown the gauntlet and she would fight to the end to prove she was worthy.

Not many women could claim to marry a gold tycoon, certainly not one who they barely knew. She chuckled at the absurdity of it all and pinched herself. No, she wasn't dreaming. She really was getting married! Even if their wedding was a bad mistake, Alex couldn't imagine ever getting married again. She suspected that all other men would pale into insignificance when compared to the virile splendor of Vitali Rossi.

She reached for the bridal magazine she'd found in the hotel lobby and thumbed through the pages. Her mother had asked for a photograph, and while she could not be there to see her daughter get married one thing Alex could do was not throw rock salt into her wounds by dressing defiantly. Where once she would have relished following through on her threats of getting married in crimson, Alex could not take pleasure in shocking her mother. Not now.

But as she flicked through the pages filled with stark white gowns she began to get more and more disillusioned. Pleasing her mother was important but it was her big day, the day she never thought she'd have. Wasn't it important that she was happy too?

Then she saw the gold wedding gowns. Delight bubbled in her heart. Gold was perfect, she thought as she thumbed through the designs Not only could she depart from tradition and still be elegant and sophisticated but a sumptuous gold gown would complement her husband's business interests. Vitali and her mother were sure to be pleased.

Since she wasn't getting married until later that evening and she wouldn't be hearing from Vitali until early afternoon she had plenty of time to go in search of the perfect dress. It couldn't be just any gold gown. It couldn't be too dull, nor to bright and shiny, but something in between. Something uniquely special. Something befitting the occasion.

She folded the page so she could find them again and called the hotel reception.

'Could you please call a taxi,' she said, giving them the Auckland inner city address of the bridal salon she had seen in the magazine. 'And I'd like to make an appointment in your beauty salon. It's my wedding day,' she said, wanting to share her news with anyone who'd listen.

'WHATEVER HAPPENS you will always have your gold dress, which unlike other gowns that needed to be tucked away and stored, your gold gown could be used again and again,' the owner of the salon told her.

But Alex was already sold. Throwing away all notions of practicality she stepped back and admired herself in the mirror. The soft golden feathers of the Marchesa dress clung to her body, making the most of her curvaceous figure. She was no longer the ugly duckling of her adolescence but a beautiful swan, she thought, happily. She did a twirl, delighting in the way the blossoms embroidered on the silken tulle skirt, flaring from just below her feather lined hips, splayed around her feet in a carpet of flowers.

'I'll take it!' she bubbled merrily. She added a pair of gold sling backs sprinkled with glittering diamantés, and a pearly-gold handbag to match, and returned to the hotel exhilarated with her acquisitions.

She spread her new purchases on the bed and took a series of photos so she could take pleasure in looking at her wedding outfit again, then placed a call to Room-Service and ordered a light lunch. She doubted the butterflies flitting around in her belly would stomach much more than the lightest of meals.

She had barely put down the receiver when the phone rang again.

'Where have you been?' Vitali demanded. 'I've been ringing all morning.'

The agitation in his voice came as quite a shock. She'd thought the call would be from room service. Alex bit back her hurt and resisted the temptation to put him and his bad mood firmly in their place by reminding him that he was phoning her much earlier than they had arranged. But this was her wedding day and she wanted it to be a happy one, no matter how odd the circumstances.

'I had the painting removed from the exhibition as you requested,' she replied, matching his brusqueness.

'*Bene*,' he said, his voice softening. 'I wanted to see if you needed any help... It's important you look—'

'Everything is under control.' She said, coolly. She felt like telling him she knew how important looks were, that she'd been indoctrinated by an expert into believing that 'looks are everything', but decided against it. 'You won't be disappointed.'

His tone gathered a sardonic edge. 'I expected nothing less.'There is one other matter.'

Something in his tone told her to expect the worse. Alex braced herself.

'*My mother.*'

She slumped on the bed and shut her eyes, pressing the phone to her chest. Please God, make his mother like me. She lifted the receiver back to her ear.

'My mother is demanding to meet you.' Vitali continued.

'Naturally,' she said more brightly than she felt. Any woman capable of rearing such a head strong, dominant alpha male would be fiercely intimidating to say the least.

'She flew in from London with her husband this morning. I must warn you, Alexandra, she is a woman with high expectations. I trust the outfit is suitable.'

Alex smiled. So, that was why he was so impatient to track her down. At least he was only worried about her outfit being a disappointment. There was hope for their marriage yet.

'My mother is a demanding woman too, Vitali. I won't let you down.'

'I'm flying our head jeweler in from our atelier in Milano. I'm sure the importance of having the appropriate jewelry for a bride of gold hasn't escaped your attention,' he drawled cynically. 'He has begun designing a bespoke piece already. I'll bring him to your hotel room at three. That will allow time for any minor adjustments before the marriage at six.'

'As you wish,' she replied coolly. Jewels meant nothing to her, but clearly Vitali thought that gold was the whole point of the marriage, and if that was how he wanted to think today was not the moment to be arguing.

'Still the consummate Ice Queen,' he said derisively. 'Have you any idea how infuriatingly provocative...? No, don't bother replying. I'm sure you know exactly what you're doing.'

Alex grinned to herself as she wound up the call and abruptly disconnected. Vitali had dropped his stoic mask, revealing that he found her façade of detached control provocative. Maybe she got under his skin in the same way he got under hers.

If that was the case...well, she might be a bride of gold who wasn't easily impressed, but she would be a wife that Vitali Rossi wouldn't shrug off easily.

She picked up her iPhone and clicked the Spotify icon, then scrolled through the *Love Lost* playlist she'd created. She selected Diana Krall's *Let's Fall in Love* and put her iPhone into the dock by the bed. She picked up her dress and, pressing it to her chest, waltzed around the room.

Call her a romantic, call her overly optimistic but she would never be called a failure. Not without putting up a good fight. She would give this marriage her best shot. What if the painting had been destined to bring them together? What if they were meant for each other, she mused as she heard Room Service knock at the door and went to answer it.

She picked over the meal which the waiter had brought to her room, her inner excitement dulling her appetite. As she placed the tray outside her door, the voice of rational doubt sanctioned that her feelings of exhilarating anticipation were totally unwarranted.

Padding over to the iPhone she pushed her nagging thoughts aside, turned up the volume, took a sip of champagne and took great pleasure in getting ready for her wedding.

15

Alex was showered, her nails painted a pretty shade of champagne pink, her neck lightly perfumed with Jo Malone's Wild Roses, and dressed in her feather and tulle gold gown by eight minutes to three. All that needed to be done was to put on her princess crown with three-quarter veil, but she had decided that could wait until after the jeweler's visit.

She had coiled the thick mass of her blonde hair into a neat chignon just above the nape of her neck. Whatever jewelry Vitali had chosen could be shown off to best affect. She glanced at the time. Five minutes to three. It felt like an eternity since she had purchased her dress, returned to the hotel spa for a relaxing aromatherapy massage, and had subtle make-up applied to her eyes by a beautician.

Alex didn't normally worry about such vanities but, mindful of the photograph her mother wanted and the high expectations of the mother-in-law she had yet to meet, she wanted to look as good as she could look without over-doing it and loosing herself in a layer of cosmetic mayhem. She reapplied her pale rose lipstick and stared at the door willing that her husband-to-be would arrive early.

Her heart gave an exultant leap as right on 3'oclock a powerful knock rattled the door. It took a major effort to keep the beaming smile from her lips as Vitali's eyes ran the length of her body and gleamed with proud satisfaction.

He was immaculately dressed in a graphite grey suit which had an appropriate air of formality about it, particularly with the silver-grey satin tie poised on a crisp white linen shirt. She dragged her eyes from her husband-to-be and observed the man who accompanied him. Next to Vitali any man would look small but this man, his thin frame sheathed in a dark three-piece 'power' suit, was unusually short.

He stood with his arms crossed, surveying her speculatively through enormous round rimmed glassed which dominated his tiny round face. His slicked-back hair was completely grey, but his blue Paul Newman eyes were sharp with youthful curiosity as they appraised Alex.

'Ricardo Allegri, jeweler,' he introduced himself with an outstretched hand. 'A pleasure to meet you,' he said with a twinkling smile.

'May we come in?' Vitali asked shifting impatiently on his feet.

'Yes of course,' Alex said, her heart racing as he brushed past her. Her heart danced an exultant jig as she caught a sultry whiff of the violets adorning his lapel.

Ricardo Allegri headed straight for the ebony desk under the large mirror in her room. He set down the slim Louis-Vuitton hard-sided case he was carrying and began to open a series of brass locks. He glanced up and winked at Alex.

Vitali paused beside Alex, his green eyes alight with

mocking appreciation. 'You've won Ricardo over,' he said in a low voice. 'But then you're very good at winning, aren't you?'

'I know what it's like to be a loser. I can't say I enjoyed the experience,' she tossed back, then walked across the room to where the jeweler had opened the case.

'Do you know your ring size, Miss Spencer?'

'No, Mr Allegri. I can't say I do.' she said, careful to ensure her voice remained a nonchalant crawl. It was all terribly exciting.

'May I?' he asked, gesturing to her left hand.

He placed an assortment of plain gold bands on her third finger until he was satisfied with the fitting.

He glanced up at her ears, noting the tiny holes in her earlobes. '*Bene*. Ears are pierced,' he said turning to Vitali, '*Perfecto*.' He reached into the case and withdrew a box and handed it to him. 'The earrings,' he murmured.

The jeweler lifted out another box from his case and opened it without ceremony. Alex's incredulous gasp as he lifted an exquisitely intricate gold necklace from the satin lined box brought a delighted smile to the little man's face. 'The Rossi Circle,' he told her proudly, as she studied the glittering array of indescribably beautiful jewels he spread before her

The necklace was indeed designed as a circle, with 16 egg shaped balls of solid gold joined together from which three elegant golden droplets dangled from a splay of beaded diamonds.

'Put it on,' Vitali commanded.

Excitement intermeshed with fear. A gift so majestic, so potent would surely come with demands, expectations, conditions she could not possibly meet. Her breath clung to her lungs as she met Vitali's gaze with a steady, stony stare.

Bewilderment and outrage imprisoned her. Ever since she'd been little people had made her a subject for their pleasure, their adornment. Starting with her mother who, when Alex was three had entered her in the first of many beauty pageants. Ironically she was thankful when puberty ruptured her face making her too hideous to look at.

Dry mouthed, her face rouged with shame as though she been ordered to strip naked, she arched her neck as Vitali picked up the exquisite necklace. With confident hands he placed the necklace around her quivering chest.

His fingers slightly brushed her neck as he reached for the clasp. She suppressed a nervous gasp, steadying herself as her body trembled. The warmth of his breath on her lobes as he leant closer toward her, pretending to wrestle with the clasp, sent butterflies to her stomach—butterflies that danced recklessly, having far too much pleasure for Alex's comfort.

A slight blush heated her cheeks as Vitali studied her with unswerving intensity. Alex was physically conscious of herself more than she had ever been in her life. Conscious of the silky feathers of her wedding dress caressing her thighs. Conscious of the gold necklace nestled above her quivering breasts. Conscious of the dryness of her throat as she swallowed a melody of stirring emotions.

And she knew her green eyes were no longer clear ponds of still water. They were hot and bothered with the awakening of explosive passions.Vitali on the other hand, she reflected painfully as he stood before her, looked consummately in control.

Alex tried to regather her composure and turned her attention back to the necklace. There wasn't anything in the Spencer family vaults that could remotely match the Rossi Circle. She doubted that there was anything to match the beauty and expense of it anywhere in the world—except possibly among the English crown jewels.

It made her nervous to think about wearing it, let alone owning it! She told her mother that Vitali was fabulously wealthy, but clearly she had underestimated his worth. The necklace had to be worth tens of millions! But what she didn't know was the value Vitali put on the expectations that came with such a gift.

'Satisfied?' He gritted.

'It's very lovely,' Alex said stiffly, not giving away an inch of just how lovely she really thought it was. His mouth curled. 'It's more than lovely, it's unique, Alexi. Rarer than toucan's teeth. A gift that should leave your family in no doubt I intend to repay my debts. And the ring and the earrings have been designed to match. There won't be a woman in the world who doesn't look at you with envy.'

He lifted a hand and lightly caressed the hollow of her throat with one tantalizing finger. Alex hoped he wouldn't feel the leap in her pulse-rate.

'At least you have the rare kind of beauty that will show them off.' His finger ran slowly to her chin, tilting it slightly. His gaze dropped to her mouth.

Alex held her breath, anticipating his kiss, but then his mouth thinned grimly and his eyes flicked up again, burning into her with fierce determination. 'Priceless jewelry suits you. But then you knew that, didn't you?'

A frightening sexual heat whipped her body into tumultuous whirlpools of passion—battling with fury and pride. Vitali Rossi might wield a powerful sexuality that had the ability to drive her emotions, but he would not crack through the layers protecting her heart.

He would have to earn her trust as she would have to earn his.

Undoing the clasp and returning the necklace to the velvet pad, she said briskly, 'I never asked for these, Vitali. And I'm not an object of art to add to your collection. Like *Lost Love*, I'm not for sale.'

'Your unwillingness to take my gifts is almost convincing.' He said, darkly.

'I told you before Vitali, I'm not trying to convince you of anything. Why won't you believe me?'

He repacked the necklace in the jeweler's case which Ricardo Allegri promptly relocked. 'I assume it won't take long to finish the ring?' he asked Ricardo as he ushered the little man out the door.

'Not long at all,' Ricardo Allegri informed him confidently.

'It goes without saying you will have it doubly checked to ensure there are no imperfections,' Vitali called after Ricardo as he disappeared down the hall.

16

'I like it,' he said.

'You do?' she said, surprised at his reaction. 'Would you like to see it on?'

'Why not?' he drawled.

She was positioning it on her head when the jeweler returned. Vitali answered the door but didn't ask him in. Alex heard Vitali thank Ricardo.

'Very elegant,' he commented as he came back to her. She stood in front of him, the short veil sitting just above her shoulder.

Unable to suppress her happiness she giggled inwardly. It was like playing dress-ups, only way more fun. Just for today she was a princess and standing in front of her was a terribly handsome, albeit richer, Gregory Peck.

Their eyes met in the mirror and for one brief moment they stared at each other—strangers who were about to enter into the most intimate relationship between a man and a woman.

'Now the engagement ring,' Vitali murmured, his face

tightening as though that moment had disturbed him in some way. He opened the smaller of the two boxes the jeweler had delivered, and lifted out the engagement ring.

Alex's skin prickled with sensitivity as he slid the ring on her finger. Alex was too entranced and blinded by the dazzling brilliance of the spectacular cushion-cut yellow diamond to lament the woeful absence of romance surrounding their peculiar engagement.

THIRTY MINUTES later Alex was checked out of the hotel and they were in the private lift which serviced Vitali's penthouse apartment. The nervous flutter in Alex's stomach had nothing to do with the speedy rise to the top of the building. Vitali's tension was affecting her badly. When the lift stopped he didn't immediately step through the opened doors. He leaned forward and pressed the close-door button, then seemed to gather himself before turning to her.

'Remember you know nothing about my mother and stepfather. You have never met them before.'

She nodded. Why was he stating the obvious? She didn't even know their names! And why was his tone so serious?

Well, she summoned her muse. For today she would be Audrey Hepburn. She would play her part and she would clean up the Academies, the Bafta, and the Golden Globe for her sterling performance. 'If that's the part I am to play then I expect you to do yours, Vitali.

His eyes mocked any necessity to be reminded.

'And you can start by pretending you and I, my groom…' the words tasted like dark chocolate and berries…'are very much in love. So smile.'

His lips curved stiffly.

'Not bad, but not convincing either,' she said as he retook control and linked her arm with his in a possessive fashion. 'A bit more warmth and sparkle would be more convincing.'

'Don't you think I've given you quite enough sparkle already,' he retorted. 'But if it's more you want then I can promise you one thing for sure *mia cara*...tonight you'll know what it's like to be my wife. All I have to do is think of our night of wedded passion and no one will be in any doubt as to my feelings.'

A tidal wave of heat surged through Alex as his eyes blazed through her with furnace-explosive intent. He was going to reduce her to just another female in the arena of their married life, even if he could never achieve intimacy in any other way. It was not so much sexual desire as a blistering need to dominate her in the age-old primal way of male control and possession. And while Alex recognized all this, and part of her mind rallied against it, the rest of her was exquisitely excited by the prospect of being conquered.

A triumphant amusement glittered in his eyes as he observed the high color of her cheeks. He even smiled as he stroked her burning skin with a light finger-touch. 'Is this the warmth you said was missing, *mia cara*?' he purred, then moved his finger to the lift button to reopen the doors.

'Just look at the gold and diamonds for the sparkle you desire, but think ahead to tonight when you and I are alone, for then the spark shall become fire.' He grinned broadly as though taking pleasure in his game of words, and Alex's intense discomfort.

She plastered on a matching smile, vowing as she did so that she would out-glitter, out spark, out fox him—even if it killed her.

As they emerged from the lift and walked towards the

archway that led into the lounge-room, Alex painted on a smile that outshone all the jewelry he clearly thought would harness her to him for a lifetime of servitude. However, she wasn't prepared for the shock that hit her when they entered the room, and the couple waiting for them rose from the far side of the sofa.

It took all of Alex's considerable self-discipline, and a performance worthy of an Academy Award, to keep the smile from shattering.

It was her! *The woman in the painting.*

ALEX'S HAND flew self-consciously to her face. She brushed her cheek with her fingers, reliving momentarily the pitted crevices that although now healed still left deep scars. Would Vitali reject her if he knew she was less than perfect, a miracle not of nature but technological intervention?

'And needless to say, since we're agreed on this route to settle the issue between us, I don't want my mother to know you're Ted Carr's daughter,' Vitali stated coldly. You are Alexandra Spencer from New York, America, daughter of Elizabeth and Charles Spencer—and we leave the pain of the past in the past. *Forever.* If that's not understood, I'm paying too much...and you will have done too little for your share.'

So, there must have been pain on both sides, Alex thought. Not only on her father's. But also on his mother's. And as much as she was dying to know what, when, why and how—and hundreds of other unanswered questions— right now it wasn't important.

'As you said last night, I'm not a fool,' she reminded him, 'and I do have integrity. I intend to fulfill my duties and comply with the terms of our agreement. Don't worry. I won't renege.'

Cold green eyes searched her assessingly. 'I wouldn't have thought so,' he said coolly. 'But there certainly will be a time when we are going to find out.'

'Yes, we will,' she said with conviction.

There was no point in telling him that she never intended hurting anyone. If she ever showed any weakness or vulnerability—or warmth of any kind—he would walk right over her.

Satisfaction took the chill out of his eyes.

'I have another request.'

Alex braced herself for another unreasonable demand.

He studied his feet, then lifted his head. 'Would it...do you...' he avoided meeting her gaze, 'Do you think you could pretend to be in love with me?'

His rare show of awkward vulnerability threw Alex momentarily.

'*Me—in love with you?*' She said the words as if loving him was the last thing she would ever feel, but her gut leapt exultantly as if confirming a truth she didn't dare admit.

'It would break my mother's heart if she knew the marriage wasn't going to last.'

Forget about your mother's heart, what about mine, Alex thought as her own stomach plummeted with a thud at the words, "the marriage won't last."

'No problem,' she said cooly. She didn't want to have a failure marriage like her mother. Once committed she would see this thing through. Till death did they part.

'So long as you can return the pretense by posing for a few camera shots of wedding bliss for my mother?' she countered mockingly. 'I promise not to leak them to the paparazzi.'

His eyebrows quirked. 'Am I to believe she has no idea what you are up to?'

'Just as your mother has no clue what you are up to either. On that point we are evenly matched,' Alex retorted swiftly. Vitali's dark brows arched. 'So...we embark on a mammoth deception together.' He gave his low throaty laugh. 'At least it won't be boring.'

'Precisely,' she returned, covering her inner exhilaration with a dry smile.

Again his gaze dropped to her mouth, and fastened on her lips for several seconds. Alex fiercely hoped he would kiss her. He wanted to. She was sure of it. But he dropped his hand, picked up hers, and almost slapped the box he had been holding in his other hand on to her palm.

'The earrings. You might as well put them on now.' He left her holding them and walked over to one of the armchairs near the window. He sat down and waved a mocking invitation towards the mirror. 'Go ahead. Aren't you dying to see them sparkling on your ears?'

'Not really, Vitali,' she said quietly.

His pupils hardened. 'Wear them,' he commanded. 'I always intended to give them to my bride...'

Alex moved over to the mirror without any further argument. She was chillingly aware of him watching as he opened the box. The tear-drop earrings glittered up at her, each an amber-gold diamond, surrounded by clusters of white diamonds. They were breathtakingly gorgeous. Her hands trembled as she fastened a large fortune to each earlobe.

'You wear them well,' he said sardonically.

'I'm glad you're satisfied, 'Alex returned dispassionately.

His eyes glittered with some dangerously strong

emotion, but the moment was brief as he controlled it and nodded toward the bed. 'Is that what I think it is?'

'It's a veil.' She said, defensively. She knew it was a bit over the top, but together with the princess crown reminded her of Audrey Hepburn and she hadn't been able to resist.

17

Her face was older, but her haunting beauty unchanged...her eyes guarded as though searching for someone...remembering someone...aching for someone. Someone that was forever lost. And now those same dark, melancholic eyes clung to Alex's face as if they were seeing a specter that filled her soul with torment.

An uncomfortable silence engulfed the room momentarily, until Vitali finally spoke. 'Alexandra, this is my mother Lucrezia—'

Alex heard the faint disquiet in his voice even as he tried to project a relaxed indulgence, '—and her husband, Simon Deloitte.'

His mother's dark haunting eyes clung to Alex's face, bringing a tension to the room that no amount of faking indifference could dispel.

Simon Deloitte thrust his hand towards to Alex hoping to distract attention from his wife's distraught state of mind, but his wrist was clasped tightly by the woman standing rigidly at his side.

'*Mia Sacre Madre...*' Lucrezia whispered hoarsely, then

spoke in slow, tortured little bursts. 'There is no mistaking her. She has his blonde hair, his pale coloring—she is Ted's daughter.' she gasped as she collapsed into her husband's chest. The sensuous beauty of Lucrezia Deloitte's face tightened and twisted in unbearable distress. 'When does the punishment stop?' she cried. Her eyes filled with tears and she turned blindly to her husband for comfort.

'Will it never end?' As though drawing upon every ounce of her energy reserves, Lucrezia drew a ragged breath and turned to her son 'You've deceived us. Deceived me.' Despair bled from her words. 'Why? Why now? Why her?'

And the past that Vitali had wanted to keep suppressed was no longer dead. It was throbbing with jagged pain.... vibrantly alive in this room.

Simon's arms came around her, gently protective in his embrace. She leaned on him, an instinctive movement that had the familiarity of long practice...years of leaning...of needing and receiving support. And the huge, solid frame of the man who gave it stood firm. Whether it was compassion for his wife or a deep personal pain of his own, it was impossible to tell, but his face was also creased in suffering.

'What are you doing, Vitali?' Simon demanded quietly. His heavy-featured round face was set on a bull-neck, and his dark brows suggested that the wispy, thinning white hair had once been dark. But the soft brown eyes, hidden beneath black caterpillar brows had an intensely comforting appeal that contrasted sharply with the toughness of his exterior. Some people may have thought him ugly, but something about him communicated "protector."

'*Che cavolo!*' Vitali thundered. 'How can *Mamma* be so certain she is his daughter?'

'Ted told Luci about his first marriage when they first became lovers,' Simon said. 'The daughter, he'd given up so that she could have a full-time father. And he confided in her what that had cost him in personal agony, how it weighed on his mind heavily. His child, the daughter he had wanted, the daughter who would never be his, the daughter he would never know. He talked a lot about Alexandra.'

A gust of emotion roared through her heart, blocking the voices debating around her. Her father had wanted her. Her father had *loved her*, Alex thought dazedly. She hadn't been wrong. The realization filled her with joy, even if she still didn't know why he had never made contact. He must had done what he thought would be best.

'We hoped it was just a coincidence,' Simon said to Vitali. 'That she would be a different Alexandra Spencer from New York...' his tone was savagely rueful. 'It was blindly desperate hope,'

Lucrezia Deloitte's sobs grew louder, smashing through the barrier of shock that for the last few minutes had held Alex's body and mind rigid. 'But that's no reason for you to sacrifice yourself, Vitali,' she wailed.

Learning how her father had felt about her had been so unexpected, sweet and bitter at the same time. But the unspoken, unnamed, unresolved trauma that coiled around them all now, triggered by the truth of her identity, was so appalling, so horrific, so hurtful. And the realization that this was what Vitali had wanted to avoid...that he thought Alex had known that her father's painting could have this terrible effect...was devastating.

And worse, that his mother thought their marriage would be Vitali's ruin. His mother thought she was out to destroy her son, that Alex's sole motive was to make him pay. She had to reverse the damage she had so blithely and unwittingly done in her ignorance.

'Mr Deloitte, I'm not after what your wife thinks...' Alex

forced her feet to break free of their paralysis and moved toward the woman who was still weeping on her husband's shoulder. Alex took Lucrezia's hand in hers and gently squeezed her trembling fingers.

'Please don't cry, Mrs Deloitte. Vitali hasn't tried to deceive you on purpose. Nor have I. Neither of us knew anything about each other's past. Neither of us wanted to upset you. Please believe me. We fell in love,' she said without a second's hesitation, instinctively knowing it was the only answer that would allay Lucrezia Deloitte's fears.

'We love each other.' Alex smiled a soft reassurance, praying inwardly that Vitali would agree.

Lucrezia Deloitte's face blanched as she turned toward her son, tears streaming down her face as her eyes drowned with painful uncertainty. 'Why are you marrying her, *mia figlio*?'

Vitali's face remained unrelievedly grim.

Alex held her breath and closed her eyes tightly, hoping that the truth of their marriage would not be laid bare.

Lucrezia Deloitte shook her head in pained incredulity. 'Vitali?'

This was the point of no return and Alex fiercely willed him to continue with their charade. To continue on, despite what had just transpired was madness, but now that they had come this far she didn't want to be rejected. She didn't want to be abandoned. She didn't want to feel once again that she didn't belong—simply because she was Ted Carr's daughter. Come Hades or high water, she was going to marry Vitali Rossi. If he'd still have her.

As the silence hovered between them Alex sought desperately for something to say that would rescue her dreams. But it was up to Vitali. He had to be the one to confirm that he wanted their marriage. Pride demanded she would not drag him to the alter against his will.

'Alexi can't be blamed, mamma,' his eyes were glinting blades of fire. 'What happened in the past was not her fault.'

There was no commitment in his words, nothing to allay Alex's nor his mother's concerns. She didn't have to look at him to feel the raging tension bristling around him, suggestive of a blaze of thoughts that he fought to suppress.

Why did she have to turn up now and ruin everyone's peace?

But then he stepped forward and wrapped a strong muscled arm around her and pulled her to his side in a show of protective support. 'We didn't plan to fall in love. It just happened, didn't it *mia cara*?'

Alex nodded and fell into his embrace, grateful to be able to rely on his strength. Her heart fizzed into merry little bubbles. He was keeping his promise. He was going to marry her!

'It's true. I didn't know who Alexandra was.' Vitali continued, 'The name Spencer meant nothing.'

'I didn't know who Vitali was either,' Alex said swiftly, settling into an acute state of alertness, keeping up her end of the deception. 'It sounds corny, but we met as strangers standing at opposite ends of a room, who looked across at each other and fell in love.'

'The connection was instant. Spontaneous. Irrevocable,' Vitali declared with such formidable conviction that Alex was almost fooled.

'Let the memory of what passed fade into the distance. Don't see Alexandra as Ted's daughter. See her for the beautiful woman she is...the woman I've been waiting a lifetime for...the woman I want to make my wife.' He dug his fingers into her arm.

Alex glanced up at him on cue, flashing a radiant smile

to meet the adoring look he was reigning on her. It was an Oscar worthy performance. His smile held a burning intensity that made Alex's heart catch and flutter. For the first time she saw Vitali's mouth soften into what could only be called a lovingly indulgent smile. If only it was true, she mused ruefully as he turned his gaze back to his mother.

If only he really did love her.

18

———

'What happened between Ted and the two of you has nothing to do with us. The past is the past. Alexandra is my present. She is my future. If you can't accept it, then I'm sorry. But whether you like it or hate the idea we are going to be together '

A painful silence swelled between them.

Lucrezia Deloitte's face grew pale. She buried her face in her husband's chest, as though trying to suffocate memories that still caused her great distress. Alex had no way of knowing what had happened to cause such angst, and there was no way to ask. Not now, perhaps never. Her father... Lucrezia....Vitali's father.... could there have been a love triangle? *And why did no one speak of Vitali's father?* But she couldn't dwell on that now.

She breathed deeply summoning every emotional force at her disposal to support Vitali's act. 'I'm truly sorry you have been so deeply hurt. We wanted...we thought...' Alex's eyes lifted imploringly to Simon Deloitte's sympathetic gaze. 'Is it so wrong for Vitali and I to get married?'

'No. No of course it isn't. Perhaps finally one good thing

will come out of this terrible saga.' Simon heaved a satisfied sigh and nodded approvingly. 'If someone had tried to arrange the marriage—no one would ever have dared hope —that it should happen naturally is fantastic!'

'Simon.' Lucrezia reproached hoarsely. 'Have you forgotten what is at stake? You can't honestly believe that Vitali should now be made to suffer!'

Simon Deloitte's eyes combed over Alex. 'Vitali won't suffer. Can't you see how they love each other.'

His mother search her son's face. Vitali shifted uncomfortably on his feet.

'I've never forgiven myself for letting Ted walk away,' Simon said, drawing a ragged breath. 'I've told myself again and again it was his choice, but I know I should have done more. I should have gone after him, made him take what he had every right to take.'

So Simon had been part of it too. *Three men...a beautiful woman...a boy and a gold mine.* Alex brushed the thoughts away. She couldn't afford to be distracted. Not now. In this moment only Vitali mattered.

Simon Deloitte drew another deep breath then turned his wife around to face him, his hands gently caressing her arms as his eyes begged her to listen. 'Lucrezia...we've come so far. Let the past go now...let it go. This is another time... another generation. Don't visit the sins of the parents upon the children. Alexandra should not be punished.'

'Oh, Simon!' it was a broken cry of reluctant acceptance. 'What would I do without you?'

His arms enclosed her gently against his heart. 'You'll never have to do without me, Lucrezia. Not as long as I live.' He rubbed his cheek over her hair in soothing reassurance, but his eyes were on Alex, urgently questioning.

She didn't know how she knew what he was asking. But

the answer slipped off her tongue without any deep consideration. 'My father died last year. His heart gave out. It's over—'

Simon's relief was tangible, yet there was an apology in his eyes for it. 'There was no way to fix it, Alex,' he said quietly. 'He must have told you that. If there was, we wouldn't have done it.'

She didn't tell Simon that she had never spoken to her father. She didn't share with him that other than the painting he had left she knew nothing of his life. Instead she stared into his great sad eyes and knew beyond doubt that what he was telling her was the truth.

Whatever had passed between the three of them had been a tragedy. Any injustice done had profited no one. Not in the way that mattered. Not even a mountain full of gold couldn't compensate for this scale of human misery.

But why did something still feel unresolved? Instinct cautioned her against voicing the questions which danced dangerously on the tip of her tongue—"*What the hell happened and what did it have to do with my father?*"

'Ted became a highly regarded artist in his latter years,' Vitali stated, injecting a note of matter-of-fact calmness into the over-fraught atmosphere, as though determined something positive should be salvaged from the torrid affair.

'Some of his paintings are hanging in the Auckland Art Gallery,' he continued. '*Te Papa,* New Zealand's museum, also holds a significant collection. He signed them Jimmie Goldie. Perhaps Mother, you would like to go and see them —after-all, you were the one after all who encouraged his talent.'

And Alex knew then why the painting had to come off the wall. If Lucrezia Deloitte had walked into the art gallery and seen her haunted face...Alex shuddered. Whatever had happened, it had traumatized her, and seeing the painting again would only bring painful memories back to life.

'I'm glad he found another way to be successful.' Simon said, and it was clear that another burden had lifted from his mind. 'Did you hear that Lucrezia? It seems that Ted found his calling. He changed his name and changed his life.'

Lucrezia buried her head against his shoulder, her weakening sobs all but drowned in Simon's corduroy jacket. Simon eased her slightly away from him and cradled her cheek in his palms, gently nudging her to meet his eyes.

'Ted's life wasn't ruined. And we're not going to ruin Vitali's and Alexandra's. We're going to wish them every happiness a man and woman can possibly share. And tomorrow we will go and look at Ted's paintings. I have a feeling that something within his art will heal the past. Seeing them will make you happy, won't it?'

The gentle consideration in Simon Deloitte's speech shook Alex. It was almost the benevolent action of a parent talking to soothe a child's worst fears. It vividly recalled to mind the lost quality that her father had painted into the portrait.

'Yes,' came Lucrezia's husky reply. Her fragile shoulders lifted and fell as she gulped in a steadying breath. The look she gave her husband was scared and wounded and sweet all at once. It was like watching something beautiful almost break.

Lucrezia turned around to face Alex and Vitali. 'I'm sorry...' Her lips trembled and she bit them, her eyes anxiously pleading forgiveness.

Alex stepped forward and took her hands in her own, pressing them warmly. 'It was the shock. You don't have to apologize, Mrs Deloitte. Please...let's all sit down...' What they needed was levity. She shot a questioning look at Vitali. 'I'm sure you have a bottle of champagne somewhere, don't you, my love?' She infused her voice with just the right amount of sweetness.

Vitali gave her a rueful look. 'Yes, of course, *mia cara.*'

It was a stiff, awkward conversation to begin with, even with the champagne that she gestured to Vitali to keep plying. Simon did his best to ease the tension, asking Alex about her life in New York. Alex skillfully led the conversation back to her career as a travel agent and regaled them with stories of her independent adventures.

'Don't you think you'll find Gold Ridge Station a bit sleepy? Will you be happy there?' Simon suddenly asked.

Alex was so used to acting as though she knew what was going on, with absolutely no comprehension of what she was really being asked, she said, 'Home is where the heart is,' she said, unable to resist a cliché and beaming a loving smile at Vitali for extra effect. 'Of course I'll be happy.'

'I wasn't happy,' Lucrezia blurted, her voice tight with warning. 'I detested every hour of it.'

Vitali's hard, capable hands clenched.

'My dear, some people suit one environment, others need something different to feel happy. Just like plants can't all flourish in the same place. Your happy place is the city. Being alone makes you wilt.'

She shook her head. 'It wasn't that. I never liked it. It's men's country. No place for a woman...' her eyes seemed to lose their focus and her voice dropped to a whisper, 'and unspeakable things happen.' Distress gave her voice a deathly pallor.

'That's enough,' Vitali declared decisively. 'Alex is nothing like you.' His serrated tone cut across the icy atmosphere.

'Vitali!' Simon warned.

Vitali strode to the windows and glared across the city landscape. 'It needs to be said,' he grunted in a tone that was barely audible.

Lucrezia's black eyes focused on Alex almost feverishly. 'Escape before it is too late.'

'History will not repeat.' Vitali growled, drawing to Alex's side. He swung a protective arm possessively around her waist. A trill of happiness mixed with fear coursed through her veins. He was making it clear she was his to keep, but what was the truth everyone desperately to keep secret?

'If you have any difficulty,' Lucrezia pleaded, 'Get away, run away...before—'

'That's enough.' Simon interrupted. 'I'm sorry Alex—the flight...the suddenness of the marriage...the unexpected—' he said, turning to Alex, 'My wife—what she's saying...she's not herself.'

Simon squeezed Lucrezia's hand firmly drawing her attention back to him. 'None of us are who we were. The situation that created—' he paused, biting down on his lip as though eating his words.

'Gold Ridge Station is different now. It's not like it was.' He said to his wife, before turning to Alex. 'You'll find it has every modern comfort a girl could possibly need. And with Vitali's helicopter on hand you could hardly call it isolated... not really. Besides,' he said, his voice softening, 'Vitali can afford to look after your happiness.'

After his mother's strained little speech, Vitali seemed to withdraw into himself. Although he continued to contribute to the conversation, it was as if he had put part of his mind on automatic pilot. His more intense concentration was channeled onto something else. Alex sensed a growing tension in him that started to play havoc as the hour of their marriage approached.

There was still time for him to change his mind about the wedding.

Her ribs squeezed against her chest at the thought of being abandoned. Was he having second and third thoughts? But his mother's fears seemed to have been allayed. The worst was over. Wasn't it? Alex's breathing raced ahead of her.

What if he had decided he was paying too high a price for *Lost Love*?

19

Alex heaved a shaky sigh of relief when six o'clock finally came and all the people with a part to play in their wedding were assembled. Vitali's solicitor arrived first, followed by the marriage celebrant and two executives in his firm who he had asked to be witnesses.

The photographer, Cinnamon Browne, a woman who Alex guessed was in her late 20's, was the last to arrive, blaming traffic snarl-ups to a very disapproving Vitali. He made it quite clear to the young woman that if he was going to play in part in helping her fledging photography career then she too had to play her part.

'Turning up late is unprofessional in anyone's book,' he growled at her, then his eyes crinkling as he gave her a playful wink, he offered her a glass of champagne as beveled flutes of champagne were handed around.

And then precisely when Alex was beginning to think that she was safe, and that the marriage was definitely on, Vitali tucked her arm around his, holding it there with purposeful determination and announced to the group at large, '*Scusarci, per favore*. Please excuse us for a few *minuti.* Alexandra and I have a few matters of privacy to attend to.'

He gave Alex no choice in the matter. He had her arm in a clamp-like grip, and, short of undoing the impression of loving harmony that had carried them this far, she had to pretend a delay was planned. If her heart could fly it would have leapt from her chest. She didn't know how she would face everyone if he dumped her now.

He steered her into a bedroom and closed the door behind them with an air of grim purpose. He released her arm, but he lifted her shoulders to ensure she was facing him as he said what he prepared to say.

Tension held her body rigid. But her mind held her chaotic thoughts firmly at bay. She was determined not to let her fears be proved real. No matter what he said she was determined to keep fighting. She placed a trembling palm on her feathered abdomen and breathed deeply from her belly, desperately hoping the fight-flight response would not drive her into paralysis.

She kept her eyes soft and calmly unwavering as Vitali frowned down at her, his green eyes sharply intent and probing.

'Firstly, I want to thank you for the way you handled the situation with my mother and Simon. It was done with finesse and compassion. Whatever else you are, I have to commend you for that.'

Alex remained mutely silent. Now was not the time to tell him that she was not the blackmail vixen he thought she was, that she would never hurt anyone—not deliberately. He would claim putting the painting in the exhibition dammed her on that score. There was only one reply to make if she was to persuade him to honor their agreement.

'I have done everything we agreed,' she reminded him

flatly. 'You asked me to take the painting out of the exhibition. You asked me to pretend I was madly in love with you,' she said, hoping he wouldn't detect the tremble in her tone.

'I did that too. *With finesse.* Everything I have said and done this afternoon is consistent with the role you commanded I play. In this matter you are the director, and I —your award-winning actress. *We need each other.* So long as we are in the presence of your family I shall keep my word.' Her lips curved in an ironic smile. 'It's a matter of trust.'

His dark brows sliced into a deeper frown. Then with a sharp jerk of his head, he released her and turned away and strode across to the huge window that looked over the city. He stood there for several moments. His back was rigid as Carrera marble. Alex knew instinctively he was not admiring the view.

'I'm letting you go.' He said with terse finality. 'Take my money and buy your freedom.'

Alex held her breath willing the words to evaporate. *This can't be happening.* If she said nothing, did nothing, perhaps he would recant.

'For whatever reason...you did something that no other woman has been able to do. You made me respect you. For that reason, I no longer feel justified in continuing with what I intended. It would be too cruel and selfish.'

It can't be...it can't be...happening to me. Defeat hammered through her heart while her mind sought frantically for an argument that might persuade him to reconsider.

'Too cruel?' She said leaping to her feet like a Phoenix rising from the ashes. 'Too cruel you say, to continue with our alliance. Too cruel to continue the charade. Too cruel to welsh out on our agreement,' she threw at him acidly, advancing toward him. 'I know what's really going on. *You're scared.* Scared you might actually feel something for me. You're a *coward.*'

He swung around, his pupils hard as cannonballs. 'I am no coward. On the contrary,' he said his mouth a sardonic twist, his eyes agleam with self-mockery. 'I am letting you off the hook, Miss Spencer. Can you see that? I thought you'd be pleased. Of course, I'll recompense you for your trouble. I'll write you an open cheque. Anything your independent heart desires. You are free to go.'

'Forgive me if I am mistaken, but where I come from the definition of partnership entails mutual agreement. I don't take kindly to being railroaded or whatever other euphemism you give to bullying,' she challenged, her head held defiantly high as she stepped closer. 'What if I don't want to walk away? What will you do then, Mr Rossi?' Alex stopped, barely a half-pace away from him, and remembering the way he manipulated her with his sexuality the previous night, she lifted her hand and lightly stroked her fingers down his taunt-bronzed cheek. The slight flinch of a muscle under her feathering touch sent a thrill of power through her veins.

His jaw tightened. 'I've just said that you can write your own cheque. I've been more than generous. What more do you want?'

Alex smiled into his fierce green eyes, gripped by a heady recklessness that dictated this one last gambit.

'I want you, Vitali,' she said, softly. 'All of you. I won't take no for an answer. You can draw a prenup and ring-fence all your money, all the gold, all your jewels, all your empire—and my answer is still, *I do.*'

His hand shot up and locked around her wrist, forcing her hand away. 'You won't win that way,' his voice was hoarse.

'Perhaps I'm not making myself clear,' her lips quivered a little at the audacity of what she was doing. 'I have nothing to lose,' she said, stating the simple truth that she knew he would never believe. She narrowed the space between them, locking her eyes upon his with seductive intensity. Their faces were so close their lips almost touched.

His Adams apple rose up and down the thick girth of his throat as he swallowed. 'Alex,' he gasped. 'I'm warning you. Give up now. Take your profit and go.'

His warm breath fanned her face.

'No,' her eyes coolly challenged him while her body blazed with desire.

Kiss me, she willed him. *Kiss me.*

She would not be the one to make the first move. She sensed his pride demanded it. Like a wild horse, he must be the one who chooses to be tamed—no matter how momentarily. Then, as though registering her consent he pulled her to him, her mouth almost level with his, his eyes ablaze.

'You'll never do to me what my mother did to your father.' he bit out venomously. 'I'll never let a woman control my life. Beauty is nothing. A body is a body. I won't ever fight for you. I will never die for you! And I won't cosset you like a child either! You will only ever be a convenience to me. Do you understand?'

'Yes,' she said softly 'I do.' She saw him now. The boy he once was. The trauma of the past that had ravaged him, hardening him like the ranges he cleaved to. He'd built a fortress made of rock around his vulnerable heart, hardening himself to anything, and anyone who would make him feel again. It was becoming clearer all the time.

He blamed it all on his mother's fragile exotic beauty. Maybe his mother had traded on her looks and her child-like vulnerability. It was impossible for Alex to know—but she herself would never trade on such a superficiality. She had never needed a man to fight for her, or cosset her, or die for her.

She simply needed Vitali to love her.

Maybe it wouldn't last long. Maybe their differences would be hopelessly irreconcilable and the marriage would prove to be a terrible mistake as her mother, and his, had warned. But until she knew for certain, nothing was going to stop her from having him.

Except Vitali himself.

'I'll leave you if you wish, but I'll take nothing—only *Lost Love*.'

'You impossible woman!' He said with an aggressive lift of his chin. And the glitter in his eyes was not wholly hostile. Alex fancied she saw a gleam of relish for the challenge she had thrown and taken up in return. Perhaps he felt he had met his match. She hoped that in her he saw a woman who would be his equal—mind, body and soul.

'Let's get on with it.'

'On with it?' she questioned, needing to hear those three important words.

'We will get married.' He added with a sharp edge of derision. Without another word or pause, he tucked his arm around hers again, marching straight out to the waiting marriage celebrant and commanded that the ceremony be performed without delay.

20

'Will you, Alexandra Anne Spencer, take this man…?

As Alex listened to the marriage celebrant's words her nerves faltered. What kind of man was she taking as her husband? The reckless certainty that had carried her to this moment wavered. She looked up at her husband-to-be, a sharp question in her eyes.

His response to her unguarded flash of vulnerability was an unmistakable gleam of cynical amusement. It served to put steel into Alex's backbone. Her gaze snapped back to the celebrant and she stared at her with fixed resolve as she came to the end of his question.

'I do!' she said firmly enough to deny any doubts whatsoever.

She had done it now, she thought wildly. For better or for worse she had gone through with it. And if she had a wolf by the tail, then heaven help her. But never would she show the slightest hint of weakness to Vitali Rossi again.

'I do,' Vitali said, unenthusiastically. He signed the marriage papers with total equanimity, exuding the air of a person resigned to making reparation for the mistakes others had made. Yet he carried himself with the air of someone who was determined he would not lose from this situation.

Triumph glittered in his eyes as he posed for the photographs, as though he was sending a message to Alex's mother. His manner throughout the supposed celebratory drinks that followed was that of a man who had won the prize of a lifetime. Alex wasn't quite sure if she was excited or frightened at the prospect of being left alone with her newly acquired husband.

What he was thinking or feeling, she had no idea. It was impossible to tell if he was still acting or not. All she knew with excruciating awareness was the blistering heat that radiated from him. Did he figure she had now played into his hands and he could do whatever he wanted with her? Or was he hiding a furious resentment at feeling trapped into marrying her because she wouldn't accept anything else?

But she had given him a choice, Alex reasoned, desperately needing to justify what she had done. Was it her fault that he couldn't believe she would walk away with nothing? Either the sense of debt to her father ran very deep or underneath all the talk of other considerations, she stirred something in Vitali that he didn't want to walk away from any more than she did.

Alex wanted to believe that. Every valve in her heart pulsed with one wish. That despite his impenetrable steel armor she had found his spot of vulnerability. For true intimacy, it was important they both open their hearts, depend on each other and support each other—no matter how raw their wounds. Wasn't this what had drawn them together, she wondered? Perhaps dreams do come true and fate can lead you to the one person with keys that fit your locks, and locks that fit your keys.

If she hadn't believed that she would never have married him. But how the next part of the charade would be played out was critical to their future relationship.

She fingered her necklace apprehensively as Vitali saw Lucrezia and Simon to the lift. Any minute now they would be alone. Her nerves were in a state of fine tension as the doors shut. The smooth heaviness of the necklace pressed against her skin as he turned to her, his eyes glittering savagely. Without hesitation, he swept her into his arms with the primal urgency of a caveman claiming the woman now branded as his possession.

The feathers of her dress spayed about her like a captive bird. His fingers tightened their grasp on the soft roundness of her hip and Alex's heart leapt. Fear left her; in its place an urgent need to have him take her in his arms and kiss her senseless, devouring any doubts about her decision. Yet even as she lifted her gaze to his, fiercely hoping to see the desire that answered what she felt, he swept his hands away, and his eyes met hers with a look of bleak mockery.

'The show is almost over,' he drawled. 'Act Two, "Meet the Parents" is complete. And now we go through to Act Three, "The Wedding Night". I must congratulate you on a stellar performance thus far. But don't count your glowing reviews too soon. Act Three will be a game changer.' He turned back into the lounge-room, pointedly separating himself from her. He headed straight for the table, opened another bottle of champagne and started filling the crystal flute with purposeful deliberation.

Alex did not follow him. She stood in the entranceway fighting the sinking sensation in her stomach. He had been acting. He didn't love her. He detested her. He hated her for forcing him into a marriage he never wanted.

She recalled the look he had given her in the lift before

she had met Simon and Lucrezia—the blazing need to dominate, to reduce her to something that could never again threaten his world. A flash of insight told her that the more Vitali wanted her, the more he would resist, the more he would deny his feelings to prove that he was in control.

She had to break that control if they were to have the marriage she wanted. And he had let it slip that he found her coolness provocative. Now, more than at any other time in her life, Alex had to be strong. She would not, could not, accept his terms of stoic detachment—or she would be nothing to him.

He offered the glass of champagne to her with mocking courtesy. 'Some liquid courage? Act Three may be grueling. Perhaps this may loosen any inhibitions.'

Every instinct she possessed told her unequivocally that this was the critical moment. If she didn't handle the situation correctly he would never respect her again. His kind of strength only respected strength.

He did not see what was coming. Had no way of anticipating it. Alex carefully controlled all expression on her face. Her grey-blue eyes mirrored nothing of her inner churning. The clear serenity that frustrated her mother so much was a well-practiced mask that could not be penetrated. She walked toward him with a slow, deliberate grace that projected absolute confidence.

She held his attention. His eyes were wary. His body had the stillness of a wild animal whose every sense was alert, suspicious and untrusting. He waited for the end-play of her move. When she halted her approach to him a half-arm's length away but did not take the glass offered, he waited for her to speak.

'Never talk to me like that again, Vitali Rossi!' she commanded frostily. 'I'm your wife. Not your whore!'

He did not move. The dangerous flare in his eyes neutralized. Emboldened she continued, 'I'm your equal. I've just become your partner—in life, in everything. And you are going to treat me that way. I won't accept less.'

Alex could feel the intense concentration of his mind as he harnessed every ounce of self-control. Was it amusement or grudging respect that twisted his lips into a semblance of a smile?

'Very polished!' he drawled. 'So refined and civilized one might almost think that lady-like indignation was true. But it's only a veneer, isn't it Alexandra? Beneath that facade is a soothsayer who wants vengeance. But let me leave you in no doubt—you won't win.'

'Perhaps it's not vengeance I want, Vitali,' she retorted. 'Perhaps it's something else entirely. But you're so stubborn, and willful and determined to hang onto your damming assessment of me I doubt you'll ever bother to find out.'

21

'God damn you!' he seethed, and the savagery in his eyes was glaring evidence that the wild animal was slipping its civilized leash. His chest heaved as he drew a ragged breath as though fighting the urge to explode. 'I'll break you Alex, if I have to, so you'd better start bending.'

Something about the rawness of his power excited her. Alex looked up at him with pleading kitten eyes, deliberately submitting to his need to dominate. He must never know that she had led him to tipping point. He must never discover that she had used powers she never knew she possessed to rattle her man of steel.

'Kiss me, you temptress!' he hissed in fierce command. 'Kiss me, my bride.' He brought his lips to within a breath of hers. 'I'm going to kiss you until I find out what you really are. And then I'm going to take you to places no man has taken you before.' His voice grew low and dangerous, 'and then we'll see how quickly you rush into your sordid divorce.'

Alex barely had time to register the blistering accusation. His lips came down to take possession of hers. She did not kiss him back. Instead, she surrendered.

There was no attempt to woo a response with sensuality this time. No intention to explore or seduce. No need to put on a show. His kiss was an avalanche, a landslide of roaring emotions, so sudden and violent that she was caught by surprise. His mouth stormed hers, ravished it, eclipsing all thought with sensations that pummeled her body. His passionate assault upon her lips triggered a surge of adrenaline that demanded an instant end to any submissiveness.

Something deep, and instinctively primitive stirred inside Alex and clawed the need to reach into Vitali, to stun and invade, take and possess, to wreak as intensive violation on him as he was wreaking on her. She met his second kiss with a blazing passion, causing him to relax his imprisoning embrace. His hands slid down her lower body meeting the desire that flamed beyond control.

Alex lifted her arms, wound them around his neck, arching her body against his with all the wanton provocation of her feminine sexuality. Their forces of opposition, female and male, sparked within each of them a wild foray of need that fought for a domination neither would concede.

A low, exultant laugh graveled from Vitali's throat and Alex stared at him with glazed eyes, frantically ordering her mind to come back to earth and anchor her from the chaos of sensation plundering it of any ability to reason. His eyes glittered over the long, snaking coils of her hair.

'*Tentatrice...*' he hissed. 'Medusa! And a devil's heart to match. Let's rid you of these deceptive trappings.'

Vitali tore her wedding dress from her body. The madness of his violent impatience to have her naked stirred an equally aggressive pride which insisted that she offer no resistance. There was no sense of humiliation, only a bubbling exultation.

He was breathing hard when he completed the frenzied disrobing and he looked at her, standing still and tall and proud before him, her hair snaking over her breasts, her only adornment the gold jewelry he had given her and a fierce satisfaction in her eyes.

'You're like some pagan queen from the past,' he said, and with a wilder laugh then before he scooped her up in his arms and marched off to the bedroom like an ancient God carrying off his conquest.

He spilled Alex on the bed, but with a graceful twist of her body, Alex turned herself onto her back, her gaze meeting his with bewitching directness. Her heart was pounding. This was a contest of power. The most ancient of powers—the battle of the sexes. Man against woman. Woman against man. Feminine energy against male energy. If he was going to take her to places she had never been with any other man, she was going to take him to places he hadn't thought possible with a woman.

'Sorceress!' he threw at her, his eyes glittering an acknowledgment of the battle she silently promised as he stripped off his clothes.

Sleekly muscled, firmly fleshed, his body honed to Herculean strength, he was a work of art as though tooled by Michelangelo's genius. A fever she had never known before heated her blood, a high pitch of awareness that sang through her body, wanting a satiation of every sense until there was nothing more to be experienced.

She couldn't suppress a smile as he knelt over her. It wasn't meant to inflame him. It was simply an involuntary expression of glorious anticipation. But it sparked an explosive reaction from Vitali.

'No!' he rasped, and snatched her hands, pinning them above her head as he lowered his formidable weight onto her pliant softness. His eyes watched her, gloating with the superior awareness of his male strength. 'You won't have your way with me. And you won't be smiling when I've finished.'

She writhed her hips in deliberate provocation, 'I will.' She closed her eyes, powerfully aware she had him under her spell. Her body slid over the silk sheets, loving the feel of his nakedness against her body, the vibrant power of his masculinity, the sensual heat of his skin, the silky roughness of his chest hair that raised an electric sensitivity as he crested her.

'Kiss me, Vitali,' she invited huskily. 'Kiss the smile from my lips.'

If there had been any morsel of sanity left before that wanton moment of provocation, there was none after it. Not one vestige of control from either of them. Any thought of contest was forgotten in a mindless need to capture all there could be between them. To tear the breath from each other, to touch and taste and exult in sensation after sensation. Exquisite, erotic, voluptuous pleasure kept building and building, fueling the explosive desire to possess all they could of each other to the most intimate depths. Past every barrier, every mask—into the unknown and beyond.

The sheer rapture of the ultimate merging of their bodies was so intense that Vitali paused to catch his breath. Their eyes met, clung, and some wordless indefinable acknowledgment was made, a pure moment of recognition that was reinforced again and again as he went on, driving himself to plunge deeper to the very center of her being, as she contracted and melted around him.

Fire to fire, force meeting force, man and woman in the

age-old rhythm of mating. Body to body, soul to soul— to the final melding that made them complete and bound them as one.

They lay together afterward, entwined in an embrace that neither made any move to break. No word was spoken. Neither made any concession to the other. But the silence they kept held a sense of peace, a truce against battling personalities as if an accord had been signed and ratified.

There would be no more fighting. Not over this. In their union, if in nothing else, they were equals...partners...at one with each other. They were both victorious.

Whether Vitali would remain satisfied with that or not Alex couldn't tell, but she was content that he showed no inclination to separate. What she had just experienced with him was what she had always dreamed she would feel.

She didn't fool herself that everything would be perfect between them from this moment on. There were too many hurdles to cross before any mutual understanding could be reached. They were right for each other, in a way that tran-scended words and all their differences, but it still might not be enough to forge the kind of marriage that would bring them both everlasting happiness.

But Alex had been right to take the gamble. She might never have known this bliss, this closeness, this joy, with anyone else. Ever.

When she drifted into sleep a smile was on her lips—not erased as Vitali had originally intended, but a smile of knowledge inked indelibly into her memory.

He was her husband.

22

The feather-light stroke on Alex's cheek raised her consciousness and the soft call of her name brought her instantly awake. Gold sunlight flooded the room and Vitali was sitting on the bed beside her, his hair dark with dampness. His jaw glistened from a fresh shave, the citrus-cinnamon scent of cologne accenting the fresh aroma of his cleanliness.

'I let you sleep as long as I could,' he said, his gruff tone contrasting sharply with the gentleness of his touch. 'But we have a plane to catch, remember? You don't want to miss out on seeing all your marriage spoils, do you?' he said drily.

Alex didn't like the hard, mocking glint in his eyes. She wondered for a moment if last night had been a dream, and then she recollected his blistering words about her divorce schemes. She didn't want him thinking that, but it was clear he would mistrust any straightforward denial from her.

If she couldn't win him over, maybe it would all end in divorce anyway. The thought of defeat bit into her heart. Instinctively she reached out to him, wanting to capture the intimacy that had flamed between them in the heat of their lovemaking.

'I'm sure you'd never possess anything that spoiled,' she said, downplaying his cynicism with an attempt at humor. She trailed a finger languidly over his bare chest, inviting a caress.

He caught at her wrist, halting her advance. His jaw went rigid and his eyes flared with animosity.

'No one ruins my life. Least of all a woman,' he stated grimly. 'Legally you are my wife. But I will not be tied. Nor will I tie you. You can do what you please. In one hour I will board my plane. With or without you.'

You are my wife.

The words were liquid honey to her ears. She gazed at him as he dropped her hand and rose to his feet like a big grizzly bear. Her grizzly bear. She would have to ignore his gruffness if she were ever to tame such a wild beast.

'You hurt my hand,' she said, rubbing her wrist, secretly satisfied that her touch had affected him so powerfully.

His eyes derisively reminded her that the power to arouse was not one sided. He leant down, and lifted her hand so he could press his lips against it, lingering there for one delicious and agonizing moment. Alex felt heat flare through her body as slowly, ever so provocatively slowly he freckled tiny butterfly kisses along the pulse-point. 'Better now?'

'Better,' she rasped.

He suppressed a smile and released her, striding to the walk-in wardrobe in an abrupt dismissal of any further physical intimacy.

She lay back on the pillow a furnace of sexual frustration as he strode past her, his towel knotted around his lean hips, the rippling muscles of his back and the lithe power of his legs ignited memories that had her stretching with a desire that he for now could not be satisfied. Tonight, she thought, and tomorrow night, and for ever more.

'You'll need to get dressed if you're accompanying me to Gold Ridge Station. 20 minutes. Don't be late.' He tossed over his shoulder.

'I'll be ready,' she said, flopping her legs over the side of the bed.

He paused in the doorway to look back at her, his eyes lingering over her naked body. 'Somehow I knew you'd want to come back to Gold Ridge Station.' Caustic sarcasm laced his voice.

She refused to let him get to her. 'I'm always up for an adventure, Vitali. I'm looking forward to this new chapter in our lives. What a fascinating book our love story would make.' She giggled, unable to contain the delicious bubbles of anticipation.

'Undoubtedly. A regular romance.' He scoffed.

'Till Death Do We Part.'

He looked at her blankly.

'The title,' she teased, hoping it might shift his thoughts away from divorce.

His reaction was chilling. His face darkened. His eyes iced over. 'You'll have to wait a long time to get your hands on my gold. I won't die like my father did.' He bit contemptuously. You'll never get away with murder. There will never be another killing.'

Alex sat deadly still, momentarily speechless. When at last she spoke the horrified questions splintered from her lips, 'Murdered?'Her gut clenched, sensing the answer was not one she wanted to hear. Who killed who?'

'I imagine your father told you it was an accident,' his

nostrils flared. 'It's interesting how people can twist things to suit their own agenda,' he said bitterly. 'Like you, your father had a talent for acting.'

'Wh...wh...what?' Alex gasped. 'I don't understand.'

His eyebrow quirked as he looked at her incredulously. 'We'll never know who attacked who,' he conceded, 'but it was my father, not yours, who wound up dead. Don't forget that when you tally up your windfall—I won't.'

Alex rocked back and forth, too dazed by the horrific revelation to rebuke his retort. She inhaled deeply and then released her breath slowly to settle the nausea slopping in her belly.

Her father had not killed anyone. Vitali had pretty much said it, and deep in her heart she knew it. Whatever had happened between her father and his parents had nothing to do with her, she reasoned fiercely. Despite this, how could he even think she would be so heartless to use his father's death for financial gain.

She would not let any of this come between her and Vitali. They were husband and wife now, through good times and bad. She had married Vitali Rossi and she was going to keep him, no matter how many times the ghosts of the past tried to haunt their marriage.

Her head lifted in defiant challenge. 'The trouble with you, my groom, is you're not used to women who can't be bought. But you'll get used to the experience. I'll wager,' she said boldly, 'you'll even get to love it.'

She made no attempt to cover her nudity as she walked toward him with all the confidence of a warrior goddess; emboldened by the power that last night's lovemaking had given her. It was as if when their bodies merged he had penetrated her soul.

She paused beside him, reached up and stroked her

fingers down his cheek in deliberate provocation. 'You're right Vitali, there will no murder,' she trailed her fingers down his throat, 'you're more use to me alive. Very much alive.' She cupped her hand over the firm mound of his member and squeezed gently. 'Now if you'll excuse me, I must get dressed.'

Alex felt his eyes boring into her every step and marveled at her brazenness. She shut the door behind her with a mix of disbelief and triumphant satisfaction. What he had told her had shocked her, and she sensed it would be difficult to find the truth; but she had also given him something positive to think about.

Something, she knew from the excitement she felt beneath her hands when she touched him, that he found thrilling— and potently addictive.

Much to his chagrin he wanted her. She had seen the unquenchable flare of desire in his eyes as she moved away. There was an explosive chemistry between them he couldn't deny. And so long as they shared that, they had a future!

She caught sight of her reflection in the mirror and realized that she still wore the gold necklace he had given her, that, along with her wedding ring, claimed her as his wife. *No*, she mused, her fingers tingling as she touched it, it was not a role she would give up in a hurry.

Let the past go. Yesterday that was what they had agreed. So, let it be. As much as she wanted to understand everything he had told her, she could do that, must do that, had to do that if she was to save their marriage. There was more to his father's death than Vitali was saying, or Simon and Lucrezia's reactions would have been different.

But worrying about the role her father may or may not have played was not going to help. Somehow she had to learn to detach. Somehow she had to learn to give up the need to be in control. It would be easier said than done, but she would try. Her happiness depended on it. Her marriage depended on it.

Even if her father was guilty of some grievous wrong, he had paid his karmic debt. Living the life of an outcast could not have been easy. And, from what she had been told, never knowing his daughter had caused her father immense suffering. The purpose of life, according to the Dalai Lama, was happiness. It was not a selfish quest.

Happiness? she questioned, staring at herself in the mirror with eyes that seemed brighter than before. Could this wild madness with Vitali be called happiness? An endless pitting of strength against strength, a duel of wits spiced by the strong attraction they felt for each other, a fight to the finish—and what was the finish she wanted?

For Vitali to love her, to need her, to want her in his life forever...

The thoughts rolled through her mind and clung with overwhelming force. She closed her eyes and concentrated on her breathing, trying, but not trying, to tame her mind by going into a meditative trance. Her heart kicked over in a funny little leap of exultation. She shook her head and opened her eyes.

He was the one!

They were meant to be together, to grow together. Mentally, emotionally, spiritually. It didn't matter why she should feel that. She just had to trust that all this madness and hurt and sacrifice had brought them together for a reason. It was pre-destined.

Of course, Vitali wouldn't see it so simply. Not yet. She was in for a ride all right. But at least she knew in her own mind why they were together and where their karmic train was taking them. How to get him to stay on board was the problem, but also the challenge, she reminded herself.

But she had the advantage no other woman had ever secured. She was his wife—Mrs Vitali Rossi.

23

Alex was late for their departure. Vitali was pacing impatiently. He had warned her he would not wait for her and meant it. He didn't even bother to glance up at her as she stood opposite him.

'I can't find the clothes you tore from me in our night of passion,' she said playfully.

It drew his attention. 'My housekeeper will have them,' he replied, his eyes flicking over the figure hugging T-shirt and jeans Alex had chosen to wear. The glossy mass of her hair was bunched back at the nape of her neck in her usual casual style. Her face was devoid of make-up, but her skin glowed and her eyes danced back at him.

His mouth twitched in amusement. 'You're quite the chameleon?'

She grinned at him. 'Just my usual traveling attire. If it's too casual, I'll change.' She didn't expect any objection. He was dressed in mustard slim-line jeans, a white T-shirt peeping out from a V-neck olive jumper—the ultimate in casual sophistication. The green complemented the color of his eyes and Alex caught her breath. Without doubt he was the most handsome man she had ever met.

She laughed out of sheer exhilaration. Not only had he waited for her when he had sworn no woman would ever control him, but she was enjoying the thrust and parry of their complex relationship.

SHE WAS on a high as they left the apartment and made their way to the airport in Vitali's personal limousine, where his private Gulfstream jet would be waiting. This promised to be a great adventure! And she wasn't disappointed.

They drove straight onto the tarmac and Vitali introduced her to the pilot and a steward who were told to look after her every need during the two-hour flight. To say the jet was palatial was an understatement.

The creamy-golden interior screamed over-the-top-opulence. Every modern comfort was catered for. There were areas for sitting, reclining, dining, and every possible need could be satisfied, including a very sophisticated galley where the crew prepared meals.

Most exciting of all was that it contained a king-size bed upon which was draped a bear-skin rug. Alex found herself wishing Vitali was being less distant with her so she could experience what it would be like to make love in the clouds.

But something about the way he bristled off to the business section and planted his nose in his laptop told her he was in no mood for passion. She heaved a sigh of disappointment and nestled into one of the down-filled leather chairs opposite him, and strapped herself in.

'You never did tell me why we have to fly to Gold Ridge Station so quickly,' she said, trying to entice him into conversation.

'I don't like missing a muster.'

'I didn't know you mustered gold?'

He looked at her bemusement. 'Not gold. Cattle. Gold mining is my job. Running one of the largest cattle stations in the world is my passion. That and collecting art.'

Alex glanced down to hide her confusion. They were flying to a mine—but he was going to muster cattle? 'You certainly know how to give a girl a great honeymoon,' she laughed. 'A mustering honeymoon. But why didn't you mention it before?' she asked hoping it would prompt him into shedding some sunlight into the contradiction.

'So there are a few things you don't know,' he said, cynically. 'I like a challenge—as you do. My mine is fully operational. . . there's no fun in that. No real skill. The loading, crushing, conveying and cleaning are all computer-controlled. At a pinch, the whole plant could be run by six people. There is no challenge in that. I need to do things. To achieve things. So I look after the international side of the gold marketing. Currently our biggest market is India, but China with its voracious appetite for gold, looks set to make this a game changer. But my real love is Gold Ridge Station. That's where I spend most of my time, and I wouldn't give up that life for anything or anyone,' he said looking at her with unswerving intensity. 'I like the challenge. I like the responsibility. I like controlling the uncontrollable.'

So, Gold Ridge Station had nothing to do with gold, Alex mused. It was a high-country cattle station! One of the vast open-range properties in Central Otago high country...a self-sufficient, isolated, frontier, with hundreds of kilometers between neighbors. Now she understood what Lucrezia had been talking about yesterday. Men's country...no place for a woman.

Vitali was watching her...watching the realization sink in.

'It's a mistress that no woman could ever match,' he said with goading certainty. 'People come and go, but the land is there forever; endlessly testing, demanding, driving a man to the limits of his capabilities and endurance; giving rewards and punishments that exalt and crush.' His eyes gleamed with mockery as he added, 'But I can hardly expect a cultured lady from New York to understand that.'

'For an educated man you really do make a lot of assumptions.' she smiled. 'You really shouldn't make such a habit of underestimating me, Vitali. It's a long time since I've lived in New York. And while I lived there I actually felt like an alien. I've got quite used to adapting to diverse environments—my work demanded it, my soul desired...desires it,' she corrected.

His eyebrows quirked, 'An alien?'

'If you're nice to me one day I may tell you about it,' she said, secretly satisfied that his mockery had been replaced with a spark of curiosity.

Cynicism curled his mouth. 'It hasn't escaped me that intrigue is a key part of your strategy.'

Alex wasn't in the mood for his sarcasm. She didn't have a strategy and never had, but if believing that kept him interested, she wouldn't look a gift-thoroughbred in the mouth. 'Let's just say that one of my better qualities is endurance. And I do so like a bit of mystery,' she said, floating her scarf across her face to reveal only her eyes.

His low gravelly laugh oozed superiority but also amusement. 'Now that we're chained together as man and wife no doubt I'll find out more about the rest of your talents.'

His gaze swept over the rounds of her breasts then trailed the length of her thighs. Every inch of her screamed, 'take me to bed, ravage me amongst the clouds,' but she was firmly brought to earth by the abruptness of his tone.

'I trust you can entertain yourself, I have business to attend to,' he said. 'Needless to say, when I came to Auckland I hadn't intended on returning married. It really has been quite an inconvenient, albeit pleasant, distraction.'

The jet had just taken off and was now leveling out. Vitali unbuckled his seatbelt and lifted his briefcase onto the table in front of him.

'Would you like any help?' Alex asked.

He looked at her with bemusement. 'Somehow I doubt you're trained for this kind of work, Alexandra.'

'There you go making assumptions,' she retorted. She had run her own travel business for years, and now owned a successful chain that spread throughout America. Having recently acquired and profitably turned around the business of a competitor who had gone into receivership, she was about to expand into the lucrative European market.

Like Vitali, she had it humming so well that the whole thing ticked along seemingly effortlessly, without her. Somehow she doubted that anything in his briefcase would faze her. Still...' she mused, twirling a curl around her finger as she regarded him, let him find out for himself. 'I'd like to think I could be your partner in everything,' she purred demurely.

He laughed, without amusement, and mockingly patted the leather seat beside him. 'Be my guest. Cast your eyes over these contracts. We're on the brink of entering the Chinese market—other than an act of God, nothing will distract me. Not even...' he looked at her with complete steadiness of purpose.

'*...not even a wife.*'

24

Alex had no intention of interfering with either Vitali's gold or his cattle business, but that didn't mean she wasn't interested in finding out more about them. She ignored the bland indifference emanating from Vitali and seated herself beside him—not so close that he could object, but close enough for him to feel the heated attraction that could not be denied. He pressed his lips together, and focused grimly on his paperwork.

Alex was used to dealing with substantial sums but the figures being bandied about were mind-blowing. No wonder Vitali hadn't blinked an eyelash over offering five million dollars for her father's painting. Alex did some mental arithmetic. His gold mine was literally a *gold mine*— staggeringly profitable.

Alex had no idea how deep and extensive the gold deposits were at Gold Ridge. Perhaps no one knew. But Alex was now sure that it was her father who had discovered them. Probably in partnership with Simon Deloitte. He certainly intimated as much yesterday.

She started piecing together the jigsaw of information

she was being handed bit by intriguing bit. The mine and the Vitali's property were both called Gold Ridge. That in itself was intriguing. What did a ridge have to do with either gold or cattle?

Lucrezia had lived on the isolated cattle station, presumably with her then husband—Vitali's father. Then along had come Simon Deloitte and Ted Carr. The open-house hospitality of the mainlanders, as New Zealand's South Coast inhabitants proudly call themselves, would have been extended to them while they prospected in the area. If the gold deposits had been found on Gold Ridge Station—which seemed highly probable-their discovery would have affected them all.

Perhaps it had precipitated the dreadful things that had happened.

Lucrezia was the center of it all—that was obvious. A beautiful woman who craved a different life, craved company and attention, who had needs that her husband couldn't, or wouldn't, fulfill. And three men who all held different choices for her.

Vitali's father, no doubt a hard, uncompromising man, like his son, who was wedded to the land more than to his wife. A man who wanted no other life but the one he'd already carved.

Simon, the aristocratic Englishman—gentle, kind compassionate, and rich. But not in the running as far as physical attraction went.

And her own father, who must have been very special for her mother to have completely lost her head over him. Had Lucrezia lost her head over him too? And her heart?

What build-up of pressures had led to the fight which had ended with the death of Vitali's father? She didn't know, and given the circumstances of her marriage, she could hardly ask. Yet it was obvious that Lucrezia and Simon had lived haunted lives ever since.

Lucrezia, particularly, was still traumatized by a sense of guilt. Had she played one man against the other...and lost both in the horror of what had happened? Had she turned on Ted when she saw her husband was dead, unable to bear the outcome of her own maneuvering?

Alex dragged her mind away from trying to figure out the past. That wasn't going to help her with Vitali, unless she could understand why he thought she wouldn't stick it out at Gold Ridge Station. He saw her as a beautiful woman, and clearly all his experience of beautiful women led him to believe they demanded indulging and admiring incessantly.

And he believed beautiful women couldn't be happy outside a glittering social life. He didn't realize that she didn't need people around her. That superficial admiration meant less than nothing to her.

But he would learn. Eventually.

Time was on her side now that she was his wife. And the thought of living with Vitali in a world of their own brought a sweet smile of satisfaction to her lips.

'I see our trading figures give you pleasure,' he remarked derisively.

Alex was still holding one of the larger contracts. 'How much does the mine produce, Vitali?' she asked, ignoring his taunt.

'About 230,000 tonnes per day.' His green eyes were hard as he mockingly added, 'Does that satisfy your greed?'

'Don't throw that in my face, Vitali,' she shot back at him. 'You could have left that gold where my father found it. No one twisted your arm to dig it out of the ground.'

His face tightened. 'The decision to mine the gold was not mine. I was only a child at the time.'

'But you didn't turn your back on the gold once it was there. So why chide me for taking an interest in it now?'

'Would you prefer I leave it buried, *mia cara*?' he mocked.

'What you do or don't do with the gold doesn't interest me,' she declared, staring straight back at him with steady eyes. 'But, as your wife, your business has just become mine. I won't be shut out. No matter what nasty motive you decide to give me.'

'You can't really expect me to believe you would have played the hand you have if there was no gold mine' he said skeptically.

'If there was no gold mine would you have married me?' she challenged.

His face slowly relaxed into a sardonic smile. 'Perhaps. You are more than just a pretty face.' His eyes simmered with more than appreciation of her ability to fight him on equal terms. 'Although I might have claimed you earlier if I hadn't seen the painting first,' he said with dry whimsy.

'Perhaps,' Alex replied just as drily, but her heart was racing with excitement. This was his first real admission that he had been attracted to her the first night they had met. She smiled, her eyes teasing his self-assurance. 'You might have been disappointed. You're right that I'm not just a face. But I'm not just a body either.'

'Rest assured I now have a healthy respect for the mind that drives it', he said with heavy irony.

Her smile broadened with satisfaction. 'All I have to do now is get you interested in my personality, and I will be the complete package.'

She sensed his conscious retreat from her even before he spoke. 'The land will reveal who you are,' he said tersely, 'it brings out the best and the worse in everyone.'

'I'm sure it's a test that I'll pass.'

His mouth twisted. 'You heard my mother. You'll be bored out of your mind.'

'We'll see,' she said, without commitment.

'Indeed.' His eyes glittered at her with some indefinable emotion, then he bent his concentration back to his paperwork, deliberately excluding her.

The Vitali Rossi's of this world, Alex mused, as she glanced down at the mountain ranges below, did not give up easily. Once they made up their minds they were as immovable as The Remarkables in her father's painting. She smiled to herself, choosing not to be offended by Vitali shutting her out, instead focusing on the reasons she had to be optimistic.

It was he who had invited her to look over his business papers, and she had scored some points. She could not demand his respect, nor hurry him in any way. To win Vitali Rossi she would have to earn his respect. She would have to become as important to him as the land he loved.

Vitali ordered brunch to be served.He put his work aside while they ate fresh crayfish accompanied by a bottle of champagne.

'Don't you drink anything else?' Alex asked.

'Peroni,' he said. 'But you can have whatever you want,' he countered.

Alex shrugged. 'I'll have what you have.'

'The advantage of champagne,' he said, 'is that the worst of it is very good, and the quality ascends from there to sublime. I enjoy drinking it.'

'Even at Gold Ridge Station?'

He flashed her an amused look. 'We have everything we want. It has every modern creature comfort—you'll even be able to make yourself a gourmet cappuccino if you start getting city-life withdrawals. What you do with your time there is up to you. You may feel that the place could use a woman's touch. Other than a few rooms which are off-limits, you can redecorate the house to suit your personal taste.'

Off-limits.

The phrase was a red flag. The prospect of defying his sanction was tantalizing. Alex contained her intrigue, while also ignoring the sexist suggestion that the only thing she would be fit for was to add a woman's touch to the décor. 'I take it you'll be an interested spectator then.'

'It will be interesting to see how you fend. To see how you will make it a home...what drives you...'

'What turns me on...' she added provocatively.

The amusement in his eyes morphed into deep-seated cynicism. 'What turns you on, Mrs. Rossi is gold. We've established that. As to the interior, it will be interesting to see what you can achieve before the isolation drives you away. Or you become bored with the game you are playing.'

She ignored the last barb. Instead she replayed the way his tongue had rolled over her new name. *Mrs Rossi.* It had a wonderful musical lilt to it, she thought happily, taking another mouthful of crayfish.

'Lovely,' she murmured. She couldn't think of a time she had felt so happy. So what if he was still gruff and unpredictable. So what if he was still a fortress, an impenetrable emotionless cold castle. Like the snow on the mountains, eventually he would thaw.

'How big is Gold Ridge Station?' she asked, glancing down at the vast landscape below, with a rare house sprinkled here and there.

'Big enough.'

She fixed him with an impatient look imploring him not to play games.

'Size, you'll find, does matter,' he said, sarcastically. 'The Station has been developed to the point where it offers 1850 hectares. Including 350 ha of finishing pastures on the flats and terraces, with 315 hectares of irrigation and 1500 hectares of hill blocks on the steeper tussock country.'

Alex watched with interest as his eyes began to sparkle, and he waved his normally wooden arms about with increased animation. He hadn't been lying when he said the High Country farm was a passion.

Like a storm cloud racing over the sun his mood suddenly darkened. 'There's nothing but timeless land all around you, and you'll be sitting smack-bang in the middle of it. Bit by bit it will start closing in on you, day after day after day...'

'It doesn't close in on you,' she said, mirroring his animation, 'just the opposite—when you talk about it you're like another person—more open.'

'It's a man's country.' He lifted his glass in a mock salute to her. 'And the isolation offers a welcome retreat from the madness engulfing the rest of the world.'

'I think that what it needs...' with poised deliberation, she reached across and took the glass from his hand, lifting it in a mock toast to him as she added '...is the right woman to tame it.'

She heard the brush of breath between his lips as she downed the champagne. Something dangerous flickered in his eyes when she passed the glass back to him. His hand closed around her, imprisoning it, pressing his dominance.

'From the start, the one thing I have admired is your coolness—'

'Even in bed?' Alex tossed in provocatively.

25

———

His smile was devilish. He used his other hand to remove the glass from her fingers while still retaining his hold on her. 'I think I shall have to refresh my memory, Alexandra Spencer—'

'Alexandra Rossi,' she corrected, barely keeping the elation out of her voice. He wanted to take her. He was going to make love to her. Which was what she had been wanting ever since he had woken her up this morning.

'I think, Alexandra Rossi...' he said with biting precision, '...that we need to practice Scene Three again...'

He moved out from the table, pulled her up from her seat and swept her into the jet's bedroom compartment. His eyes glittered with relish for the task he had set himself as he closed the cabin door behind them. 'Even if we are at thirty-five thousand feet, nothing's going to stop me giving my best performance,' he promised her.

Alex fought to keep a grin from betraying her delight. He must not think it is what she wanted all along. She would wantonly let him put on his best performance, she mused, biting her lip as he strode out of his jeans. This was going to be a repeat performance she would relish.

But it wasn't respect on her mind by the time they were sated with lovemaking. More like awe .They were so incredibly attuned to each other.The pleasure she had sampled with him last night was not a one hit wonder. He packed plenty of pleasure.

She lay back on the bed contentedly. Enough pleasure to last a lifetime.

Vitali didn't say anything about respect either. In fact, for a long while he didn't say anything at all. Eventually he pushed himself away from her, off the bed and on to his feet.

'I don't understand you. I don't understand who you are and what you want. But I do know that I don't trust you and I never will. But to your credit, I also know that tangling with you is one hell of an experience.' He stared down at her and gave a slight shake of his head.

The admission intensified Alex's satisfaction, but she repressed the impulse to lay her true feelings bare to possible mockery. Instead she gave him a slow, languid smile.

'You're a worthy—' she searched for the right word. Opponent wasn't right. She didn't want to highlight their differences. 'Leading man,' she said, satisfied he would like the idea of being the one in control of their performance.

She stretched out, enjoying the delicious sense of languor in her limbs, and savored the smooth co-ordination of Vitali's muscular body as they made love.

The performance was short but fulfilling and when it was over he turned aside to pick up his clothes and pulled his jeans back on. He took his time, moving slowly with an air of dogged determination.

Vitali paused in the doorway and looked back at her, a

taut, driven expression on his face. Something in his eyes— a flicker of hungry possessiveness—made Alex's heart leap with hope.

He didn't want to leave her.

'You have an hour before the plane lands. And I have work to finish. Please yourself what you do,' he said curtly, then stepped into the next compartment, pulling the door shut behind him.

He could keep putting walls between them all he liked, but one way or another Alex was going to prise open the door to his heart. One by one she would break down his barriers. Even if it took her the rest of her life.

26

———

'The Jewel in the crown,' Vitali mocked, as Alex's first view of the mine appeared.

It was a tiny, lonely scar on an arid landscape, as disembodied and ugly as a crater on the moon. Yet people had fought and died because of it...with the passion only a woman could stir. Somehow it couldn't excite Alex at all. If the gold had never been found, perhaps her father would still be alive.

Alex turned her head away from the window and met the hard glitter of his green eyes with a quiet determination that she would allow nothing to shake. 'I'll wait until you want to show them to me personally. Until then, I'm far more interested in the home where we'll begin our life together. Where we'll live is far more important to me than the gold you covet.'

His eyebrows quirked in obvious skepticism. 'In that case, I'll instruct the pilot to continue to the homestead airstrip.' He accepted her word without argument.

Alex returned her gaze to the landscape below. It reminded her of other wildly barren vistas she had seen in her travels, like the Sahara Desert—fickle places that were at once blazing hot, then relentlessly cold. Not so unlike her husband.

'How many cattle do you run on Gold Ridge Station?' Alex asked as Vitali returned to his seat.

'Depending on conditions, it varies from four thousand up. '

Alex frowned. She'd visited cattle ranches in Texas and while she was no expert the numbers seemed low. 'That makes it ...what ...about six for every square kilometer? '

Vitali's eyes widened. 'A good guess,' he drawled. 'The summers can be very dry and the temperatures soar. But in winter they drop to below freezing and everything is covered in snow in winter. The numbers are dictated by the climate and what we can feed. But the herd naturally increases in the good years. That's why we have regular musters. To brand the calves and cull out the wild bulls.'

His mouth moved into something like a smile, dangerous and edgy. 'Not the kind of life you expected as my wife, is it?'

'I didn't have any expectations. But if I had, I can honestly say you've exceeded them,' she replied truthfully. 'You've left me hungry for more.'

His shoulders tensed. 'More?' his tone was steely as though he was bracing himself for her exorbitant demands. His eyes narrowed as he held her gaze, looking like some pagan god of war. 'What is it that you want more of, Alexi?'

'More of you.' she said, staring at him with unflinching certainty. 'Much more.'

'We'll see,' he muttered dubiously.

Her stomach lurched with a strange mix of excitement and trepidation as the plane began its decent and Gold Ridge station came into view. The size of the place made it look hugely prosperous. And backed by the wealth of the mine, it had to be.

Everything seemed meticulously organized; squares of fenced stockyards, rows of buildings with galvanized iron roofing, strategically placed water-tanks, pipe lines running up from a large waterhole that had been dammed into a creek, avenues of shade trees and shelter belts. It was nothing like she expected. Isolated it might be, but there was a hive of activity.

In the distance she made out several men on quad bikes, riding up the rugged terrain, men on horseback milling around what appeared to be sizable stables, and a group of people were standing around the airstrip. Clearly Gold Ridge Station was a thriving community of people who helped run it and who would provide her with company if she ever needed it.

Whatever the life was like here, she would adjust to it, Alex vowed, as the plane touched down on the airstrip. As she stepped onto the tarmac Alex gazed up at the ancient alpine ranges, towering thousands of meters tall in the near distance. They were the bright, mysterious mountains of childhood dreams and fantasy. This was an enchanted Enid Blyton landscape, full of magic and blurred boundaries and snowflakes in winter which fell from heaven.

Her heart pulsed, so great and immediate was her love for the place which meant so much to her husband. She understood now the hold this land—his mistress—had on Vitali. Nothing could surpass her wildly exotic beauty.

A baby deer peered at her from amongst the wild mountain tussocks, its bright eyes regarded her with primal wisdom. She half expected it to speak in this charmed, magical place. Something was calling to her. As clear as a clarion bell.

Call it intuition, call it magic—call it love. She didn't know what it was, but its impossible message was plain. "Stay," it whispered. "Stay in the foothills of these magic mountains. Let nothing tear you away."

The first people Alex saw when she and Vitali stepped out of the plane were a group of Maori boys perched on a nearby fence. They were waving madly at them with huge grins on their faces. Alex laughed and waved back, and in the next instant they jumped off the railings and scampered away, up towards the houses, giggling

'Who are they?' she asked Vitali.

'The children of our stockmen, part of George Whiti's extended family. They were here before the English ever colonized this country. As far as I'm concerned this is their home.' He gave Alex a warning look 'This is where they stay for as long as they want.'

'Of course,' she agreed.

His eyes probed her with sharp intensity. 'No racial prejudice?'

'No. Why should they be?' She said matter-of-factly. What a strange thing to ask.

He shrugged and Alex saw the tension ease from his face as though she had passed yet another test.

'First impressions will count with your people,' she whispered, tucking her arm around his.'Kiss me, Vitali and show them I'm the woman you love.'

He gave a low laugh and pulled her arm more firmly around his and kissed her on the cheek as a sleek black Range Rover Sport, dust billowing behind it, came to halt at the bottom of the aircraft steps.

'Alexandra, this is Robert McKee. He and his wife, Dara, manage the place in my absence. Robert, this is Alexandra, my beautiful wife.'

How long would he manage to keep projecting a lovely indulgent manner? I may as well enjoy it while it lasts, she thought as she snuggled into him.

'Please call me Bob,' Robert McKee said, holding out a freckled hand. His lips and eyes beamed in heartfelt approval. 'I never thought I'd see the day,' he laughed, 'You must be some lady, melting that steel heart of his. Me and the wife look forward to getting to know you more.'

Bob Rossi was well into his fifties, a lean, wiry man whose weather-beaten face was creased in mirth. His hair was ginger-gray, his eyes sparkling clear blue. Alex took his hand and smiled as his hand closed around hers, giving her a gentle squeeze of encouragement.

'I'm very pleased to meet you, Bob. Very pleased indeed,' she said as he released her hand and gave Vitali a playful pat on the back. 'American?' he remarked in surprise. 'You're a long way from home, I hope you'll be happy here with us, Mrs. Rossi.'

'Thank you. You know, I really do feel quite at home already, Mr. McKee,' she said, warmly.

Bob McKee flashed her an approving grin. 'I didn't think Vitali would pick a wuss!'

'Wuss?'

'A wet blouse...a....' then registering her confusion, Bob McKee came right out with the question that seemed to be on everyone's minds, 'a quitter!'

'Oh, I can assure you, I'm no quitter. '

Alex felt Vitali's arms gently squeeze her waist, before he dropped them stiffly and reached for their luggage. 'Enough standing around,' Vitali said, impatiently. 'There's work to do.'

Alex's suitcase was packed into the Range Rover while Bob chattered on about how delighted everyone was with the news of their marriage. Vitali had sent word ahead, Bob informed her, and every man, woman and child—and deer, he chucked in, enjoying his own humor, on Gold Ridge Station was waiting to meet the woman that had claimed the bosses heart.

And they were there to look her over too, Alex though with a flutter of nerves.

27

Alex worried briefly about her choice of clothes, then reminded herself that she didn't want people judging or evaluating or responding in any way to what she wore, but to the person she was and the person she was choosing to be—the loving wife of Vitali Rossi. And in this last point alone she was relieved to have an advantage.

The staff were obviously fond of Vitali and held him in high regard. Surely everyone was ready to like her because he had chosen her to be his wife. Still, she was certain that winning their affection on her own account would be another test she would have to pass if she was to win Vitali's respect.

Alex was too preoccupied with the task ahead of her to take in everything as the Range Rover bumped along the rough terrain between the farm buildings, stables, barns and staff houses. They were all built of local stone, and their natural beauty and affinity with the landscape impressed themselves briefly in her consciousness until she caught sight of the big house.

No big was not the right word. Ginormous didn't even do it justice!

Vitali had told her the property was set over 1850 hectares of land across a glacial valley. He had told her it was an award-winning home, designed by a pre-eminent New Zealand architect specializing in eco-architecture. But what he couldn't possibly have begun to describe, was the raw power of its natural beauty. The house was created from stone reflected the schist and moraine boulder deposits from the substructure of the surrounding land. It blended seamlessly within the rugged setting of the glacial valley with 180-degree views of the surrounding mountains.

Surrounding it was an incredible array of flora including native brown top grasses and wild native mountain tussocks. Sculptures crafted by New Zealand and international artists complimented the natural beauty of the property's lakes, waterways and wetland areas.

'*The Wolves are Coming*', Bob McKee said, following Alex's gaze as she studied a sculpture near the entrance of the house. 'A hundred and ten life sized wolves, cast in iron', he said, gesturing to it.

Alex's gaze locked on the lone man, forged in iron, standing his ground, his sword raised, as the wolves snapped and snarled at his feet

'When Vitali first saw it in Beijing he was instantly captivated,' said Bob. 'It's a major work from China, the start of expanding his sculpture collection internationally.'

Captivated was one way of putting it, Alex mused as she studied the disturbing yet fascinating fortified steel. There stood a man, a David amongst a Goliath of wolves. Their lips bared back from piranha-like teeth, yet he showed no fear. His face was a mask of steel, his body and soul seemed battle-weary from the unrelenting duel for survival.

You are what you art.

If this was the case what did the piece her husband had chosen reveal about Vitali—his personality and the wounds of his past? The sculpture reminded her of man, a warrior, a knight who would not be overcome, nor possessed, nor defeated. A man, like the wolves who refused to be tamed.

'It's an interesting piece,' she said, turning to Bob McKee, 'My agent told Clive Gagos that when you choose a work of art it's as much an expression of who you are as the artist that created it.'

She lifted the tone of her voice toward the end of the sentence as though her statement were a question. Bob was a man who perhaps could help her unlock the mystery of her husband, and help her open the door to his troubled past and impenetrable heart.

Bob McKee laughed. 'You know there may be something in that.'

'When you think of wolves what comes to mind?' She pressed.

He regarded her thoughtfully, then glanced back at the sculpture. 'This may seem strange, but for some reason all I can think of is those children that you hear about in the news sometimes—you know, the ones that are raised by wolves. Isolated from human contact from a very young age, with little experience of human care or love...' His words trailed off.

'Even the fiercest of wolves will embrace a stranger as their own and from then only through death do they part,' he said, as though reading her mind. 'Anyhow, we'd best rattle our dags—your husband will be wondering where we got to.'

Alex's stomach knotted as she reflected on his words. Was this what had happened to Vitali? Had his father died trying to defend himself, the goldmine, or the woman he loved?

Had Vitali, then at a vulnerably young age, been abandoned by his mother, neglected and left in this isolated place, devoid of love. Did this painful yet fascinating and powerful statue remind him of the past and affirm his solitary guarded nature? If so, what hope was there for her?

28

Alex had little time to contemplate the questions. A crowd of people were lined up on the sweeping deck perched atop craggy rocks like the rim of a flying saucer. They waved and called out excited greetings to her and Bob as the Land Rover came to a halt in front of them.

The next hour was an exhausting one for Alex. She was introduced to some fifteen families and she tried hard to remember the names and the various occupations of all the adults-a mechanic, governess, book-keeper, horse-breaker, cook and on and on...white faces and brown and every shade in between, all expressing a friendly welcome. Vitali, to her intense relief and pleasure, gave her every support, exhibiting the quiet pride expected of a newly-wed and doting husband.

If only he wasn't acting, she mused sadly. As soon as the courtesies were over, he stated that he and Bob had business to discuss. He smoothly passed Alex over to the care of Dara McKee, Bob's wife, who was instructed to show her through the house.

Alex bit back a protest and hid her disappointment that

Vitali didn't see fit to show her through her new home himself. Now was not the time to make a stand with so many other people around, but sooner or later she would make him recognize that she wasn't going to be fobbed off and cut out of his life with such pastimes as interior decoration.

She was going to be his in partner in every sense. In the meantime, she did need to get her bearings and make friends with Dara McKee. She had gained little insight from Bob, but perhaps his wife would be less reticent in sharing all she knew about Vitali and his life.

The older woman was eager to be as accommodating as possible and Alex quickly warmed to her cheerful and open personality. She was a big-boned, wide hipped woman with white hair and lively brown eyes. Her thick hair was pulled back from her strong face and tied in a practical, no-nonsense bun. She smiled and laughed frequently with the easy confidence of someone who was adored, and who loved her life here.

As they toured the massive property it was clear that Dara was as proud of it as though it were her own. Which it was in a way. She and Bob lived in the western wing.

'How long have you been at Gold Ridge Station, Dara?' Alex asked.

'Oh, we've been here ever since Vitali was a boy. I practically raised him after his mother—' she pressed her lips together. 'Some thirty-odd years now,' she said, glancing out to the glacial peaks. 'Our two boys were only youngsters liked Vitali when Mr. Rossi, Vitali's father, asked us to move in and manage the place. He used to bring Vitali across from his boarding school in London for his holidays.' She looked at Alex solemnly, 'He was always too busy with work to stay here with the boy himself.'

Dara shook her head in bewilderment. 'Bob and I were born and bred around here. We love it. So does Vitali. But his mother...Do you know, she's never been back...all these years?' She frowned and darted an anxious glance at Alex. 'I suppose you either love it or hate it. I guess you'll find it very different from your life in New York.'

'Yes, it's quite a change—thankfully. I think I love it already. Just like I fell in love with Vitali the first time I saw him.'

She wasn't exaggerating. The feelings she felt for Vitali had been instant and now this house of his...' she pondered as they continued the tour of her new home, a home that accurately reflected who he really was and what he valued. It exulted an equally powerful and instantaneous effect.

The rooms were grand and lofty—full of light, and revealing surprising vistas. Mysterious, unexpected shadows interplayed against the pristine white walls adding layer upon layer of depth. Naturally the house was adorned with beautiful artworks—once again all landscapes, an eclectic and interesting mix of old and modern juxtaposing naturally.

The furniture was designed equally for show as it was comfort—this was not a museum, a show-pony of a house, nor a machine to be lived in, but a home to be loved, to be embraced, to leave an imprint upon a person's soul.

'Vitali gives people he cares for free-range. He only asks one thing—to respect his private space.' Dara said, nodding to the north-facing wing.

As Alex continued her tour of the house she could think of only one room she would like to bring her woman's touch. The wing that guarded the passage to her husband's heart. The North Wing. Vitali's true north. His inner sanctum—the area where access was denied and fiercely guarded. But while she was impatient to break down his walls, she knew better than to hurry him. Little by little she would win his respect, then his trust and then his heart. Of that she was certain.

Almost.

'Vitali has arranged for you to have your own room,' Dara said, avoiding looking at Alex.

'Of course,' Alex said quietly, not wanting to reveal her hurt surprise. 'I enjoy my space and privacy as much as he does.'

Like the wolves of his sculpture Vitali remained an unpredictable beast. While he had been true to his word and there appeared to be every modern comfort she could possibly desire, there was another thing she would never care for—their separate bedrooms.

It was archaic. Medieval. Primitive. Hurtful. As though he was the king and she was a wench who would be at his disposal should he command it; or worse, as though she was a wife he did not want to bed.

When Dara left Alex to settle in by herself, she did some serious rethinking of her position.

The separation of the bedrooms seemed to be symptomatic of the separation of responsibilities at Gold Ridge Station. The division of labor was very definitely drawn. The women ran the domestic chores; the men worked the farm. Of course, they were interdependent; one without the other would never survive. Normally Alex would not have considering meddling with a system that by all accounts seemed to suit everyone well.

Well enough for everyone except her.

She wouldn't be able to develop the sense of working together with her husband unless she did something that would be of very real value to him. Something positive that met the challenge of the land itself. That was what he cared about. That was his pleasure. His passion. Controlling the uncontrollable, Vitali had said so.

If she didn't come up with some workable plan that would impress him, he would keep her on the periphery of his life. She would be just a convenient woman—and an inconvenient wife. And she desperately wanted to be at the heart of everything, with him standing proudly at her side.

29

———

Alex took a shower and changed into her lace dress in deference to the fact that this would be their first dinner in their real home. Her suitcase of clothes made little impact in the cupboards in the dressing-room, and she made a mental note to ask her mother to send out the rest of her clothes. Then, she went into Vitali's room entering through their common bathroom and dressing room.

Her heart hammered against her ribs as she stepped into his sacred space. It was wrong to go against his command, but there would be no sense of togetherness at all if Vitali insisted on keeping separate bedrooms. That had to be settled before anything else and here was a domain in which she may be able to bring some womanly control. Control which she must demonstrate right now.

It was only a few minutes before she heard him striding along the deck. Her pulse instantly quickened. She had made a fair fist of regulating what happened between them so far. She couldn't afford to let him make all the rules at this critical point. Acting on sheer instinct, she sprawled across the bed in a pose of relaxed nonchalance.

The moment Vitali walked in, his body stiffened at the sight of her. 'This is my room, Alexi,' he said curtly. 'You've got your own room and I told you there were somethings that are off limits. This is one of them. So, if you're thinking of changing anything, forget it. You're wasting your time.'

'I was just trying out the beds to see which was more comfortable for us to sleep in,' she said. 'Or were you thinking of sleeping alone? '

She felt the touch of his lips as his dangerously beautiful mouth curved. 'The bed you can share, whenever you like. Like you, I intend to make what I can of this marriage. Just don't interfere with anything else,' he gritted. 'Is that understood?'

'Understood. But, there are a couple of things *you* should understand, Vitali,' she began purposefully.

'Don't push me too far, Alexandra. I've given you free rein to do what you want with the rest of the house. With the exception of the North Wing, which houses my private study.'

'You won't have to worry about me snooping around in your absence. When you're not here I don't intend to be here either. Where ever you go, I'll be with you.'

'That *mia cara*, is your prerogative on any international trips I have to take. But you're not coming on muster with me. For one thing, I don't take passengers in the helicopter during the round-up. It's too dangerous. I need total concentration. There's always a chance that the engine may stall on some of the close maneuvers.'

His eyes flashed with derisive determination. 'And secondly, you'd only be a liability on the ground. Apart from the distraction to the men who need to keep their minds on the job, I doubt you could sit in a saddle day after day without causing everyone concern over your well-being.'

He didn't wait for a reply. He headed straight to the bathroom and shut another door between them. Alex repressed the impulse to chase after him and argue. She didn't have a rebuttal for him. She didn't know they used helicopters for mustering, although she could see now how useful it would be when there was such a vast territory to cover.

A thrill coursed through her. Perhaps she could learn to fly. That would make him sit up and notice her. Surely that would gain his respect. Something to think about, she mused, as she sat on the bed and waited for Vitali to reappear.

As for the riding, she liked horses, but she wasn't sure she wanted to be stuck to one and she doubted her butt would handle being on a horse for 8-10 hours, day after day. Still, if that was what it took to win Vitali over and show that she could handle country life, she would sacrifice her thighs for the ride. By the time the next muster came around, she would be ready. She reasoned that by then all the men on the station would be more familiar with her. She would be less of a novelty and therefore less of a distraction.

At least she had some possibilities to work on, but instinct told her she needed something meatier. The thing her husband valued most was making money, she mused. What if she could match him in the business stakes, show that she was capable to contributing income to the Gold Ridge coffers and of making a considerable profit.

Then she would win on two accounts. If that didn't earn his trust and respect nothing would. She needed to familiarize herself with the way the station ran before she would be able to come up with any brilliant ideas about just how she would do that.

'It didn't take you long to regret your decision,' Vitali said, sensing the thoughts that weighed on her mind.

Alex had been so absorbed that the mocking question startled her. He had already washed and was emerging from the dressing-room, buttoning the cuffs of a sky-blue shirt. His eyes moved across her face, intensely watchful, as he waited for her confirmation.

'On the contrary.' She smiled and rolled off the bed, deciding to close the physical gap between them if nothing else. 'I have no regrets at all. I was just thinking about our new life together and all the wonderful challenges to be solved.'

Alex sauntered towards him and slid her hands up the walls of his brawny, powerful chest, her eyes teasing at the guarded reserve in his. 'Why should I regret anything when I have you, my groom.' She stood on her tiptoes and kissed his lips with a fervor she hoped would short-circuit his brain.

His mouth momentarily softened, as though he was surrendering to the passion storming through then both, then clamped shut as though regretting his momentary lapse of control.

'What do you expect from me, Vitali,' she said softly, masking her hurt with a smile.

His hands grasped her hips, halting any further attempt to draw closer. 'I have no expectations of you, Alexandra. Expectations only lead to disappointment. I discovered that a long time ago,' he said bitterly.

'What are you afraid of Vitali?'

30

Something savagely vulnerable flickered in his eyes. 'I'm not afraid of anything.'

'It's me. It's me you're afraid of, isn't it? I would never do anything to hurt you.'

'Afraid of a woman? Are you mad? Certainly not,' he bit out scathingly.

'Then why are you holding me at a distance?'

He dropped his grasp. 'You cost me dearly,' he said, and the tone he used reminded her once again of the layers of steel wedged between them.

'But I will minimize the damages, as far as is in my power. And don't think I can't live without you, Alex,' he growled, his voice heavily accented as he retreated from her.

'You don't have to live without me, Vitali. I'm your wife.' she reminded him.

He bit back a harsh laugh. 'Now let's see you put on another Oscar-worthy performance and play your loving role through dinner, *mia cara*.'

And that's just what she did. Much to the McKee's delight. Vitali had invited them to share a meal with them in the elegant dining room with panoramic views across the lake. But she didn't have to act. It felt so lovely, so honest, so truthful to share with the couple how much she really loved her husband. And there were moments when she was sure than even Vitali was uncertain whether she was acting or not.

He did not argue when Alex suggested they retire early. This was their honeymoon after all. The McKee's immediately said they farewells and disappeared into the ebony dark night.

Every step toward their bedroom was charged with electricity. There was no way they were going to separate beds. The door to Vitali's room was the closest. He swept Alex inside and held her in an embrace that throbbed with uncontrollable desire.

'Medusa!' The words hissed from his lips as they claimed hers, but they lost any venom in the passion that surged between them.

Alex didn't care what names he called her. She cared for nothing but the sweet-honeyed taste of his kiss.

'Say you want me. Say you need me!' his voice strained in the extremity of his own need.

'I want you,' she gasped. 'I need you,' she urged. 'Now!' she demanded, unable to contain her desire. She was beyond talking, beyond thinking, beyond games. She barely heard his hoarse cry of triumph as he laid her on the bed, and took her in another peak of tantalizing sensation.

'Say you've never had a man like me before in your life.'

'Never.' she cried, acknowledging the truth.

He took her again and again, from peak to higher peak still, and then when she thought they could go no further they both climaxed in unison to the summit.

.   .   .

How much time had passed since they fell into a blissful embrace, their bodies quietly entwined, she didn't know. Nor did she know what had driven Vitali to command her to say the things she had to him.

Ego? Pride? Doubt? How would he respond if she demanded that he do the same, that he swear that he'd never had a woman who pleasured and excited and aroused him like she did. She couldn't bear to think of any woman making him feel more than she did. Perhaps he felt the same. Maybe that was why he forced her confession. If so, she wasn't just a convenience any more. She was more special than that.

But still the attraction was still largely physical. She had to reach further...make Vitali see that she was capable of matching him in every way.

And as she glanced out at the moon lancing off the mountain peaks the idea came to her! She had to investigate it and see if it was possible. And she needed money. A lot more money. Certainly more than she had in cash reserves. The acquisition of the European travel chain had eaten into that.

Alpacas! Of course, they'd be perfect, she thought as memories came gusting back of a night she'd spent on summit in the Andes. She had been leading a group of people interested in eco tourism, and after a day digging channels for irrigation for the villages, the beautiful mountain creatures had milled around them. She remembered the the achingly beautiful sound of the children calling out the names of their pet Alpacas. The beautiful creature with their big brown eyes, and soft, fleecy coats of fur, came running like big teddy bears.

Alex pulled the crumpled sheets over her and snuggled contentedly in Vitali's arms. She didn't need to do any analysis. She already knew enough from her time amongst the villagers to act. A little more research would confirm what her intuition told her so strongly. If she fell on her face, if it couldn't be done, so what? Not trying was the real failure. What was the worst that could happen? While there were no guarantees, something deep in her gut told her she was onto a winner.

She turned toward Vitali and watched him for a long moment as he lay sleeping beside her. His long, dark lashes rested peacefully on his smooth cheeks, his cupid lips were curved in a gentle smile as though he was still relishing the intimacy they'd shared. Her heart did cartwheels in her chest.

Tall, dark, and entirely too handsome, what drove her husband was to control the uncontrollable, to achieve the unachievable, to conquer the unconquerable—that's what he respected. The greater the hurdle, the more she had to prove, the more Vitali would admire and respect her. Well, that was the theory, and tomorrow Alex would put her hunch to the litmus test.

31

———

The blast from the alarm clock shocked Alex from her sleep. She woke to find Vitali fully clothed, tucking the sheets around her. The room was still dark, while outside the slither of the moon was still visible.

'Go back to sleep, Alexandra.'

'Vitali? Are you leaving?' She murmured drowsily.

'I'm sorry I didn't mean to wake you. I forgot to turn the blasted thing off.' He said striding to the bathroom. 'You wouldn't have been disturbed if you'd done what I asked and slept in your own room,' he tossed over his shoulder.

'You should have insisted.' she said

He grunted.

'Besides, I wanted to be woken up. I have something I need.'

His silhouette in the bathroom door stiffened. 'Tell me when I return,' he said autocratically.

She propped herself up on her pillow and tapped the sensor light beside the bed until it dimmed to a soft, gentle light. 'I'd prefer it if we could discuss it now, Vitali. You did say I had only to ask and you would do all you could to ensure my comfort.' she said, ensuring her voice sounded firm yet demure.

'Note to self, you're not only incredibly strong-willed but you have a memory like an elephant,' he said, splashing aftershave on his face.

She bit her lips. *Dear God, please let me succeed.*

Alex decided to come straight out with it. No matter what she said, how creatively she framed it, she needed him to invest in her venture and she doubted he would regard her idea favorably. Far better to set about it under the cloak of secrecy and aim to wow him. He already thought she was a gold-digger, but she would return his investment a hundred times over.

'I need some money,' she blurted.

He flashed her a contemptuous look. 'That didn't take you long,' he spat bitterly. 'At least my perceptions weren't unfounded.'

His cruel words speared her heart. She took a deep breath and reminded herself that beneath his hardened exterior was a wounded hero. Her wounded hero. And she would do everything in her power to show him she was his heroine, worthy of his trust.

'I'd like my own bank account,' she continued. 'With some money in it?'

'How much money, Alexandra?'

In truth, she had no idea how much her venture would cost. Better to shoot high, she decided. She could always repay any extra, but the last thing she wanted to do was go cap in hand begging for more. It was already demeaning to have to ask him for it in the first place. All her life she had stood independently. But if she was going to make this idea happen then she needed to think big.

'Three hundred and sixty-three thousand.' The figure came to her intuitively—her lucky numbers.

He blanched then flashed her an acid look. 'I'm surprised you are settling for so little. Dollars, I assume?'

'U.S.,' she bit. Let him think what he will, but he deserved to suffer for thinking badly of her and her motives. Part of her hated herself for being so childish and feeding his belief. But then they had got off to a bad start and Vitali didn't look like he was going to change his mind no matter how altruistic her motives.

'That's some serious coin. Going somewhere nice?' he said, mockingly.

'I'm not leaving with your money, Vitali.'

'Well, what then?'

'You said I could do some decorating—add my woman's touch.'

'What are you going to do? Repaper the house in 24 karat gold?'

'Actually I was thinking of exterior improvements rather than interior. I'd also like to learn to fly.'

Vitali thrust his foot into his boot, then looked up at her sharply. 'What are you up to, Alexandra?'

'Nothing,' she said. 'You can fly a helicopter and I think it would be fun to learn too. How else am I going to fill in my time?'

'You won't need money for that. I'll teach you myself, he said gruffly.

Alex felt a thrill of triumph. He was offering to spend time with her. Finally she was making progress.

'That would be fabulous. Thank you,' she said leaping from the bed and planting a kiss on his lips.

'Is that it?' he said fixing her with a wary look as he stood up.

'That's it. I hate to appear pushy, but do you think you could put the money in my account straight away. I'd really like to make a start on my project without delay—especially if you're determined to go away.'

'You pushy?' he said, throwing his camel jacket on. 'What project?' he added, suspiciously.

'Nothing to worry about. I promise. In fact, I think you will be pleasantly surprised.' she said smiling extra brightly at him in the hope of melting the deep ravines of worry creasing his brow.

He sighed an exasperated breath. 'Whatever makes you happy,' he said with an ironic twist. 'Just make sure it doesn't make me wild. I'll speak to Bob. He'll make the necessary arrangements immediately.' he tossed at her as he headed for the door.

'Vitali—'

'What now!' he said testily.

She raced to him, throwing her arms around his neck before he could stop her. 'You forgot to kiss me goodbye.'

'For God's sake, Alexandra. I'm through with the charade. Stop playing games.' There was a ragged edge to his vehemence. His hands curved around her soft, warm nakedness as she clung to him. He drew her body even more intimately against his.

'One kiss.' she purred, thrusting her fingers persuasively through his thick, coal-black hair. 'It won't hurt. I promise. And I was a good wife last night, wasn't I?' she purred.

His chest heaved and his mouth possessed hers in angry compliance. His hands splayed over her body, grabbing her with crazed urgency. When he finally wrenched his head up, a raging conflict glittered in his eyes.

'I am going,' he pronounced with glacial resolve. He pushed her away from him. 'You've had your proper goodbye, now let me get on with my work, wife. I'll see you when I return in a week or so—if you're still here.'

He slammed the door shut after him. His boots boomed along the deck, as though the wolves were snapping at his heels. Alex grinned and leapt back into his side of the bed, drawing the covers up to her face, and inhaling the sultry memory of the passion they'd shared. She writhed in sensuous delight. He was her man. Soon she would convince him that she was his woman.

He wanted her to stay. He hadn't said it? Well, not exactly. But he wouldn't have offered to teach her to fly his beloved helicopter otherwise. And though they'd had a testy exchange he hadn't balked at giving her the money.

"Whatever makes you happy." Those were his words. "Just don't make me wild." She would show him that she was committed to his happiness. She would prove that together they could achieve their mutual joy.

32

Alex drifted back to sleep and didn't wake again until eight. Outrageous, she mused, smiling as she stretched. She never normally slept so late. Despite everything, she felt relaxed. She buried her face in the pillow inhaling his sultry scent. If only she were in his arms. She glanced out the window and felt her heart tremble with excitement. She was on a new journey. A new chapter in her life.

She swung her legs over the bed and skipped towards the shower. This was her first morning at Gold Ridge Station and life was full of beautiful possibilities.The hot, dry, shimmery heat of the day enveloped her as she dressed. She slung a loose shirt-dress over her head and strapped sturdy sandals onto her feet, twisted her hair into a single plait, and danced onto the deck.

She looked up at the endless blue sky; the parched brown and grey hills; the shimmer of sun on the lake and schist; and inhaled the scent of summer fruit trees laden with sun-ripened apricots and shiny crimson cherries. Once again she counted her blessings. Life was beautiful and she intended to enjoy it to the max.

Here she belonged.

The yummy gold smell of freshly baked bread wafted in the air, intermingling with sun-ripened fruit and grapes from Vitali's vineyard. The shouts of children blended with the barks of farm dogs.

Alex had never felt less isolated in her life. New York, with its teaming throngs of stressed out people and thugs, had always made her feel alone.

She stretched her hands to the sky and inhaled the sweet air. There was no way she would ever be lonely here. Or bored. Her project would see to that, she mused happily as she went in search of Dara McKee. She found her in the kitchen with the two Maori girls who helped in the house—Aroha and Hinemoa. Alex insisted on having her breakfast at the kitchen table so she could chat to them all, but the girls were so full of shy giggles they could hardly speak. So Dara answered Alex's questions on their behalf.

'I thought you must be baking bread,' Alex remarked questioningly, looking around at the ovens although there was no smell of it in the kitchen.

'Everything's cooked down in the bake-house,' Dara explained. 'I'll show you after you've eaten. If you like.'

Alex nodded. 'Yes please. I'd like that very much.'

Dara laughed. 'Everyone's looking forward to strutting their wares in front of you at the Farmers Market. But be warned, they can talk the hind legs of a stag when you get them started. You won't find us lacking in passion.'

'I'm glad to hear it.'

Hinemoa served her a plate of fresh fruit—plump pinot grapes that popped in her mouth, fat plums, the juice of which threatened to slide from her spoon, sweet, succulent cherries and sun kissed orchards. She really was in heaven, she mused, eating the fruits of the gods.

'Do you fly these in?' she asked.

'Good heavens, no!' Dara chuckled. 'All home-grown. Mr Rossi is big on self-sufficiency.'

Alex almost choked on her mouthful of fruit as she gagged back the temptation to declare, '"aint that the truth." Instead she nodded her head in admiring approval.

Everything in New York seemed to be out of season, imported from some exotic locale, and none of it was anywhere near as tasty as this delicious bounty. When Aroha disappeared outside and returned shortly after, grinning proudly, with a bowl of freshly laid free-range eggs Alex didn't have the heart to tell her she couldn't possibly eat anything more.

As she tucked into the most sumptuous omelet she had ever tasted, Dara told her about the meat-house and the store where all the dried and tinned foods were kept, as well as other maintenance necessities. Clearly, Dara had been tasked with filling Alex in on all the domestic things which went into ensuring the house ran smoothly. Alex listened patiently, feigning interest.

A bell clanged in the near distance and Dara immediately answered Alex's unspoken question.

'The school bell. It's nine o'clock.

'You have a school here?'

'Of sorts. This year we're home schooling fourteen kids. Most of them are the sons and daughters of our employees, but Vitali is passionate about making sure all kids, regardless of economic circumstance have the right to quality education. If it wasn't for him,' Dara said proudly, half the Maori kids round here would still be illiterate.'

Alex shook her head in amazement. Her husband really was multi-faceted and generous. Her admiration and love for him notched higher.

Dara left the girls to clean up while she and Alex embarked on a grand tour of the places they'd just spoken about. Bread was baked in the bake house every second day. The store was open every morning for anyone who needed supplies. The radio correspondence lessons in the school were very personal, each child speaking to the teacher in turn. The meat-house looked as if it could feed the whole community for weeks.

Alex reacquainted herself with most of the people she had met yesterday and thoroughly enjoyed herself, inspecting the produce that was destined for the farmers market. Their last stop was the stables. She arranged with Matt, the head stable-boy and horse-breaker, to select a very obedient horse and have it ready for her to ride later in the afternoon. If her bum and thighs were going to survive a muster they'd better start toughening up now.

They returned to the house for lunch and Alex took the opportunity to ask Bob if she might have a private chat with him in Vitali's study. Ever since a fall from a horse had aggravated an old back injury he could no longer ensure long hours on a horse. Instead he busied himself with running the business end of the station in Vitali's absence. Alex noticed with interest he looked at his wife, as though seeking her approval, before consenting with a broad smile to join her in Vitali's study.

His very private study.

'I never thought I'd see the day,' he chuckled. 'He's met his match in you, that's for sure,' he said, punching in the code which unlocked the study door. He hesitated before turning the handle, 'He does know what you're up to?'

'He told me you'd help me,' Alex said, peering past his arm.

'Time he started opening some doors, anyhow.' Bob muttered as he allowed Alex to enter.

33

Vitali's study was nothing like she'd imagined. This room was inconsistent with the pared back modern simplicity that permeated every other corner of his house.. It was warm and cosy and almost cluttered.

In the center facing the view was a massive antique desk, feather-filled, worn, butter-soft leather chairs sat around an ornately carved coffee table, in the middle of which sat a sulphur yellow work of art. She immediately recognized it as a piece by New Zealand's most eminent ceramist Len Castle.

Against one wall was a large showcase of trophies, and above it hung an impressive number of blue ribbons showcasing a variety of awards for venison and wine. Floor to ceiling bookcases held rows of magazines and books, and there were several business-like filing cabinets.

'I assume it's about the money?' Bob said matter-of-factly. 'I called the accountant as Vitali instructed. I'm assured the money will be available by close of day.'

'Thank you, Bob. I doubt I'll need the full amount.'

'More is more. Alex.' he grinned. 'A drop in the Pacific to

Vitali, and besides, I get the impression he wouldn't leave you wanting.'

Her embarrassment about asking for the money subsided as she realized how easy Vitali and now Bob were making it for her.

'Vitali tells me you have a special project. Sing out if I can be of any help.'

'There is something I'm hoping you can assist with,' she said, brightening at the prospect of not having to wade through the detail on her own. 'It's experimental,' she cautioned. 'No guarantee that my hunch will work. But if we don't try we'll never know.'

'Go on,' he said, his eyes sparkling.

'Do the names Suri, Cara and Lanuda mean anything to you?'

'I think the wife might have mentioned Suri while flicking through the gossip mags,' he scratched his head. 'Yes, that's it. Tom Cruise's daughter. As for the rest, nah.'

Alex laughed. 'Nothing as famous as Tom Cruise. What if I told you they were different breeds of Alpaca? What if I told you we could breed them here?'

'Honestly?' he asked. 'I'd say you were trying to make possible the impossible.' Which I take it is just the point.' he said chuckling. '

'Exactly.'

'Don't take this the wrong way Alex, but it seems a bit fanciful for around here.'

'Not at all,' Alex said fired by his interest and the hope that her plan could be a success. 'The thing about them is that they can survive longer than most animals in drought conditions—like their relatives the camel they've got well-developed sweat glands. Plus, they can survive in frozen terrain. I'm sure Central Otago feels warm in winter compared to the Andes.'

Bob McKee nodded his agreement. He sat down in one of the plump leather chairs, and stretched out his legs, his hands clasped behind his head. 'You have my undivided attention,' he said, nodding toward the opposite chair.

'Not only are they more fitted to this country than deer,' she said, sitting down, 'but if I overheard you correctly last night you told Vitali that deer farming is on the wane as it's not as profitable as it was a few years ago. The market is saturated and demand is tailing off is it not, Mr. McKee? But the market for exotic fur, on the other hand, is ballooning. And then there is the challenge, which is after all what motivates my husband.'

Bob looked dumbfounded. He slowly shook his head as if needing to clear cobwebs from his mind. 'I thought...' he paused, and made a helpless gesture with his hands, then gave her a lop-sided smile. 'Looks to me like Vitali's got himself one hell of a wife. Does he know the details?'

Alex decided that discretion was the best strategy. 'Vitali said I could go ahead and do anything that makes me happy. He said I could, what was the term he used—free-range? This is what will make me happy. Hopefully it will make Vitali happy too.'

Bob McKee chuckled, his blue eyes crinkling with amused delight. 'Don't get me wrong, Alex. I'm with you all the way. There's just not too many women, or men, for that matter, who'd come up with a whacky idea like this—and be certain to pull it off. It sounds good to me. Worth a shot. Regardless of the outcome.'

'Thank you, Bob,' Alex said leaping from her chair and swinging her arms around his neck. Thank you so, so much.' She breathed a sigh of relief as she released him and walked to the panoramic window.'Let's just keep it to ourselves for now. No need to bore Vitali with the details. I want it to a wonderful surprise.'

'Mum's the word,' Bob said, tapping his finger on his nose.

'I'll be honest—I really don't know where to start.' She confided. 'I don't even know how you go about importing Alpacas. I'll need your help on what channels I have to go through. Government departments and then of course there's the bigger picture', she said looking at the awards Vitali's deer had won. 'We'll have to figure out how we're going to win prizes.'

'Prizes?'

'I figure if we are going to make Vitali happy we'll have to cater to something he cares about. He's too rich to be in deer farming for the money—these are what is important to him. Accolades. Prizes for being the best.' She spun around to face Bob. 'Our Alpacas, mine and Vitali's—and yours, have to surpass all others.'

'I like your thinking, Alex. Think big and get the job done! Why not? I'll get straight onto it. One thing's certain. Whatever you import will have to be quarantined. It's not going to be quick, Alex. You'll have to be patient.'

'So you'll make those enquires for me? Get the ball rolling?'

'Right away,' he promised. 'I'll certainly have some concrete information by tonight.'

'You're a gem, Bob!'

Bob laughed outright. 'I reckon you're the marvel around here, Alex. A gold-nugget in the rough. Now I know how Vitali got snared. All these years women didn't seem to mean anything to him. But you...' Again, he shook his head. 'He must have detected a vein of gold in you. I'm glad he's been able to play a part in enabling you to bring your talents to the surface. Well. Good luck to you. I'm glad for you both.'

Alex wished it was going to be as easy to convince Vitali of her good intentions as it was Bob, but she was pleased with the initiative she had taken, and the feedback Bob had offered. He was now her firm ally, and together they would get the project active as soon as possible. Hopefully, before Vitali got back from his muster. She wanted something definite in hand to show him that she could be a true partner in every sense of the word.

Luck was on her side. Bob called some personal contacts and found that the MAF security department was running an experimental operation on Matiu Somes Island off the coast of Wellington. They were importing frozen embryos of these breeds from Argentina, and transferring the embryos into local Alpaca from Waiheke Island.

'We've got half a million dollars, Bob. Let's buy whatever we can with that,' Alex instructed without a moment's hesitation. Not even by a flicker of expression did she betray her nerves. Could she really pull this off?

34

The days that followed were packed with activity for Alex. Most mornings she spent with Bob, pressing for a resolution about the Alpacas she wanted. Forty females and ten males would be airfreighted from Matiu Somes Island to Gold Ridge Station within the month.

While all this was being negotiated Alex learnt a great deal about the running of the station under Bob and Dara's coaching. Then every afternoon she spent more time in the saddle. It didn't take long for the aches and pains to subside and she began to enjoy increasingly long rides.

The horse which Matt had chosen for her was a very well behaved golden mare called Chardonnay, and Alex loved riding her. The head stable-hand, cautious of the boss's wife's safety, always insisted that someone ride along with her, so Alex made the acquaintance of the Maori boys who had waved to her from the fence that afternoon.

She particularly liked two of them, Rangi and Jack, who kept her entertained with stories of their skills of survival and self-sufficiency, fending for themselves on the land. They both boasted they could survive anything, anywhere, any time and they were going to be the best stockmen that had ever sat in a saddle on Gold Ridge Station.

Alex was inclined to believe them—they handled horses expertly as if they had almost been born in the saddle. Gradually Alex mastered their skill of riding bareback and she loved the thrill and exhilaration of feeling at one with the animal. She was pretty sure that Chardonnay also loved the freedom of being unencumbered by a weighty saddle, and a horrid bit in her mouth.

HER WEDDING PHOTOGRAPHS arrived on her sixth day at Gold Ridge Station. Vitali hadn't bothered about choosing from the proofs. He'd left them on her writing desk in her bedroom. Large prints of every shot taken were bound in two identical albums—one for her and one for her mother she assumed.

Alex leafed through the album, studying the photos of her and her new husband, looking to see if their deception would be picked up by her mother. But as she looked at the image they were so incredibly convincing that she almost believed that their marriage was not one gigantic lie.

She trailed her fingers over the large close-up of their kiss, his head bent to hers, their foreheads touching, his sensuous lips pressed to hers.

As though they were one.

Looking at that photo she could almost believe that Vitali had married her because he loved her with all his heart and that their marriage would last. But photographs could lie, and she was well aware of Vitali's agenda.

She started to have doubts about sending the album to her mother. Vitali had made it clear he wanted no publicity. She wrote a long letter to accompany them asking her to keep the photos private, and telling her about their life together.

She wanted her mother to understand the life she had chosen with Vitali, but held little hope. The South Island of New Zealand was a million kilometers away from her mother's glittering life in New York—the life she'd wanted her only child to follow.

Yet Alex yearned to recapture the brief wave of empathy they had shared on her wedding-day. She wanted to reach out to her mother again. Just as Alex wished she could have reached out to her father. She'd attended too many funerals and heard too many stories where people had left it too late to tell the people most important to them that they were loved.

Thumbing through her wedding photos, and recalling loved ones no longing living reminded her of the photographs she had printed and placed in a small album in her suitcase...the close-up ones she had taken of her father's painting *Lost Love*.

She fetched them and spread them on her writing desk. Alex's heart pounded then took a dive as her mind raced. She knew now who the woman in the painting was, but what was the significance of the setting?

It had to have been inspired by somewhere on Gold Ridge Station, she decided, glancing out at the craggy ranges in the distance. But where?

When she went out riding that afternoon she described the painting to Rangi and Jack. It would have been easier to show them the photo but Vitali had made it bitingly clear that on no account was the painting to be shown to anyone.

'Do you know anywhere with endless velvet plains of golden tussock and Rātā trees clinging fiercely to craggy rocks? Somewhere that looks like it could be a painting, somewhere beautiful with rough soaring peaks that look as though they could be troughed on the canvas? Lit from the dying sun with a hurtle of blue and ochre and gold. Do you know anywhere around here like that?' she asked, careful to inject her voice with only mild interest.

'Yeah, why?' Jack asked, a puzzled line creasing his brow.

'I saw something like it in a travel article once. I'd like to see it for myself,' she said.

'Fair enough. Heaps of places. We'll show ya a few of 'em if ya want.' Rangi crowed in his cocksure knowledge of the land.

Alex's pulse quickened. 'I'd love that.'

'It's pretty far,' Jack cautioned, as though conscious of their responsibility to look after the boss' wife and the fact she had only recently learned to ride.

'Come on Jack, stop being a wet blanket,' Rangi argued. 'We can be there and back before dusk— heaps of time before anyone notices we're missing. What are ya worried about?'

Jack regarded him skeptically, then shrugged. 'Nah, it's all good,' he smiled weakly.

'Sweet as' grinned Rangi. 'We'd better get a hurry on if we're to get back before dark.'

35

―――

As the horses crested the hill a little over an hour later Alex paused triumphantly, then gazed in awe at the breathtaking view. Her heart spasmed as her eyes lingered on the spot where her father had stood, not far from there, so many years ago. The spot so indelibly etched in her memory. The spot like a beauty mark on her soul.

Her eyes pooled with tears, and every hair on her body stood on end as she looked around her at the setting that was so achingly familiar. She lifted agonized eyes to the craggy ranges, imagining the place where her father had painted Lucrezia's face. A warm wind danced around Alex, calling her name, drawing her deeper and deeper into the painting's mystery.

'You alright, missus?' Rangi asked. 'You seen a ghost?'

'Yes...yes—I'm fine,' she said absent-mindedly. It gave her an odd feeling to know that her father had stood on this very spot. That this was what had burned in his memory all those lonely years he'd spent in self-imposed exile.

More than anything she wanted to be alone. Alone with her father, with his memory, with his spirit. He felt so real to her—as though she could almost reach out and touch him. She decided that tomorrow she would return on her own and camp overnight so she could watch the sunset that he had painted and spend time with his memory. It was probably as near as she would ever get to the father she had never known and she wanted to feel his closeness.

Perhaps he might even give up some of the secrets which haunted the man she loved.

'Better get a move on before the sun goes down,' Jack said, insisting that they head back to the homestead. He frowned as he looked at the sky.

'What's up?' said Rangi.

'The boss's chopper.'

'But he's not due back for two days?' Alex said, as at last the helicopter broke through the low cloud.

'Must be some kind of trouble,' said Rangi.

'Trouble like we'll be in if the missus ain't back safe and sound before the boss,' Jack said.

Alex immediately urged Chardonnay into a gallop. Why was Vitali home two days early? What kind of trouble would cause him to return home to her? She didn't know. She simply didn't want to miss a second of being with her husband.

It was fortunate that they did turn back because they were still a fair ride away. The horse responded with enthusiastic urgency and they sped home.

She raced up to the big house, and handed her horse over to the boys to return to the stables. Her heart was galloping as she dashed along the deck to Bob's office, expecting Vitali to be there. But only Bob and the bookkeeper were in the room.

'Vitali?' she asked breathlessly. 'What's happened?' Dread wormed through her gut.

'Nothing's happened—he's come home early and gone to make himself handsome for you. Must be missing his new bride' Bob teased with a wide grin.

'*Really*?' She beamed a happy smile.

'Did you tell him about the shipment of Alpacas?'

'Nope—didn't want to spoil your surprise.'

'Thanks,' she said, then shot away to the kitchen. She wasn't too sure that Vitali was sprucing himself up for her, but she could use the extra time to her advantage and make his home-coming extra special. Luckily Dara and the two girls were in the kitchen preparing vegetables for dinner.

'Have we got any Bluff Oysters, Dara?'

'Sure do. When they're in season and Vitali's at home we get them flown in daily.'

'And some of Vitali's favorite champagne?'

Dara nodded. 'Yip. Cellar's full.Always.'

'Would you mind fetching the most expensive bottle he has. Something really, really exquisite.'

Dara whistled. 'Me oh my. Looks like you're in the mood for a celebration.'

'I am, Dara.' she beamed happily. 'I am.'

TEN MINUTES later Alex carried a tray of oysters, champagne and crystal flutes to Vitali's room. The thought that he might have come home because he missed her put an extra lift in her step. Why else would he have come back early from his beloved muster? Whatever the reason she was going to make the most of his return and show him how sincerely his wife had missed him. And, of course she was bursting to share news of her project.

Strange, she thought, standing in the doorway to their room. She couldn't hear running water. Perhaps he had already showered. Maybe he was getting dressed. She walked through to the walk-in wardrobe. The connecting door to her room was wide open. Vitali was standing at her writing-desk, studying one of the wedding photos. She stood still, watching his face.

She wanted to say "we look good together.". Instead when at last she spoke she said, 'They came out well, don't you think?'

His head swung toward her, and for a moment there was a sharp question in his eyes, as if he had seen something in the photograph that made him wonder about her. About them. Then his gaze dropped to the tray she was still carrying and his mouth curved in amusement.

'A woman bearing gifts spells danger.'

He wore a sumptuous thigh-length black silk robe which grazed his long, powerful legs. The robe was loosely tied, revealing a deep V of his bronzed bare chest, from which spirals of dark hair peeked. Freshly showered and shaved, he oozed masculine virility, and Alex caught her breath.

She glanced down at her riding boots and jeans and fiercely wished that she had thought to clean herself up after her long, dusty ride. She hadn't even stopped to think about her appearance. And it was too late to dash back, put on the lippy and transform herself into a goddess.

But something about the way his eyes met hers when at last she lifted her gaze to his told her he would take her *au natural.*

She let the delectable thought linger between them. He said nothing about the wedding photos. Instead he just stared at her, undressing her with his eyes. She tilted her chin and drew a purposeful breath. She had to get his mind away from sex and back on the challenging track that would make their relationship sustainable.

'You're very photogenic.' He said as Alex carried the tray over to the table beside the bed.

She put it down, and picked up the image he had been studying. 'Thank you. So are you.'

'Your mother will be convinced you love me.'

Perhaps I do.

His hands slid around Alex's waist and pulled her back against him. 'But we both know better,' he murmured into her ear, moving his lips over it with teasing sensuality.

A delicious tingle of excitement spread through her. Perhaps Vitali really had come home because he couldn't get enough of her. Eager to see some need in his eyes, she tried to turn around, but he tightened one muscular arm around her waist, pinning her back against his chest.

'Stay right where you are my little seductress.' The need for dominance over her graveled through his voice.

His free hand roved up over her breasts to the top button of her shirt. She felt the stirrings of his desire that no words could hide or diminish, and she knew there was no dominance. Nor did she feel in any way threatened by her body's response to the exquisite caressing of her bared flesh as his hand explored her hardened nipples beneath her shirt.

She willingly surrendered to his need to hold and touch her with such erotic finesse. She did not fight the waves of pleasure that rippled through her in increasing strength, melting her bones so that it was only his support that kept her standing.

It was Vitali who could no longer bear not to take what she could give him. With a guttural cry, he swung her around and pressed her heated flesh to his, arching back at the sheer impact of the long-deferred intimacy.

36

Alex didn't remember how they got to the bed. She recalled only that first sweet thrust of him inside her and the incredible storm of sensation that followed, holding him tightly when he finally collapsed on top of her. She remembered kissing each other in an ecstasy of feeling that had nothing to do with power games and never would.

And when eventually he spoke, Vitali made no mention of games or charades. He said, with a dry intonation, 'Let's have that glass of champagne now.'

'Yes,' she replied huskily. 'Will you do the honors? If I pop the cork I might take out your eye.'

He gave that low, throaty laugh that hit the pit of her stomach in a wave of tingles, and slowly untangled his limbs from hers. Alex rolled on to her back and watched with immense pleasure as he padded butt-naked around the bed.

He lifted the bottle from the tray on the bedside table and popped the cork with the finesse of a French sommelier, and filled two crystal flutes. Alex hitched herself up onto the pillow as he held out one of the glasses to her.

'So, have you managed to get through the half million yet?' he asked mockingly.

'Not quite,' Alex answered, and sipped her champagne with every appearance of blithe unconcern. 'But I do have to discuss fencing with you.'

His broad brows furrowed. 'Fencing?' he asked skeptically, and proceeded to pick up an oyster still in its shell. He passed it to her, and held it up to let it slide into her mouth as she opened her lips. Then taking one for himself he sucked it into his mouth with what Alex could only sum up as a slow purposeful tease. 'What do you want to cage, Alexi. Not me I hope.'

'Alpacas.'

The oyster he just downed nearly came splurging out of his mouth. 'Alpacas?' His green eyes flared in disbelief.

'Fifty of the world's finest.' She replied enjoying his reaction. 'They cost me– us—a lot of money.' she corrected. 'But let me assure you that as my financial partner in this venture you can be assured not only do I intend to return your investment within 3 years, but to double the return.'

She proceeded to tell him exactly what Alpaca's she had purchased and what she intended to do with them. 'I have full capital and financial projections—but now's not the time to be looking at Excel and Power Point,' she said, trailing a finger down his chest. 'Work-life balance is an important part of business success, don't you agree, my love?'

The disbelief and mockery quickly neutralized. Calculations and speculation grew in their place, and when Alex had finished informing him of the length and breadth of her venture into Alpaca breeding, Vitali stared at her for a long time before speaking.

'You...are one hell of an opponent, *mia cara*. You're going to ride me all the way, aren't you?'

'Yes, I am,' she said, placing her glass down and straddling him. 'With pleasure.'

His mouth twisted in dry irony. 'I think I'm going to enjoy the return on this investment.'

'And I'm taking this land on. Just like you. Not against you. As far as I'm concerned, your business is my business. And if there's any way of making our dealing better, I'm willing to do it. Do you have a problem with that?' Alex demanded.

It was a very deliberate challenge, and on it hung the future of their relationship. If he refused to accept her interest, there could only be the most bitter conflict ahead.

For what seemed like an eternity the green eyes searched hers with fierce intensity. 'This is a long-term project you've embarked on, Alexi,' he stated, without any inflection at all.

'Don't you think I'm aware of that? I intend to see our partnership through—Alpaca or no Alpacas. But obviously, I'd prefer your cooperation,' she said just as flatly.

He nodded slowly, as if feeling his way with great care. 'I would prefer, in future, that you don't make any more decisions without my knowledge.' His tone was stern, yet his eyes betrayed his struggle. Was he struggling to admit that he respected her, admired her—loved her? Despite himself?

A knot twisted in Alex's gut. She couldn't be sure. But control was not something she was not used to sharing or ceding. But with Vitali it was a lesson she was willing finally to learn.

Perhaps they would teach each other how to share control and care for each others' mutual interests in business and in life.

And importantly—*to trust.*

'I would prefer, in future, to be accorded the same respect.' She said, summoning a counter statement.

His mouth twitched in dry appreciation and Alex knew she had won a significant victory.

'Are we looking towards a long future, Mrs Rossi?'

Her lips curved in quiet triumph. 'Yes, I do believe we are, Mr Rossi.'

'Tangoing with you grows ever more stimulating, but don't let it go to your head, Alex. Because I'll keep my head, no matter what surprises you flash at me,' he warned her mockingly. He brought his arms around her neck and pulled her toward him. For the first time she sensed he was happy to relinquish control. The thought made her smile. *He loves me, even if he's too proud, too stubborn, too afraid to admit the truth.*

'I'd hate you to lose your head, Vitali.' Alex said, kissing him. Even their earlier kisses hadn't prepared her for the sheer need that welled within her as Vitali made love to her mouth with his.

'I do so enjoy the taste of your lips, the smell of your skin, the feel of your hair—and I adore looking at your beautiful face.' she said breathlessly.

For the first time, he gave a full-throated laugh. His eyes danced at her in pure joy as he lifted her arms above her head and moved his body over hers with slow, sensual deliberation.

'What else do you enjoy, Alexi? Tell me, you wanton seductress, *mia tentatrice.*'

'Everything about you,' she teased. She wanted to tell him that what she wanted most was for him to tell her that he loved her, not just with his body, but with his heart.

Maybe he would always guard that vulnerable part of him closely.

But at least she was no longer a wife in status only. He had accepted her as his partner, and importantly, as his equal. That was more than enough to forge a solid and lasting future. Wasn't it?

Now that she felt more secure she could even start thinking of having a baby, a child, a family. Alex was sure that Vitali would heartily approve. Hadn't he told her that night of their strange proposal? "We will marry and you will have my child."

Surely he still wanted that—after all, what was a kingdom without heirs? She had only to look at the way he was with the children on the Station to know that. He might never allow himself to admit he loved her, but Alex had no doubt he would openly confess his love for their children. She pressed her palm against the flatness of her stomach and felt it flutter.

What if she was pregnant already?

37

The honking horn of the Land Rover woke Alexandra the next morning. She and Vitali had slept in her room far too ensconced with each other to think of setting the alarm. She heard him mutter something under his breath, then a possessive arm arched over her breasts and swept her back against his chest. He nudged her onto her back and peppered delicate sensual kisses down her neck as his fingers encircled her nipples.

It was more than half an hour later that Alex remembered the beeping horn. The tempestuous blazing intensity of their lovemaking obliterated the noise from her mind.

Vitali lay half sprawled across her naked body in relaxed abandonment, devoid of any cares whatsoever. She tried to remonstrate with him as her fingers teased across his chest. He had the most amazing upper body. As for the lower half...she ran her hand down the fine hair that snaked from his chest to his loins.

His stomach contracted under her feathering touch.

'Your driver has been waiting a long time, my groom.' she said, continuing her descent.

'I haven't slept in for...I don't know how many years. I feel so relaxed. I guess I must have been tired.' he said with a slight trace of guilt.

'The benefits of being the boss,' she whispered as she kissed his neck. 'Along with the other benefits' she said, reminding him of their lovemaking last night.

'Tongues will be wagging,' he grinned, 'there won't be a person on the station who doesn't know what I've been up to.'

He showed no remorse and Alex couldn't suppress a merry little giggle, which Vitali clearly found provocative, because he found the energy to silence it, cupping his mouth over hers and planting a lingering kiss on her lips. Hence the driver was forced to wait longer.

ONLY AFTER VITALI left did Alex finally stir herself to rise. The muster wouldn't be finished for two days. It was unlikely that Vitali would break his work schedule again. She could return to the place her father had painted, stay overnight and return before Vitali was back. She found herself breathing fast.

There was nothing she wanted to do more than to be alone in that special place her father had found so inspiring. Not only was the setting intrinsically beautiful but, even though she had only experienced it briefly, she had felt something deeply spiritual.

Alex had never thought of herself as a spiritual person but a powerful feeling deep within, convinced her that if she sat silently, for long enough, beneath the crimson Rātā tree her father had painted, the secret of the painting may be revealed.

The only challenge would be convincing Bob and Dara

to let her go alone.

'I've travelled though India, Mexico, Jordan and Egypt and a whole bunch of places on my own. I know how to look after myself,' she told them. 'I've even trekked through the Sahara on a camel.'

Bob sat impassively, his arms folded over his chest. 'Your husband would never forgive us if we let you go wandering off on your own. Especially overnight.'

'Bob's right,' said Dara. The high country isn't some benevolent tropical destination scattered with tourists and travel agents, and people who will cater to them. It can turn on you, quick as a wild bull—just like Vitali will turn on us if anything happens to you.'

'Nothing will go wrong.' Alex insisted. Then sensing they would not be swayed she added, 'Rangi and Jack can come. They'll look after me.'

AFTER GETTING Rangi to pinpoint on the Station map exactly where they were headed, all objections were promptly dropped.

Alex and the boys set off on their horses after lunch, giving themselves plenty of time to reach their destination before sunset. A pack-horse loaded down with what Alex thought was an unnecessary amount of camping gear trailed after them.

'Can't let the boss's wife rough it,' Jack said, as they tracked up the steep bush-clad gully.

'I'm not the Queen,' she said, 'I would've been perfectly happy sleeping under the stars in my sleeping bag.'

The boys looked at each other and laughed, 'Yeah right.'

Alex silently contented herself with the thought that soon enough they'd see for themselves she wasn't a prima donna and would report back to everyone that "the missus could rough it as well as anybody."

The boys laughed and joked and were in high spirits. As they rode they entertained Alex by identifying all the plants and wildlife they saw, and telling stories about them—including ones about how traditional Maori medicine was made from many of the trees and bushes they encountered along the way. There was one underlying theme in everything they said.

Survival in a hard country.

The strong lived, the weak died. There was nothing in between.

As they rode further and further into the golden plains her father had painted, Alex was too overwhelmed with sadness to be a good listener. The boys quickly sensed her change of mood and chatted quietly to each other.

The track in places was narrow and rocky, dropping steeply even in the relatively tame descents of the mountains beyond. After an hour of riding under the scorching Otago sun, ducking under arching native bush and trees, and carefully picking over slabs of schist embedded in the dry earth, the track leveled out onto a thick fur of golden tussock.

When they reached a water-hole nearby the boys advised Alex it would be best to camp there. Alex patted the neck of the champagne mare before dismounting and handing the reigns to Jack. The horse turned her great chocolate eyes to her as though understanding her sadness and gently nuzzled Alex's hair.

Tears prickled Alex's eyes as she wondered, had her father been alive, how he would have comforted her. 'I'd like to be alone,' she said, not unkindly. 'Will you stay here and set up camp while I go for a walk?

The boys looked at each other uncertainly.

'Sure, boss,' said Rangi nudging Jack. 'No worries.'

She left them to it and walked through the tussock, her breath catching, as she headed towards the giant rātā tree which had been depicted so hauntingly in the foreground of her father's painting. Standing defiantly alone, the gnarled bulbous trunk, with incredibly twisted limbs exploding in a blaze of crimson brush-like flowers, seemed to claw at the sky in tortured longing.

She remembered the staccato flourishes her father had used as though each dab of paint had stabbed at his heart. Had the tree been to her father a visual expression of his own innermost feelings—the love for another man's wife that was tearing at his soul? Had he too felt a deep empathy for this land? Had it torn him apart when he had to flee, she wondered?

She trailed her hand around the trunk of the rātā tree, pressing her back against it, and stared at the ancient mountains that stood like sentinels to untold lifetimes. She had no trouble identifying the giant outcropping of craggy rock from which Lucrezia's face had emerged. It had probably been there for centuries and would stay the same through centuries to come...indestructible...timeless, like the Great Sphinx of ancient Egypt. An eternal symbol of her father's love for Lucrezia.

'*Speak to me*,' she cried out to the rugged stone range that jagged across the skyline in the distance. 'Speak to me. Tell me what happened here?'

Tears gathered in force and spilled down Alex's cheeks. For the first time in her life Alex didn't try to stop them. *Her father had remembered his daughter.* And he had left her a legacy of love...and pain.

She slid down the tree-trunk to sit at its base, a sob

tearing from her mouth. All those lonely, needing years... they might have been so close if they had known each other. For so long she had fought her own battles, made herself self-sufficient, but there was still a child inside her that cried out to be wanted, and to be loved—no matter what she looked like or who's child she was. To simply belong to someone without question or reservation. Why did her father have to die before she'd even heard of his existence?

The thundering sound of an approaching helicopter hammered in the air. Her mind screamed in protest against what it meant and sought frantically to explain it away. The mustering was being done a long way from here, but Vitali could be just passing over.

Surely he wouldn't be coming for her. He didn't miss her or need her that much, he'd made that clear. And after last night surely his sexual appetite was sated.

Tension played havoc with her nerves as the noise came closer and closer. The sound built up to a crescendo, dry grass caught up in the tornado of the wind it created spewed across the sky. The noise lessened then cut out altogether. Her gut lurched.

He had landed.

Probably near the water-hole where the boys were setting up camp. And he would come looking for her if she remained hidden. She would have to go to him to minimize his wrath.

He was sure to be annoyed once he realized why she was here. But how did he know? He must have been to the homestead and found her gone. As soon as he had been told by Bob and Cara where she was heading...she could well imagine the significance he would put on her coming here to the scene of the painting!

Would he be furious she'd brought the boys with her,

fearing that somehow they may piece the significance of why she was here? She didn't know—she only knew that she was too upset right now to take on another battle. She was a mess; her face streaked with tears, her emotions in tatters.

How was she going control Vitali when she wasn't even in control of herself? Any other time or place she would have welcomed Vitali's company, but not here. Not now.

It only felt like an intrusion.

She fingered the photo of *Lost Love* buried in her pocket. Why did so many people want to deny the truth? Why did her father and his painting have to remain a secret? Why did nobody care what she wanted or what she felt? The answer drifted in her consciousness like a soft breeze.

Because you must open you heart, you must confide your feelings, to love deeply you must risk being hurt.

No, she resisted. This was an intensely private matter to her, and Vitali wouldn't understand, wouldn't be sympathetic, couldn't be sympathetic. He thought her father had killed his father—or as good as. She had to remember he'd inferred that.

Even trying to explain anything seemed hopeless, but she had to cope somehow. Vitali left her no other choice. Alex pushed herself to her feet and leaned against the tree-trunk as she rubbed over her face with the sleeve of her shirt. She took several deep breaths in a desperate attempt to compose herself. She took a couple of steps around the trunk to get a view of what was happening at the campsite where the chopper had landed.

Vitali was covering the ground towards her in long, lithe strides. His workmanlike jeans and shirt did nothing to diminish his strong aura of raw power. He came to a halt a few paces short of her, his hard warrior-face looking as if it were carved from granite, the green eyes seared hers with bitter questions. The tension emanating from him in a cloud of distrust almost choked her.

'What the hell are you doing up here, Alexandra?' he demanded curtly. 'I thought we agreed not to drag up the past.' The lowering sun glinted like blades of fire on his hair.

'I'm not bringing it up, Vitali,' she said in an attempt to appease the bitter accusation in his green eyes. 'I'm just looking at it.' An ungovernable wave of sadness brought another welling of tears and she half turned away as she fought for composure.

'Alexi?' his deep voice was barely a whisper, weighted by concern. His hand grasped her arm turning her around to face him again. 'You're crying.'

'I can't help having feelings about my father!' she protested, unable to stop the tears from trickling down her cheeks. 'I'm not a cold, unfeeling piece of rock. I can't just shut off my emotions like you do. And I'm not hurting anyone or anything. I know you don't have reason to care about him,' she sobbed, 'But he was my father. And this...' she said pulling the photo of *Lost Love* from her pocket and sweeping it toward the ranges, 'this is my only link to him'.

She bit her lip and shook her head, but it was as if all the bottled-up feelings of her childhood were clamoring for an outlet, and the tears just kept rolling.

'Alex...' he stammered.

Her blurred vision didn't allow her to see the expression on his face, but the concern in his voice was her total undoing, unleashing a floodgate of pent up tears. Tears she'd never cried when she found out her father was dead. Tears she'd refused to shed when her mother told her that her whole life had been a lie. Tears she wished weren't spilling down her face now.

'Please—' she said, in gasping sobs, struggling as his arms encircled her in a soft, protective embrace. 'Please, just —' she sobbed. 'Just...just leave me alone...'

She was swiftly drawn into a warm haven of strength and mountainous support. Keeping one arm around her, he folded her head against his chest, and stroked her hair until at last the turbulence of her emotions faded into limp exhaustion.

Somehow she couldn't bring herself to be concerned about the debilitating emotion that left her dependent on Vitali's compassion. It felt so good just to rest her head on his broad shoulder, to feel his cheek rubbing softly over her hair, to be wrapped in his arms, and sag against him and know he wouldn't abandon her or let her fall.

The game she had played, the deception that had rolled on and on gathering an untenable life of its own, the fight to survive, to keep on top, in control—somehow it had all collapsed on her and become meaningless. She wanted the truth—craved it, whatever price had to be paid.

'Vitali—' She didn't lift her head, not wanting to see if she was treading on forbidden ground. He would either answer her or not. And if not...there was nothing real between them anyway. 'Was my father...was he to blame for what happened?'

38

'No!' His voice sounded like a grenade as an explosion of feeling roared from his lips. Everything that he had kept deeply suppressed, that hurt him to admit it, demanding to be cleared.

'You said...you implied...murder...do you truly believe that...?'

She felt his chest expand as he dragged in a deep breath and there was a note of pained searching for truth in his voice when he slowly added, 'How does one apportion blame? Who can untangle all the threads that led to tragedy? A meshed web of circumstances, passions and raw unbridled emotions driven to breaking-point...'

He sighed and his breath wavered through her hair like the soft stirring wind of change. The words that followed were slow and measured, weighed in the balance of what was known and unknown.

'Your father was probably no more to blame than mine. There are some women with the power to twist men's souls. My mother is one of them. Even Simon...poor damned Simon, hungering for the crumbs she gave him...does give him...and I hate seeing it. I hated it then...what I felt was happening all around me...but I was only a boy, Alex. There was nothing I could do to stop it. Nothing anyone could do...'

Only a boy...caught in the middle of something he didn't understand...and his father ending up dead. A wave of sympathy for his lonely fears and the terrible loss he had suffered stirred Alex from her own anguish. She lifted her head, bleak grey-blue eyes meeting and understanding his pain.

'I'm sorry about your father, Vitali,' she said softly. 'You must have been very close.'

'Close?' The slight twist of his mouth mocked himself, not her. 'How close does anyone ever get to another human? My father was not an affectionate man. Yet he was everything I wanted to be.' His gaze trailed off to the horizon. 'A son's blind love for his father. Obviously, he was not everything my mother wanted.'

'Vitali...' she hesitated, aware that she was scraping over old wounds, yet her need to know pushed the plea from her lips. 'How did your father die? What happened? You intimated that it wasn't an accident. That my father—was he a murderer?'

'No,' he confessed gently. 'A violent fight broke out between my father and yours. My mother was screaming. She ran and got a rifle. God only knows why. Perhaps to frighten them...to stop them from brawling. She yelled at me to get Simon, who had walked away when the arguing started. We heard a shot. By the time we'd run inside, my father was dead. My mother was sobbing hysterically over his body, and Ted was standing there, staring down at them, the rifle in his hands. Simon asked what happened. Your father didn't answer. He just handed the rifle to Simon and walked away. He never said a word. No explanation. He packed up and left within the hour and we never saw him again. My mother kept crying that it was an accident. She said there had been a struggle for the gun and it had gone off.'

'Oh my god—but you, you saw all that?' Her stomach knotted sickeningly. She looked at the tortured man before her, read the trauma in the set of his shoulders and the stiff, controlled tilt of his head. 'How horrible.'

He simply nodded, his mouth pressed in a grim line. 'Later, I heard talk that my father had killed himself. That your father had wanted to save our family from the scandal of his suicide...and the financial ruin—all insurance null and void, the loss of business confidence–the scar on my future. So, he took the blame and walked away. Looking at my mother and I, only reminded him of the destruction their love had caused—this is embodied in the painting, that and perhaps also the freedom that comes from doing the right thing—not giving into selfish yearnings...sacrifice.'

Vitali gave an apologetic grimace. 'It was all a blur, but even now, as it did then, the whole thing seems strange—as though nothing was what it seemed. But no one, other than my mother and your father, knows the truth.'

Alex, squeezed his hand 'I'm sorry...I didn't mean to bring the trauma...'

'All I know is it just seemed so surreal...the whole thing....as though orchestrated in some way. The fact that Ted went away, turning his back on everything...I guess I always interpreted it as guilt. But it might have been shock. It might have been trauma. It might have been disbelief. It might even have been the only thing he could do to protect us from a truth too horrible to bear. I guess I've always felt that in some way I owe your father a debt.'

The kind conciliatory tone of Vitali's last words floated over Alex's head. What if it had been Lucrezia's finger on the trigger? Or what if they had been arguing because Lucrezia had told Vitali's father she was going to leave with her father? What if he had killed himself to stop their dreams dead? What if her father had left in order to protect the woman he loved, taking the guilt upon himself? And Lucrezia might well have let him, only to be eternally haunted by the weight of his sacrifice. No wonder she looked so miserable.

Lost Love was both poignant and painful, infused as it was by blood and beauty.

However, there was nothing to be gained by sharing Alex's wild leaps of imagination with Vitali. It was not for her to speculate or to judge. Whatever his mother's role, whatever her sins, she had certainly suffered for them. Ted Carr had taken their secrets to the grave and it was in everyone's interests that they remain buried. If Alex had known any of this she never would have exhibited the painting.

Still, some good had come, she mused looking at Vitali with increasing admiration. And even if it was not the story she wanted to hear, she was much closer to understanding the life and passion that drove her father.

She gazed up at the barren, desolate rock face of the mountain ranges he had painted so poignantly. She was sure her father would agree, despite the pain, that it was better to have lost in love than never to have loved, or been loved.

Perhaps, if he hadn't channeled all his emotions into his paintings, she wondered, would he ever have reached the status, received the acclaim he had, touched people's lives, if he hadn't suffered?

She was reluctant to open Vitali's wounds further but

having come this far she couldn't repress her unsatisfied curiosity. Again, her eyes lifted to Vitali's in searching appeal.

'What was my father like?'

He frowned. 'Don't you know?'

Alex felt her jaw tighten. She heaved a deep, shuddering sigh and pulled out of his embrace, feeling too raw and vulnerable to stay in the comfort of his arms. The wounds to them both went too deep. Her legs felt weak and shaky so she backed up against the rātā tree.

If there was a time when the truth had to be spoken, whatever the consequences, it was now.

39

'I never knew my father,' she confided. 'My mother hates to be reminded of her first marriage. It grates her to even mention my father's name. As far as she was concerned he never existed. All my life I thought another man was my dad. Then, bang, like a wrecking ball thundering into my life I finally find out who my real father is—but he's dead.'

The memory of how cheated and robbed she had felt shadowed her eyes. 'All my life I felt different. All my life, even in a room full of family and friends, I've felt alone. All my life it's as though I've been searching for something... and it was here all along...*with you*...within my grasp...but my family, the people who were supposed to love me kept the truth hidden...until it was too late.'

Alex exhaled a shaky breath, and the sense of release escaped. Finally, she could talk honestly about how she felt, and trust her pain to someone who wasn't trying to load her with guilt or make her feel ashamed.

The setting sun blazed a river of molten gold over the infinite-canopy of the colbalt-blue sky, and Alex felt her tears and her sadness and her pain disappear as she stood, wrapped in the warmth of the enormous and immovable love of her husband.

Vitali was staring at her…as if he was seeing Alex for the first time—not the ice queen façade she had so skillfully engineered, but the seam of glowing gold that coursed below her surface veneer. Suddenly she desperately wanted him to understand.

The anxiety she'd felt about confiding in him, that he may think she was an emotional train-wreck, or that he wouldn't care, now melted away like ice warmed by the sun.

She swallowed the boulder of emotion that lodged in her throat. 'You see…I never fitted in with the glittering life my family led in New York. I was not the daughter my mother wanted. And I was most definitely not the child my step-father considered an asset. So, when I received the letter telling me of my inheritance it was the only link to my past. I desperately wanted to believe that somewhere, someone loved me. That, had things been different, I might have felt I belonged…that I was loved. *Unconditionally.* Not because of the way I looked, or how much money my family had, or for who I might marry—but for me. *Just me.* But It was hard. *It's still hard.* Because if my real father had cared, why didn't he come for me?'

'He couldn't come to you, *mia cara.* He was a wanted man. After my father died, he never surrendered himself to the authorities. He simply vanished. Now we know he changed his name and assumed a new identity. If he'd tried to leave New Zealand, chances are he would have been arrested for manslaughter. Maybe even murder,' Vitali explained carefully.

'And that would have dragged my mother and the whole messy tragedy into the public eye,' he said. 'I'm sure he did think…you were better off without him. We all were. What sort of life would you have had if there was the merest suspicion your father was a murderer? He made the ultimate sacrifice. For you. For me. For all of us.'

'I know that now,' Alex said painfully. 'I guess I knew it when I went in search of him, and *Lost Love*. I knew something dreadful had happened to him...' her eyes begged his belief as she added. '...but I didn't know how much you had suffered, Vitali. I truly didn't. I'm sorry. I just wanted...'

'To take from us what we had taken from you and your father,' he said as Alex floundered for words.

'No!' she shook her head, helpless to explain exactly what she had wanted. 'You can't get what's forever lost. I thought if I came here...' She looked up at the mountains. 'If I watched the sunset...'

Vitali stepped forward and turned her face to his. His green eyes questioned without any hint of the skepticism Alex was accustomed to seeing in them. 'You really don't care about money—or gold. That's not why you married me, is it?'

'No. It's not. I wanted other things, Vitali. Things that I've been looking for my whole life.' Her mouth curved in a dry half-smile. 'I guess...somewhere...a place for me. And to be wanted...unconditionally. The driving need to be wanted...and to belong...somewhere.'

'And is this the place you want, Alex?' he asked, quietly, seriously.

'Yes,' she answered truthfully. She wanted to add "home is where the heart is – and my heart is with you." But it sounded too clichéd, too corny for the seriousness of the occasion. She couldn't make Vitali love her, but he was her husband. And she was falling desperately in love with him. Now that she had found him, she didn't want to live without Vitali.'

He picked a piece of dried tussock from her hair, gently tucking a disheveled blonde coil back from her face. He had a strange, almost whimsical look in his eyes. 'Perhaps Simon was right,' he said. 'And this is the resolution.'

He gave a little shake of his head, and his expression became more resolute, his voice flat but not unsympathetic. 'It was your father who found the gold seam, Alexi. As far as I'm concerned, you had the moral right to his share. Except we could never find it to give it to him. If Ted had wanted to find us he knew where we were. But he never did. And we thought...let the past go. It seemed the only resolution. But I wasn't expecting *you*. How could I? The daughter I didn't even know existed.'

His thumb grazed softly down her cheek. 'You keep surprising me. I had you figured with no feelings at all. Except revenge. And now...I have to concede that I was wrong.'

'I should have confided in you earlier,' she said, relieved to finally be dropping the pretense. 'I guess I've always had a problem with trust.' she shrugged. 'If I'd opened up to you earlier...of course I must have seemed that way to you—not knowing what game I was playing until it...Oh, God, Vitali... it's not too late for us is it?'

'No, Alexi. It's not too late. In fact, I sense it's just the beginning. We were both to blame. Both lumping our baggage and tortured pasts around,' he said softly. 'I don't know about you, but I'm ready to create a new life story. Something that ends with "happily ever after."

The unexpected emotional intimacy erased the fears and inhibitions that had been devouring her confidence. But she sensed that to firmly close the door on the old they must both first make peace with the past. 'Please, Vitali... please help me understand a little of my father.'

'From a child's perspective?'

'Yes, who was the man you knew as a young boy?'

'He had a great imagination—always telling us stories. But what I remember most about him was his smile—he always had a smile. I never heard him say a cross word to anyone. He was the kindest man I ever knew, Alexi. I guess I was stubborn. I wanted to believe the worst of him to block out the memories of that horrible night—and the truth I didn't dare face. He didn't deserve my hatred. You would have loved him. He was a lot like you.'

'Thank you,' she said, huskily. 'It means a lot to me.'

'You're welcome,' he said gruffly. 'At least I had some years with my dad even if he wasn't a gold medalist in the father-of-the-year department.'

His hand trailed from her cheek and he moved away from her. He took a few steps to the side of the Rātā tree, then stood staring up at the mountains her father had painted.

'If it hadn't been for my mother your father and mine would have been lifelong friends instead of rivals. They liked each other. It was the liking that made everything so much worse. Because it made the passion more intense. I understand all that now. I didn't then.'

The graveled tone of his voice carried painful emotions and Alex moved instinctively to his side and touched his arm in tentative sympathy. 'I didn't mean to bring it all back to you, Vitali.'

He looked down at her, and for a moment she saw, mirrored in his eyes, the same aching loneliness that she herself had known for so long. His arm lifted and curled around her shoulders, pulling her close to him.

'You came halfway around the world to see this sunset, *mia cara*. Look. It's starting.'

The flaming sun had turned the mountains to molten gold. The blazing oranges and golds eventually subsided into violet shadows which saturated the sky before creeping over the land. Slowly, the reflection of the dying blaze turned the landscape to sleepy blues. It was an awesome display of nature's alchemy. Alex could see why her father had painted it as he had. She hoped he was at peace now, just as they were.

It felt good...deeply companionable...watching it together...sharing. For once there were no barriers between them. When Vitali turned back towards the camp, Alex was content to go, to finally put the past behind her and match her step with his wherever he led.

Jack and Rangi had a billy over a fire, and dinner was well on the way to being cooked. Their grins stretched over their cheek as they showed off their outdoor culinary skills to Vitali, and grabbed the opportunity to ply him with questions about the muster. Alex listened to his replies, happy that he kept her at his side, his arm still curved around her. He didn't let her go until they sat down to eat their meal.

A slow and eerie new moon cast an entirely different light over the landscape ...dreamy and full of new beginnings. Alex was glad when the meal was over and Vitali quietly invited her to share his sleeping-bag. And that was different too. He made no attempt to make love to her—instead he held her almost as if she were a child needing comfort.

'I'm glad you came,' she murmured. 'I didn't think you'd get back until tomorrow.'

'I'd finished all that I wanted to do and the men all reckoned that a new wife rated a higher priority than any help I could give them.' She could hear a smile in his voice. 'I was inclined to agree.'

She snuggled closer and he rubbed his cheek over her hair in a sweetly tender manner.

'Do you still resent marrying me?'

'Something good might come of it yet.' His voice hummed with smug satisfaction. 'And if my memory serves me correctly, it was you who married me. I proposed you accepted.'

'Only after suitable deliberation,' she countered, smiling to herself. 'I did check out your form first.'

'I stacked up then?' he asked, clearly amused.

'You seemed a good bet.'

His arm tightened around her then slowly relaxed. His hand ruffled gently through her hair. 'I'm glad I came to find you. It's strange...but I feel at peace with everything...even myself.'

'Yes,' she sighed, feeling a wonderfully warm glow of satisfaction.

'You know—we have something else to be grateful to your father for,' he said, after a moment's silence.

'What's that?' She murmured.

'If it wasn't for your dad protecting us all like he did, people would be gossiping about our scandalous marriage.' She could well imagine the headlines.

He said no more and Alex didn't break the silence. Eventually she fell asleep to the soothing rhythm of his contented heartbeat.

40

———

When they finally arrived home the next morning after a wonderful night of getting to know each other more deeply, they went into Bob's office to talk about the area they were going to fence off for the experimental breeding of Alpacas. There was a detailed map of the whole station on the wall, and, while Alex had studied it before, it was far more real to her now that she could visualize the terrain.

She listened to Vitali and Bob discuss the pros and cons of various sites, and both men made her feel very much part of the discussion. They even looked to her for agreement when the decision was finally made.

Alex felt it was probably the happiest day of her life, and the new sense of togetherness that had been forged with Vitali grew in the days that followed. They took time to understand each other, and their conversations became less and less guarded.

The men came home from the muster, and as was the custom, a day-long *hangi* was held at the homestead. Huge sides of beef were lowered into smoldering knee deep pits which had been filled with wood and piled high with volcanic stones and heated for hours beforehand. Flax baskets were lowered on top, full of potatoes, *kumara*, carrots and onions, and then covered with clean damp hessian sacks, before being completely covered with a mound of soil. It was then left to steam in the smouldering earth for three hours. It was a huge feast that everyone thoroughly enjoyed. Alex had never tasted food so succulent and tender.

Vitali introduced Alex to all the stockmen and good-humoredly laughed at the coarse jokes lobbied his way. It was plain that they were glad to see him happy, and they all welcomed Alex with open-hearted friendliness. After all, any woman who could rope and brand their boss had to be extra special.

And, much to Alex's joy, Vitali's changed attitude towards her gave them no argument on that score. Gone was the indulgence of a dominant male to "the little woman." In its place was the easy camaraderie of partners who were attuned to each other.

Pride there certainly was, just as she was proud to have him as her husband. And as far as any physical expression of their relationship was concerned, Vitali had no reluctance whatsoever about demonstrating that he loved her, whether it was simply a hand at her waist or an arm around the shoulders.

As the day wore into evening, the men brought out an array of musical instruments including guitars, accordions, harmonicas and banjos. The stockmen played with considerable skill and the Maori men had voices that brought tears to her eyes. It was simple entertainment but Alex couldn't remember having enjoyed an evening more. As she and Vitali walked back to the house she knew she was happier with tonight's entertainment than any of the sophisticated cultural events available in New York.

The next few days were busy for them both. Vitali began giving Alex the flying lessons he'd promised. The new fencing for the Alpacas was in full swing. Alex was persuaded to talk to the school children about the Andes and the way of life there.

They enjoyed it so much the school mistress suggested Alex give "The Art of Travel" workshops, sharing with the children her travel journeys and boosting their awareness of the fascinating cultural diversity and opportunities that exist in the world.

Alex was delighted. Maybe some of the children may be inspired to raise their horizons, she thought, and set forth themselves, whilst others would get a taste of places and people they may never see. She combined story-telling with plenty of hands-on activities, such as cooking and art, reflecting the chosen country's culture.

And to everyone's pleasure, Alex also gave the children photography lessons. She taught them how to take panoramic photos of the landscape, capturing the rugged beauty of the terrain using the best light, and experimenting with unusual angles.

Her workshops soon became a regular fixture, and Alex was pleased to be helpful and inspire others. Other than these journeys back into her past Alex has virtually forgotten about the life she had left behind.

A call from her mother upended that.

41

S he and Vitali had just finished breakfast one morning and were about to set out to inspect the progress of the fencing when Bob called out from his office.

'Alex...there an international call for you. It's New York.'

'My mother,' she said to Vitali as she hurried along the deck, toward the phone. 'She's probably calling about what clothes to send me—or with more questions about you,'

'Maybe I'd better monitor your answers,' he teased as he strolled after her.

But Alex was wrong on both counts. And Elizabeth Spencer was very decisive about what she wanted.

'Alexandra, I've booked a flight to Christchurch. It gets in early Sunday morning. Charles has arranged for a limousine to pick me up at the airport and take me to a hotel. I'll spend several days there to recover from my trip. I want to know how to get to Gold Ridge Station after that.'

Alex was so thrown she was lost for words. Why on earth would her mother even contemplate getting her Manolo Blahniks dirty in the high country? Surely they could Skype instead?

Vitali, who had heard the conversation, took over the call.

'Mrs Spencer, this is Vitali Rossi. I would be pleased to arrange your transportation. I'll have one of my men contact you and confirm. My jet will be standing by to fly you here. It is no trouble. In fact, it will be my—our absolute pleasure.' he added winking at Alex.

Alex's brow furrowed as she wondered what possible reasons her mother had for suddenly wanting to travel half way around the world to visit her.

'Oh! That's awfully kind of you...I do hate to be a bother.' Her mother sounded flustered by his willingness to go out of his way.

'It's no trouble at all. We look forward to making you feel at home here at Gold Ridge Station. I'll hand you back to Alex now. Goodbye, Mrs Spencer.'

Alex still hadn't recovered her composure. 'Mom? Did you get my letter?'

'Yes, dear. And the photographs. I've never seen you look more radiant.' There was a slight catch in her voice.' You looked beautiful—and happy.'

'Thanks,' Alex managed weakly.

'I've packed the things you asked for,' her mother added briskly. 'I'll bring them with me.'

'It's a long way to travel just to bring jeans and socks,' Alex said.

'I want to see how you are—where you are. I must confess I'm more than a little intrigued. And of course, I'd like to meet my son-in-law in person.' Alex thought she heard the tiniest tremble in her voice.

'Of course,' Alex affirmed, pulling herself together. 'My husband and I will look forward to seeing you too, Mom.'

It was only after she had put down the receiver that the

full ramifications of her mother's visit hit her like a sledge-hammer. She shot Vitali a look of urgent appeal as they left the office. 'There are some things I have to tell you. Some things I have to explain.'

Vitali raised a quizzical eyebrow. 'I doubt there's anything your mother can throw at me that I can't handle, Alex.'

'It's not that. She's far too polite to say anything critical to you. Although she has an ingrained snobbery and social-mindedness that will probably test your patience. But it won't be a long visit. This isn't her kind of world. If you know Manhattan society at all.'

'*Mia cara*, she either accepts us and the way we want to live, or she doesn't,' Vitali said firmly. 'I will extend every courtesy to your mother. How she reacts to Gold Ridge Station is her business. I hope her reactions will be favor-able. If not, she can leave whenever she wishes. Her visit is not a problem to me.' His eyes were sharply watchful as he added, 'I didn't marry your mother. I married you.'

'My mother doesn't know anything about my father's connection to this place. Or to your family. Or to the gold mine. Only about the paintings. So there's no point in mentioning the past.'

'I agree. But if your mother ever mentions Ted.'

'I very much doubt it,' Alex interrupted, hurt bleeding from her words 'My father has always been a black smudge on my mother's finery.'

Vitali eyed her curiously. 'You have my attention.'

Alex's mouth twisted in bitter irony. 'He was a mistake. *I was a mistake.* They married because of me. Having an ille-gitimate child was hardly respectable. Especially for a woman of my mother's breeding. I was the daughter they never wanted.'

She dragged in a deep breath and tried to shrug off the negative image. 'Don't misunderstand me—my mother tried to do her best. We're just so different. I like freedom, she likes security. I love adventure, she clings to safety. I balk at conformity, she clamors for acceptance. At any cost.' Alex felt her old hurts rise, as though demanded to be exorcised.

'She's my mother and I'm her daughter but all my life I wondered if I was adopted. Like I told you up at Gold Ridge, out of the blue I find the man I thought was my father is...' she chose her words carefully...'an imposter who never wanted me. No wonder we never got along. At least she's coming alone. But you know...deep down I'm glad. Maybe this place will work its magic on her too and finally we can let go of all our pain.'

Vitali drew her into a gentle embrace. A twinkle of amusement overlaid something else in his eyes. 'How did a beautiful flower like you cover her true colors in Manhattan society?

'It wasn't easy,' she replied, striving for levity to cover the rush of her pulse.

'You must confess,' he murmured, and kissed her with a slow sensuality that somehow imparted more tenderness than primal desire. When he lifted his head, his eyes held no amusement at all. They held a look that seemed both possessive and protective.

'Don't *ever* think of yourself as a mistake,' he commanded, softly but firmly. 'You're no mistake, Alexi. Not to me or anyone on Gold Ridge Station. And this is your home. You keep that in mind...*this is where you belong...*' his lips curved into a smile '... partner!'

The words, "I love you, Vitali" almost slid from her lips. She barely caught them. How would Vitali react? He had kissed her; but had he come to love her? She would never know. Even if he did feel love, admitting it would reveal a certain vulnerability. She knew better than most that it wasn't easy to give your heart.

She resigned herself to being content with their relationship just the way it was. She had everything she wanted, and it was actions, not words, towards her that mattered most. She didn't need four letters to define "*love*." Her mother wouldn't find any fault in Vitali's manner toward her daughter. They were friends and partners, and lovers. And she couldn't think of anyone she knew that had all those things in their marriage.

42

The week leading up to her mother's visit raced by. When the jet flew in on Monday afternoon, Alex and Vitali were at the airstrip in the Range Rover, ready to meet and transport their visitor to the big house.

At the homestead children were either sitting or dangling over the stockyard fence, eager to see "Miss Alex's" mother from the American city of New York. Alex had pointed out where her mother was from on the huge wall-sized map of the world which Alex had sourced and pasted onto the wall in their classroom. She was pretty sure they were expecting the queen herself when her mother arrived and she didn't' disappoint.

Dressed toe nail to perfectly coiffured hair she emerged from the jet looking like royalty on safari in Uganda. She wore a stylish wide brimmed linen hat, tied elegantly beneath her chin with a flowing silk scarf in a black and tan leopard print, which in turn matched the shirt under her round necked jacket. Her face was beautifully made up, her nails perfectly manicured. She looked all class, right down to her black and white walking shoes. Alex glanced at her own dusty sandals and wished she had worn something more elegant.

The children instantly started waving to her mother and after a moment's hesitation, and much to Alex's relief, Elizabeth Spencer raised her hand and gave them her best royal wave. But her smile to Alex and Vitali looked stiff and a little uncertain as she came down the steps of the plane. The tension in her body eased ever so slightly when Alex gave her a hug and kissed her cheek.

They never hugged.

'It's lovely to see you, Mother,' she said as warmly as she could, knowing how uncomfortable her mother was with public displays of affection. Alex then turned to Vitali and kissed him on the lips and proudly linked her arm around his. 'And this, of course, is my husband, Vitaliano Rossi.'

'Vitali' he said, flashing a smile designed to charm and disarm. 'Welcome to Gold Ridge Station, Mrs Spencer —*mother.*'

Elizabeth Spencer stared up at him for several long seconds, her face blanching, before she collected herself and took his outstretched hand.

'Forgive me,' she said, flushing in painful embarrassment at her lapse in manners. 'You just reminded me so strongly of—of someone else. Not in looks but...Oh, my! I am making a hash of this.' She swept her silk scarf away from her cheek. 'I'm very pleased to meet you, Vitali. Gosh —a son-in-law. How wonderful. And do call me Lizzie,' she finished in an awkward rush.

Alex shook her head in disbelief. Was she hearing things? Had the altitude affected her mother's attitude? This over-friendliness was so unlike her mother's usual polished and guarded composure. It was to prove to be one of many surprises.

Not one word of criticism about anything passed Elizabeth Spencer's lips. The big house was "most impressive" she said; and the room Alex gave her "simply fetching"; Bob and Dara were the "nicest people." It was all strange—but pleasantly welcome.

When Vitali casually informed her during the course of dinner that they were preparing for a shipment of Alpacas, the experimental breed that Alex had suggested, Elizabeth Spencer beamed proudly. And when she said, "My daughter is such a clever, enterprising girl," Alex almost choked. She decided to stick to mineral water for the rest of the evening in case the alcohol pickled her brain and made it all seem even more surreal.

'Well, you mustn't let me take up any more of your time,' her mother said after dinner. 'Both of you go right ahead with whatever needs doing. I'm so fascinated by all that Alex wrote me about the life here that I'll be very happy just pottering around.'

Vitali took her at her word, but Alex struggled.

However, the next day her mother went out of her way to make the acquaintance of everyone at the station, and not once did she emit the slightest hint of snobbishness or prejudice. She even found Rangi and Jack "charming boys", and said she would certainly take up their offer to go riding with them. They promised to show her everything like they did with "the missus."

'You don't have to babysit me, dear,' her mother gently admonished. 'You go along with Vitali. Dara said she'd look after me, and Bob's going to explain how the working year is organized on a large station like Gold Ridge. It's all rather fascinating. So you don't have to worry about me at all.'

As astonished as Alex was by her mother's attitude, she was also intensely gratified. It demonstrated the kind of acceptance that she had always wanted from her mother, and certainly created a very relaxed atmosphere that she had never enjoyed in her presence before.

For the first time in her life Alex wasn't made to feel that something more was expected of her, that she wasn't a disappointment, that all her life choices were wrong.

'It must be you,' she told Vitali that night. 'She took one look at you and decided you were a man she'd better not tangle with.'

'Unlike her daughter,' he commented smugly, running a teasing caress along her thigh which was pleasurably entangled with his.

Alex laughed. 'Has anyone told you you're irresistibly sexy.'

'Well, if all I am to you is a body—'

He rolled her onto his absurdly chiseled chest proceeded to use his hardened body in a way that obliterated any further thoughts about her mother.

The day before the Alpacas were to arrive, Vitali took them both on a tour of the gold mine. He presented Elizabeth with a magnificent natural gold nugget, promising to have it made into a bespoke piece of jewelry, of her own design by his Milanese atelier, if she wished. Alex was deeply touched when her mother's eyes filled with tears.

'Thank you, Vitali. That's very generous. But I'd like to say that you've already given me the best gift. I'm thrilled to see Alex so happy. It means more to me than all the gold in your hills, and all the money in my husband's Wall Street vaults. I was so afraid...' She smiled at Alex through her misty eyes. 'But it's all right. I thought you'd never find what you were looking for. But I see you have. My daughter's a keeper and she's loyal—I know that she won't let go.' She turned a rueful look back at Vitali. 'She's tenacious, you know—and exceedingly loyal.'

'Yes, I know,' Vitali answered drily, and moved to hug Alex close to him. He looked down at her as she snuggled under his arm. 'This daughter of yours is utterly unrelenting, Lizzie. Once she gets her teeth into something, there's no stopping her. She used me quite shamelessly to get what she wanted.'

Elizabeth laughed. 'I haven't seen you looking heartbroken about that, Vitali.'

'She's a sorcerer, Lizzie. She cast a spell on me. I was powerless,' he laughed uproariously in his low, sultry Italian accent.

And instead of denying what he said, or even correcting him in any way, Alex laughed with her mother, rejoicing in her mother's delight, marveling that underneath the disapproval of all those years there had been a very deep and constant vein of caring for her, a vein of gold she kept well-hidden but now at last it was seeing the light. It was only afterwards that Alex wondered if Vitali really did think she was using him to get what she wanted. The thought sat uncomfortably, like a nail in her shoe. No matter how she tried to ignore it, it pricked her confidence.

They were happy together—weren't they?

43

They were both in particularly high spirits the next afternoon when the freight-plane from Matiu-Somes Island touched down at Gold Ridge Station. Everyone at the homestead was down near the airstrip to see the Alpacas arrive.

The stockmen were there on their horses, ready to direct the small herd into a nearby stockyard. Here they would be fed and watered and allowed to settle down after their long trip. Alex and Vitali were standing by the Land Rover, eagerly awaiting first sight of their investment.

A ramp was fitted up against the plane and finally the door was opened. One by one the alpacas came streaming out, jumping and kicking playfully with the excitement of being released from close confinement. As Alex looked at their woolly, umber coats she thought they looked like giant toy bears.

Vitali smiled at them as though he was thinking the same thing, and her heart swelled effervescent bubbles of happiness. Alex clambered over a fence to get a better look at them. As she walked across the open paddock a massive wild bull emerged from the thick native scrub to the left of the airfield.

Whether the scent of the Alpacas had evoked his territorial instinct Alex didn't know. All she knew was his gaze was fixed on her with purposeful fury.

Her body froze in terror at the sight of 2000 pounds of dangerous sinewy muscle, menacing horns and a temper to match. The black beast glared at her. Then he lowered his solid neck and powerful shoulders. He pawed the ground with his sharp cloven hoof.

Everything happened so fast. Vitali yelled her name.

He leapt in front of Alex and shouting at her to run, grabbing at the bull's horns with Herculean strength.

Enraged the bull thrust his head and tossed him in the air. Alex screamed as Vitali fell to the ground. He rolled and try to scramble away.

The bull pursued him trampling over him with furious hooves. Then turning, he scooped Vitali's limp body in his horns, and charged at a low stone wall. She heard the chilling crunch as the bull crushed him against the stones.

The men rushed to Vitali's aid. Rangi hung onto his tail while Jack ripped off his red checked shirt and distracted the bull with a blaze of color. Finally, a carefully aimed rifle shot ripped through the air, ending the beast's horrific rampage.

Bob dragged Vitali by his feet to safety.

Alex broke free of the arms that had restrained her. 'Vitali! Vitali! Vitali!'

He lay lifeless, the only movement, blood streaming from the deep gash in his face.

She felt the faint whisper of his gurgled breath on her face. Thank God. *He was alive.*

He lay motionless, his eyes flickering in and out of consciousness.

'Oh my darling, I'm so sorry, so, so, so sorry. It's all my fault'

Fear and guilt washed in her gut. If anything happened to him...' she pushed her anxiety firmly aside. She sat on the dirt beside him and gently dabbed her shirt at the gaping gash on his face. 'You'll be ok. You'll be ok,' she whispered, projecting her voice with confidence, desperately willing him to live.

Then Dara was kneeling beside her, and applied pressure to stem the bleeding. Alex squeezed Vitali's hand and gently stroked his hair. She didn't know how long they'd been there when his fingers slowly flexed under hers.

'Alex...' It was the tiniest of whispers. He didn't open his eyes, but a line creased between his brows as if he was struggling towards consciousness.

'I'm here, my darling. I'm here,' she cried.

'Don't...' he whispered breathlessly.

She bent closer to his lips to catch whatever he was trying to say.

'I'm badly hurt...if I die...'

'Don't! Don't say that. You're not going anywhere. Not without me. I need you, Vitali,' she insisted passionately. The words she had wanted to say for so long now poured forth in a tidal wave of emotion.

'*I love you.*'

He barely registered the words.

Why the hell hadn't she said them before?

His eyes flickered partially open. Pain glazed his eyes... excruciating pain. 'I can't move my legs.' His eyes clamped shut. His head rolled back in despair. 'I can't live like—'

Her gut twisted with the knowledge of what he meant.

He would rather surrender the will to live than be left a cripple, caged in a body that couldn't pleasure her or do what he wanted.

'Let me go. Let me die,' he implored. His breath rasped as though his lungs pooled with blood.

'No...' she moaned. 'No...'

'Get on with your life. This place...it's yours.'

'It means nothing. Not without you.'

Bob kneeled at Vitali's side and inserted a hypodermic syringe into his arm. Then another. Shooting him full with emergency morphine.

'*I will not let you die,*' Alex said fiercely. She must summon the strength for the both of them. For the three of them, she corrected, pressing her palm upon her belly.

'I'm carrying your child,' she blurted, 'Vitali, I'm pregnant—we conceived a child on our wedding night. *You can't die, do you hear me? You can't die. I won't let you.*'

There seemed to be a slight flicker of recognition in his dulling eyes.

'Our baby must know their father,' she said with desperate vehemence. 'You've got to live.'

His lids dropped shut as if they were too heavy to hold open. Alex didn't know if he had heard. She had held back from telling him until she'd passed the twelve-week mark and was absolutely sure the baby was safe. Now she regretted her decision. She should have told him. He should have known. At only ten weeks pregnant she never thought she'd be praying both her unborn child and the man she loved would live.

'*Our baby needs you,*' she called after him as strong arms wrapped around her and lifted her to her feet as the man who had come to mean more to her than life itself, was loaded onto a make-shift stretcher.

He remained locked in a slumbering drug-induced unconscious silence.

EVERYTHING HAPPENED SO FAST and morphed into a foggy blur: The Lear Jet screaming in from the mine and taxiing to a halt; Bob yelling instructions as the men carried Vitali on board; her mother accompanying her as she followed the stretcher on which Vitali lay so still and lifeless. They had to get him to a hospital, and as quickly as possible. Christchurch, Bob said was 484 km away.

Did she mean anything to Vitali? Would he fight to live?

Had he heard her tell him about their child? Surely, knowing he was going to be a father would give him the will to survive? It had to mean something to him—his very own kin and blood. *A mini-him. Or her.* A son or a daughter who needed a father. It had to make living count, even if— she paused as the tragic reality pressed down on her—*even if he wasn't the man he was before.*

Vitali had told her he would never fight for her. Yet when the moment had come, he had risked his life to save her. Did he love her? Did he still believe that she only wanted his body and the wealth he could give to her?

Maybe it wasn't only his despair at being left caged, and confined to a wheelchair, his body no longer able to do his bidding? What if he couldn't be what he thought she wanted any more. Sexy.Irresistible. Better than any other man she'd ever bedded.

The memories ripped across her mind like storm clouds...the night he had made her tell him he was better than any other man. What she'd taken as flippant remarks might have held his innermost beliefs, she thought as the

Lear jet soared into the sky. In just over one-hour help would be at hand.

'One hour. Live for one hour, Vitali. Please, my love. Live for us,' she said, clutching his hand.

Alex's painful whirlpool of thoughts churned relentlessly as they flew north towards Christchurch. Nothing was certain yet, she consoled herself. Don't imagine the worst. After they got to a hospital, and the doctors had examined him thoroughly, when the options were made clear—*then panic.*

But she also saw Vitali's angst. Even if they could put him back together again he would be scarred. She knew what it was like to live with disfigurement. She knew better than anyone else, even if, or when, the facial scars healed, what it was like to still feel fatally flawed.

Of course, she found him compellingly handsome, but that wasn't why she loved him. Superficial attraction didn't flame the fires of her heart-felt passion. She couldn't remember if she'd told Vitali that or not, but if he lived, she had to make him believe the truth.

He would have to undergo a trial of strength, just as she had endured all those years ago. And she would help him as best she could, aided by her own experience.

She turned to Bob, who kept vigil with her. 'Tell the pilot to radio ahead. We need the best surgeons in the country. In the world. Anywhere,' she commanded.

And as he headed to the cockpit, she gave another silent command to the man who was her life. *Love us, Vitali. Love us enough to want to live.*

44

Vitali was strong enough, Alex kept arguing to herself. Stubborn enough too. If anyone could pull through the shock and the trauma of the surgery, he could. On a purely physical basis he had the stamina of an ox.

Those doctors had the fittest, healthiest body they could possibly have to help them in their task. But the will to live —did Vitali have that? Did he want her badly enough to survive?

How many hours had it been now? Eight? Nine? The flight to Christchurch...the emergency treatment to ensure he was stable enough for reconstructive surgery...the transfer to the Spinal unit...the scans, the X-rays...papers to sign that committed Vitali into the skilled hands of the finest surgeons. They were papers he might not have signed himself—but as his wife, Alex had made the decision. Whether he wanted it or not, she would do everything in her powers to keep her husband alive.

'Coffee, Alex?'

She looked up at her mother who had quietly kept her company all these hours, unobtrusively doing things for her.

The shirt and jacket she wore were what her mother had handed to her. The uneaten sandwiches that had been purchased from somewhere. Even soup had somehow materialized from mid-air. She had barely acknowledged these things.

'I'm sorry I haven't thanked you...' Alex shook her head as tears swam in her eyes. Her mother gently squeezed her shoulders. 'I don't expect you to talk, Alex,' she said softly. 'You never did...not when things were hard for you.'

'I didn't mean to shut you out, Mom. But I couldn't...I can't ...express how I feel.'

'I know. We're the same you and me,' she confided. 'If I'd done a better job sharing my feelings you wouldn't be here.'

'Don't say that. *Not now*. If things had been different, I never would have met Vitaliano. Please don't feel guilty. You did the best you could.'

Elizabeth Spencer heaved a deep sigh, 'Don't think I haven't thought about my mistakes, Alex. It's too late to change them now, but...there are some things I'd like to tell you...things I've kept locked inside myself all these years....and they might help you feel...less lonely. One thing I've learned these past few months is that it's never too late to change the past. You taught me that.'

Alex nodded, touched by the sympathetic understanding in her mother's eyes.

A sad smile curved her mother's mouth. 'You're very like your father. You have his eyes. And his expressions. Even as a child, you looked at me as he did.' Her smile turned down into a rueful grimace. 'I tried so hard to forget Ted. But you never let me. Every time I looked at you I saw him. Your gestures, even the things you said...so like Ted. I guess, you can't fight genes. You only have to look at the way your second toe is longer than your big toe,' she smiled sadly as she looked down at Alex's sandaled feet.

'Your father always said it was the mark of artistic genius. Leonardo da Vinci had toes like yours too, you know.' Her mother laughed, her eyes trailing down the corridor as though savoring a distant happy memory. 'I felt I had to keep repressing my feelings,' she said, becoming serious once again. 'I had to fight and deny my passions or the choice I'd made would have been unbearable.'

Alex shook her head. 'Mom, you don't have to explain to me what went wrong between you and my father. I know you didn't plan to have a baby. I know I was a mistake.'

'You couldn't be more wrong.' Her mother paused as though weighing up the consequences of what she was about to say. 'I wanted you more than anything in the world, Alexandra. I loved your father with all my heart. And I wanted our child. *I wanted you.* But my father wouldn't hear of it. He told me I had brought shame upon our family. I should have stood up to him. I'll regret that I didn't for the rest of my life. I can blame my young age, or my father's domineering presence—but if I'm honest, I've always blamed myself. I failed all of you.'

Alex put her coffee cup down and wrapped her arms around her mother, signaling her forgiveness. For a moment her fears for Vitali disappeared. Her mother had wanted her. *She had not been an accident.* She loved her.

She had always loved her.

As they fused closer she felt her mother's body soften and knew this was a turning point, a water-shed moment in all their lives.

'No man ever measured up to Ted. He was one of a kind. He was...well, he was like your Vitali. When I stepped off the plane at Gold Ridge Station that first afternoon my heart somersaulted. Vitali has exactly the same pride, a driven, yet deeply caring air, and the same intelligent, inquiring eyes that could render one defenseless.' She smiled. 'And those same powerful thighs. A body built for stamina and endurance.'

'Mom!'

'Your husband's a survivor, my darling. 'Stronger than a herd of elephants, fiercer than a pride of lions, more determined to win than all the world's greatest Olympian medalists. Trust me when I tell you he will never leave you.'

Elizabeth Spencer glanced out of the hospital window, her gaze drifting south to the formidable hills in the distance. 'When you wrote and told me where Gold Ridge Station was, I had to come,' she continued. After years of saying not a word about her father Alex was happy to just sit and listen as her mother explained and tried to make peace with why she had done the things she had.

Alex hoped that perhaps with harmony between them restored the positive energy would reach out and heal Vitali too.

'I told myself I was coming purely to see you both—and it was partly. But I was curious. I wanted to see where your father went when he left me. I knew that Central Otago was where he was heading...he had wanted me to come with him. I'd never heard of the place. And New Zealand was so far away. I wouldn't leave New York. *Couldn't* leave New York.' She turned to Alex, her eyes pooling with tears.

'My father threatened to disown me. I couldn't leave him, or my mother. And Ted wouldn't stay. He wouldn't even try to fit in. He just kept saying that America, and New York in particular, just wasn't his kind of place. He wanted to find a place where he belonged,' she gave a sad, resigned laugh.

'"His spiritual home", is what I think he said. He scorned

the life I led. He said it was too narrow and confined, too full of senseless rules and the punitive division of people according to wealth, and lots of other stupid conventions that had no meaning for him. But Alex, it was the only life I knew. He wanted to find a place of equal opportunity where a person wasn't judged or given precedence because of their money, or connections or the color of their blood. He was a free-spirit. Like you.'

Alex's mind shimmered like the still waters of Lake Wakatipu. Her mother's words about her father's deepest yearnings mirrored her own. But her heightened understanding of their similarities was double-edged—comforting on the one hand, but sharply increasing her bitter sense of loss.

Please don't let Vitali be taken from me too, she said silently.

Elizabeth Spencer's eyes refocused on Alex's in painful self-mockery. 'I didn't understand until I came. I didn't realize how captivating and totally mesmerizing this country is. Not until I flew over it. It's so small, compared to the US, but so very, very beautiful. Once I saw it all—the mine, the cattle station, and those stark and velvety blue peaks rising from the lake—I understood immediately why Ted couldn't be happy in New York.' Her mouth twisted into a grimace.

'*I finally knew*. Just like I know how right it is for you and Vitali to be together. I knew I had made a mistake. Your father had the courage I didn't. He followed his dreams. But I had made my choice and I set about justifying it in every way I could. Marrying Charles. Making all the right connections. Doing all the right things. And I wanted you to do the same, Alex. To be like me because...' she pressed her lips together and studied the high gloss linoleum floor. 'I was wrong.'

'It's okay, Mom.'

'No it's not okay,' she said lifting her head. "I'm so sorry.' Her eyes swum with shards of angst. 'I was so, so selfish. You see, I wanted you to be like me because in my own stupid way I thought that would make me more right.'

Her mother's obsession was rooted in the pain of a love that hadn't met her preconceived expectations. No wonder she froze Ted Carr out of her life. It hurt too much, Alex realized, and with understanding came a ready forgiveness for her mother's driven need to be successful in her chosen world, to prove that she hadn't made a mistake.

'I'm sorry I disappointed you.'

Her mother clutched Alex's hands. 'No...no...you must never think that. I would have been more disappointed if you had followed in my footsteps. You see, I hated Ted for not settling for second best and doing what I wanted. And I was frustrated with you for turning your back on the life I felt I was building for you. *I felt rejected.* Rejected by you and your father. You both turned your back on the things I'd convinced myself I valued.'

'You always had that far-away look in your eyes that he did, widening our distance. As if you too yearned to be in another world. And the truth was I wanted to be part of that world too. *If only I'd had the courage.* If only I hadn't fought so hard to deny the truth. If only I had held onto love. But now that I've come here I'll never feel the same. Even your father —I can forgive him now.'

Who knows what drives any other human being? Alex thought with deep humility, finally letting go of the need to judge her mother. Who hasn't made mistakes? What gives anyone the right to judge another? She looked at her mother, feeling a depth of compassion she'd never felt before, for the woman who had lived her own private hell because she didn't have the courage to follow what, in her heart, she knew would give her happiness. Instead Elizabeth had settled and tried to live a life others expected, and all the time she tried to prove to herself that her life was worthwhile.

'Are you happy with Charles, Mom?'

'We understand each other, it's been comfortable.' Her voice trailed off.

'I always thought perhaps you married him because of me? So that I'd have greater security.'

'We'll never have what you and Vitali have. Not even close. You can't manufacture passion. You can't turn it on and off like a tap...but I've been lucky—at least I had a taste of that with your father. Some people spend a lifetime never being truly, deeply loved. My only regret is that I threw it away. I lost his love. But I'm glad you have that, Alex. Despite all our misunderstandings, deep in my heart all I ever wanted for you was the best.'

'I know, Mom. Alex wrapped her arms around her mother and squeezed her tight. 'But thank you for telling me. And for telling me about my father—who he was and how you loved him and why it didn't last. Who knows what might have happened if you'd made a different choice? Even though leaving my father was so painful, if you'd stayed perhaps in time you would have felt like Vitali's mother did living here, isolated and cut off from everything she valued. You know, New York isn't really so bad.'

Her mother gave a half smile.

'All that culture, amazing concerts, great parties, award-winning food, stunning architecture. Europe's a stone's throw away, coffee to die for. To some people living with all this quiet, natural beauty can seem like hell on earth. I guess, what I'm saying is that we're all different and we all have different hopes and dreams, pasts and futures. One of the first things Vitali said to me was, "let the past go. It doesn't matter. It's beyond our control. What matters is now. Now and the future."' Alex shut her eyes as tears as hard as pins pricked them.

If Vitali died...what future would there be?

She had to stay strong. She had to be tough. She had to make him want to live.

45

———

'I don't have a great track record...but I want you to know I'm here for you, Alex...if you want to talk. It might help.'

Her mother's distressed offer grabbed at Alex's heart. Her mother had bared her soul to help her daughter. Saying nothing to her now would be cruel...yet another rejection...but sharing her innermost feelings was something Alex had no experience in.

She wished she was one of those expressive, emotional people who could lay their heart bare. She wished she wasn't so private and contained. Words failed her. Feelings swam like torrential rain then began to hail, pelting her insides. It shouldn't be so hard.

If only she had told Vitali she loved him before...

'I'm afraid,' she cried out. 'I'm so petrified. I'm so scared that he'll give up. That he'll feel a ghost of his former self and that I won't be enough for him to stay in this world. I know him—if he can't walk again he'll feel like his whole life has ended. He doesn't want to be caged in a body that isn't perfect.'

'Alex, it may not come to that. The doctor said there's still hope. There's always hope.'

'It was my fault. If I hadn't been so stupid...what if he hates me for being so stupid?'

'No! It was an accident. And Vitali knew exactly what he was doing. You didn't make him put himself in harm's way. He wanted to. I saw it in his face. The look of unrelenting purpose as he leapt to take the bull's charge away from you. It wasn't an impulsive, instinctive leap, or some uncalculated move of madness. His fear, his horror, his terror of losing you...was so real...he would have given anything to save you. *Even his life.*'

Alex searched her mother's face—desperately wanting to believe her. 'It won't make any difference to me if he's crippled or disfigured. I fell in love with the man inside. How he is on the outside doesn't matter. I love him, Mom. I really love him,' she clutched her hands to her stomach.

'I know,' came her mother's soft reply. 'And if anyone can convince Vitaliano Rossi that his life is worth living, that you love him just the same, it's you, Alex. His wife—the mother of his unborn child.'

'Do you really believe that, Mom?' Doubt wobbled through her voice.

Her mother smiled and tenderly stroked her curling hair back from her temples. 'When have you ever given up, Alex? Even when you experienced so much suffering yourself, you challenged the world and those who thought you weak— including me. You're strong, Alex. You've gone through things that most people will never experience in a lifetime. But you're not alone. Not now. Alex, you can lean on me. I'll give you all the support you need.'

Tears flooded Alex's eyes as the dam of stoic vulnerability came crashing down. For years she had convinced herself she was a rock standing alone from the island of her family. That even in the most over-populated cities, she existed in isolation, fending for herself.

She let the tears run down her face, only this time they were not of sadness but of the happiness of healing her fractured relationship with her mother. Exhausted with the effort of her fierce self-reliance and doing everything on her own, she felt the tension in her shoulders release. Her mother had thrown her a life raft when she most needed it. And she was both happy and relieved to be offered help, and to let go of her unrelenting need to prove she didn't need anybody.

'Thank you,' she whispered huskily, then hugged her mother with all the warmth she could muster. And her mother hugged her back with a fullness of heart she hadn't felt before.

Everything would be all right. Alex was certain of it now.

The sound of footsteps thundering down the hospital corridor fractured their peaceful moment, sending her soaring to her feet. Her heart started drumming. Whoever was approaching had something serious on their mind and the prognosis didn't sound good.

46

———

The two people who turned the corner into the waiting-room were not medical staff with news of Vitali. They were his parents.

Lucrezia glared at Alex with wildly accusing eyes. 'This is your fault, isn't it? If you hadn't interfered—'

Simon severed the outburst, cutting in front of his wife and offering his hand to Elizabeth Spencer. 'It's been a terrible shock. Forgive our lack of manners. I'm Simon Deloitte, Vitali's step-father and this is his mother, my wife Lucrezia. I'm sorry we're meeting like this.'

'You did this to my son,' Lucrezia spat.

'Luci! Pull yourself together. You're not helping anyone,' Simon snapped. He turned back to Elizabeth and Alex, 'I'm sorry, she doesn't mean that.' His hesitant tone betrayed him.

Lucrezia began to hyperventilate, spewing out a tirade of accusations in short, shallow, angry bursts, too distraught to heed his sanction. 'I knew this would happen. The family is cursed...and you... you never loved him, all you wanted was the gold.'

'Don't you dare—' Alex roared, unable to bear her hurtful abuse any longer. All her Buddhist meditations, all her calming aromatherapy tinctures, and all her theories about loving kindness, erupted in a volcanic ash cloud of anger and pain. 'Don't you dare tarnish me with your guilt.' Her voice shook, as she unleashed her agony.

Lucrezia Deloitte hissed more abuse. 'The wedding was a lie, a sham, Vitali never wanted to marry you—he only did it to protect me.'

Alex's control completely broke from its tenuous hold. 'You selfish, self-centered, vile woman.' Exhaustive tension strained her words as she exploded in a passion-fueled tirade that finally silenced the woman.

'Who the hell do you think you are?' she continued. Newsflash! The world does not revolve around you, Mrs Deloitte. Vitali married me because he wanted to. I don't care about your dammed gold mine. I don't even care about your torrid past. You're so absorbed in your own world you haven't even bothered to ask how he is. All his life you've been so focused on what you want, what your needs are—you never even saw his loneliness. You never stopped to think about his needs—just like right now you're so blinded you can't even see his pain. You're the only one who's ever counted—aren't you? You don't care.'

'Alex!' It was a hoarse protest from Simon but Alex was on a roll. She doubted she'd ever feel so liberated to say what she wanted to say.

'Live your life how you want. But don't you dare...don't you dare pour your poison on ours!' She fired her finger at the exit. 'Leave! Go back to your life. I'm Vitali's life now. He's my husband and I love him. Love will heal Vitali. Not your accusations and your hatred.' A huge boulder swelled in her throat. Tears pricked her eyes then flooded down her face. She rubbed her cheeks helplessly. 'No wonder he doesn't want to live.'

Her mother's arms wrapped protectively around Alex and drew her to her chest, soothing her like a child. 'I don't know what's going on here Mr and Mrs Deloitte, but I do know it's not helping. My daughter has suffered a terrible shock. We all have. But those things you're accusing her of —' she leveled her gaze at Lucrezia Deloitte like a lioness protecting her cub, '—I can assure you have no substance. My daughter is one of the most honest, loyal, trustworthy people I know. If she was the gold-digger you seem to think she is, you're wrong. There are men in New York with more money than all the Vitali's of this world. And Alex didn't want a gold bar of any of them.'

VITALI'S EYES OPENED SLOWLY, struggling to clear the hazy film that clouded his vision. Where the hell was he? He looked around the room at the sterile white walls, devoid of art works or anything personal, absorbing all the details in the room as his vision came back into focus.

The horrid ceiling panels and harsh florescent lights made his skin look green. He took in the washbasin surrounded by boxes of surgical gloves. He looked down at the drip taped to his arm, then registered the thick leather restraining belts buckled around his body. 'What the...'?

Then he remembered. He remembered running toward Alex. He remembered the crazed eyes of the bull glaring down at him, hard and black as cannon balls. He remembered looking into his bovine face and thinking he'd met the end.

He remembered fearing for his life as the bull flung him

in the air. He'd grabbed on to the horns as the bull rushed at him again and hung on as though he were in a rodeo. Then he recalled the ugly crunch as the bull charged at him again, pinning him against the stone wall.

Jesus. No!

He tried to move his legs. He tried to kick the sheets free. He tried to fling his feet over the bed and get the hell out of that place. Nothing.

Dizzy with horror he glanced at the maze of beeping lights, tubes and machines monitoring every bodily movement. Yet there was none. Not below his waist, he realized with sickening horror. He wanted to puke. He felt nothing. As though his legs had been torn from him. They may as well have been, he thought angrily. With no legs, no feeling he may as well be dead.

He glanced around the sterile white walls. Why did hospitals always make you feel like you were in a morgue? He gripped the alarm and forced his finger down on the call button. 'Get me out of here!' he thundered.

He slumped against the shapeless pillows and closed his eyes. He willed himself to be swallowed by the darkness. But Alex's face came to him in a vision. Her voice soft like feathers, so full of fear and concern yet full of promise. Had he really heard her correctly? Had it been a dream? Had his own Florence Nightingale arrived in a mystical apparition— giving him a reason to live.

'I'm pregnant. I'm going to have your child.'

47

The weeks passed in a blur. For days on end Vitali was x-rayed, poked and prodded. Just when he thought it was over, it started again. Finally the diagnosis came back.

'Your T8, T10, and T12 vertebrae are fractured,' the doctor said impassively.

Vitali contained a violent impulse to censure the doctor. He wanted to yell, show some bloody empathy, man. He may be familiar with this sort of thing, but Vitali most certainly was not. Instead he patiently asked: 'Is that the good news or the bad news?'

'They're the main vertebrae in the middle of your back. They're also the hardest to break.'

'Just tell me straight Doctor, will I ever walk again?'

The doctor studied his clipboard. His silence was ominous.

'Can you operate?' Vitali pressed.

The doctor put the clipboard down and drew closer to Vitali's side. 'It's a bit unconventional, but do you know what I would do if I were in your shoes?'

'It sounds like you're about to prescribe something

unconventional. I'm liking the sound of this already.' Vitali said, his tone bright with hope.

'You're young and fit. Super fit. We could operate, but there's a danger—instinctively I feel your best chance of recovery is to wait and see how the injury responds naturally.'

'What are the odds?'

'It's a gamble.'

His biggest gamble yet, Vitali thought ruefully as the doctor presented the facts. High stakes didn't come close to capturing the consequences. If he chanced it and had the operation, gave in to the side of him that just wanted to get on with it, there was a chance he could end up with permanent paralysis.

If he waited patiently, allowed his body to attempt to heal, things could worsen. The pain for one thing. He grimaced as a flare of agony splintered through his upper spine. At least some feeling was beginning to return, he thought ruefully.

Not knowing was the worst. Either way, he decided he was screwed, as he wrestled with his dilemma.Things like this didn't happen to Vitaliano Rossi. He was a warrior, a fighter, a defender.

Not a pathetic victim.

He clung to Alex's optimism, and her hope and the promise of the baby that grew in her belly. They were his only rays of sunshine in a landscape that had never looked so bleak. He had come to rely on her. When she was not there, even before the accident, he felt desperate and alone.

But he knew with gut-wrenching certainty that this would either be the making of them or the final death knell. If she was really a gold-digger she would walk away. She would leave him to his miserable fate and find herself a more manly, billionaire tycoon.

'Take me home,' he commanded. 'If I'm to have any hope of recovery I have to be at Gold Ridge Station with my wife.'

TWO DAYS LATER, accompanied by a private physiotherapist, he was taken back to Gold Ridge Station to commence intensive rehabilitation.

When no one was looking, he couldn't stop crying. Angry hot tears masking his fear.

Look at yourself, Wolf. Look at yourself. You're stuffed.

The days passed too slowly. His parents and Alex tiptoed around him, exhausted from worry and steadfastly refusing to give voice to his fear that he may never heal. On top of his physical pain he felt gut-wrenchingly guilty for causing so much grief.

He slid from his bed into his purpose-built wheel chair. Somehow he had to rise above his self-pity and despair. He had a family to care for and protect. People needed him. But he was painfully aware that now, more than ever, he needed them. He had to get on with his life.

48

Animals, farming and being outdoors made him happy and, until the accident, had been his whole life. But now that he was in a wheelchair the cattle and the horses were too dangerous in their unpredictability.

No one could trust them with their biting and kicking and everyone agreed that somehow they always sensed when you were vulnerable. How could Alex have possibly been able to predict that, while he couldn't go safely in the paddock with the cattle and the horses, her Alpacas would come to the rescue?

It was as if those fantasy-like creatures with their big black eyes and long lashes looked right through Vitali, right into his soul. They could tell if you were a good one or a bad one. And even if Vitali didn't admit it, they knew he was "a good one", and Alex knew they were an important part of his healing.

She should do. She'd researched high and low looking for a cure and then, fortuitously, she stumbled upon a book about the extraordinary passions of New Zealanders. In it she read about a lady they called the Llama lady, an ex-jockey paralyzed in a fall, who credited llamas with saving her life.

'It's the Alpaca affect,' Alex said happily, as she watched them run after him as he zoomed around the paddock in his motorized chair.

'Goldie don't be so pushy,' he called out, grinning. Alex put her hand on her stomach as she felt their unborn baby kick 'Daddy's happy. You can feel it can't you,' she said, as she rubbed her belly. In just a few weeks the baby would be able to see so for itself.

'Did you see that, *mia cara*?' Vitali called out to her, laughing. 'For a four-legged animal, Marilyn has a wonderful sense of mischief.'

Alex chuckled as she watched a blonde Alpaca sneak up on one of the farm dogs and blow on her tail, then skip off and hide behind a tree as though nothing had happened. As the indignant dog approached Marilyn jumped out, her long teeth stretched into a huge grin.

'Loosen up, mate,' Vitali yelled to the dog, 'Take a leaf out of Dalai's book' he said pointing to one of the other farm dogs lying in the shade of a tree. 'Go with the flow, zen out!' Vitali looked up at Alex.

Alex gave him the thumbs up and nodded her approval.

'There's so much to do. I don't have time to die.' Vitali said, wheeling to her side.

In less than seven months their Alpaca business had bloomed. They imported a further 30 alpacas to boost their base herd. Not only were they making a roaring trade from the sale of their exotic and luxurious Alpaca wool but their first live exports had been dispatched with great success—to Holland, of all places. Other orders promptly followed, from clothing and textile manufacturers in Milan and China.

Nobody knew Vitali was in a wheelchair. Through the

Internet they ran their business together. He left Bob to run the station and his other business interests, pushing his past life to one side and relishing all the new challenges.

Alex glanced at Vitali as he stared out at the mountains, so proud and stoic like himself. He did a good job of masking his pain. But no matter how much he tried to hide it as her belly grew with the promise of their child, Alex knew he yearned for the mobility he had lost. To kick a ball, or ride bareback across the hills with his son or daughter.

'I'd love to climb the summit of Mount Cook. That's something I've never conquered, 'he said unexpectedly. 'I'd like to think that one day I could tag team with our son or daughter, and share with them one of New Zealand's greatest treasures.'

WHETHER IT WAS the Alpacas and their playful zest, fierce intelligence and enthusiasm for life, or the pristine surroundings that beckoned, she'd never know. Deep down Alex preferred to think it was her love and the deep love Vitali felt for his wife.

But little by little the feelings in his legs returned and he regained his strength. She had no idea how much feeling had really returned until the day their baby was born. He wheeled to her side as she cradled their son in her arms.

'May I? he asked, stretching out his arms to hold his son as he wheeled to her side. And then suddenly he stood. Strong and stable and proud.

Alex's mouth fell open. She stared at him with disbelieving eyes as tears of relief streamed down her face. 'I never thought—'

'Don't think about the past. From now on we only have

our future. He bent his mouth to hers and kissed her fears away. '*Te amo. I love you.*'

'*Anche io ti amo.* I love you too, my darling,' she said, and passed their son, Edwardo, to him. Vitali nestled him in his arms, and stared down at his sweet face, then pressed a kiss to his forehead. Lifting the baby higher, he pressed another kiss to his chubby cheek. 'My son.'

The love that was lost, had blossomed again—and this time they all knew it would be forever. Happily ever after.

THE END

BY MOLLIE MATHEWS

GEMSTONE BILLIONAIRE BRIDES:

THE ITALIAN BILLIONAIRE'S CHRISTMAS BRIDE

THE ITALIAN BILLIONAIRE'S SCANDALOUS MARRIAGE

GEMSTONE BILLIONAIRES 2 BOOK-BUNDLE BOX SET

GEMSTONE BILLIONAIRES 3 BOOK-BUNDLE BOX SET

PASSION DOWN UNDER:

MARRIED BY CHRISTMAS
BRIDE OF GOLD

TRUE LOVE:

FLIGHT of PASSION

***PASSION DOWN UNDER SASSY SHORT
     STORIES:***

TWIST OF FATE
LOVE ME FOREVER
LOVE ME FOREVER
FOREVER and ALWAYS
*PASSION DOWN UNDER 2 BOOK-BUNDLE
     BOX SET (Books 1 & 2)*

First New Zealand eBook and Paperback Edition 2017, 2019

Cover Design: © Steven Novak

ISBN Print: 978-0-9941410-3-3

ISBN ebook 978-0-9941411-9-4

(First published 2016 as The Italian Billionaire's Scandalous Marriage)

Published by

Blue Orchid Publishing

New Zealand

Visit www.molliemathews.com to read more about all our books and to buy them. You will also find features, author interviews and news of author events, and you can sign up for e-newsletters so that you're always first to hear about our new releases.

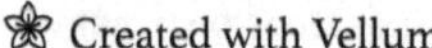 Created with Vellum

ABOUT THE AUTHOR

MOLLIE MATHEWS writes fun, sophisticated, passion-filled contemporary romance. She is known for her "sensual, beautiful, empowered stories enveloped in true romance" (5-star review). Her books have resonated with a global audience. She has been featured in magazines, television, and radio.

A former child and family therapist Mollie passionately believes in the power of romance to transform people's lives. She loves Mother Theresa's words, *"We are all pens in the hands of a writing God sending love letters to the world."*

Her stories are unashamedly positive, optimistic, full of fun and passion.

She is graduate of Victoria University, in Wellington, New Zealand and has given keynote speeches at romance writers conventions and international seminars.

Mollie follows the sun, dividing her time between New Zealand and exotic locations—wherever she intends setting her next romance novel. She lives with her very own romantic hero, Lorenzo—tall, dark, terribly handsome and fluent in Spanish!

Follow her on BookBub https://www.bookbub.com/authors/mollie-mathews and on her blog https://molliemathews.wordpress.com

and sign up for Mollie's newsletter at www.Molliemathews.com and receive her FREE gift.

Follow Mollie on twitter at www.twitter.com/molliemathewsnz

Join Mollie on Facebook at www.facebook.com/molliemathewsnz

Be inspired by Mollie on Instagram www.instagram.com/molliemathewsauthor

Check out her inspiration board on Pinterest www.nz.pinterest.com/molliemathews/

Writing as Cassandra Gaisford (www.cassandragaisford.com), she is also an award-winning artist and bestselling author of self-empowerment books. Cassandra is celebrated by her readers as, "The Queen of Uplifting Inspiration."

AUTHOR'S NOTE

The idea for this story was sparked when I inherited a painting from my aunt—the sister that my father never knew existed. My father was abandoned by his mother into the care of a private boarding school when he was only four-years-old.

Needless to say, he grew into a very self-reliant man. When he was in his 70's he received a letter from a woman in her 80's telling him she was his half-sister, and requesting that they meet. They got along famously—but sadly she passed away a few years later, and my father, soon afterwards. They shared the same dad, but different mothers.

It struck me as incredibly sad that they had not met earlier. I wondered why my dad's mother had never told him about his sister. I wondered why his father never told him either. Later, I began to notice and read similar stories of people, some famous, other's not, who found out as adults, that the people they thought were their fathers or mothers, weren't.

I began to think about all the secrets many families have. The lies they tell each other. And all the lost loves.

And I wondered, what if two people were attracted to each other but trust issues kept them apart? What if a painting had the power to bring them together, to shed healing light on the secrets of the past? And what if a painting had the power to rekindle lost love?

And I wondered, what would it take, in spite of fear, anger, and distrust, for a man and a woman drawn together by tragedy, to open their hearts to love. You'll discover the answers in *Bride of Gold*. I hope you love this story is much as I loved writing it.

If you'd like to learn more about these characters, gain inside tips into the writing process, or be the first to know when a new book is released, subscribe to my newsletter here: http://eepurl.com/ghM501. Please email me and I'll be in touch personally—I promise...mollie@molliemathews.com.

ACKNOWLEDGMENTS

I'm very blessed with some wonderful cheerleaders and writing friends. Amongst those instrumental in bringing *Bride of Gold* to life, are Sandy Johnson and Rae Waterhouse. Having your help made all the difference in finishing and publishing this book.

Cate Walker, thank you again for being a very enthusiastic proof-reader. Your emails telling me how much you loved the story and couldn't wait to read the rest—asking me when were you going to get the next chapters to edit-kept me moving forward.

And to the love of my life—Laurie Wills, my Templar Knight. Thank you for believing in me. Without your faith, support, commitment, inspiration, and love, I could never have written this book.

And Finally

Thank you for purchasing and reading my books. You are more than my livelihood-you let me live my passion. Without your love of romance and belief in the power of love, this book would never have been born. I really hope you loved this book as much as I enjoyed writing it. Here's to an extra-ordinary level of love and happiness in all our lives.

With love,

THANK YOU

Thank you for reading *Bride of Gold*... I hope you loved it. If you did...

1. Help other people find this book by writing a review
2. Signup for my new releases email to find out about the next book as soon as I release it, sign up here http://eepurl.com/ghM5o1
3. Email me at mollie@molliemathews.com with a copy of your honest review and let me know if you'd love to join my dream team and of advance readers
4. Follow me on BookBub, https://www.bookbub.com/authors/mollie-mathews
5. Stay in touch on Facebook, https://www.facebook.com/molliemathewsnz
6. Follow me on Twitter - https://twitter.com/Molliemathewsnz
7. Be inspired on Pinterest - https://nz.pinterest.

com/molliemathews and Instagram - https://
www.instagram.com/molliemathewsauthor
8. Follow my blog - https://molliemathews.
    wordpress.com

Keep reading for a preview of other passion-filled stories including *Flight of Passion* and *Claimed by The Sheikh* (available in paperback and eBook)

EXCERPT: FLIGHT OF PASSION

FLIGHT OF PASSION

BOOK ONE IN THE TRUE LOVE SERIES AVAILABLE NOW

Past love and the obsessions that bind them.

Devastatingly handsome Oliver Hart is used to getting what he wants. Single, thirty-five and a committed bachelor, he plays by his own rules. On a personal quest to catch a rare, elusive and very valuable butterfly, he's unwittingly distracted by a former flame, Ruby Diaz—a woman who callously abandoned him eight years earlier.

Deciding he wants to reclaim the beauty as his own, in his mind, it's as good as done.

But Ruby is not his for the taking. Promised to the son of a wealthy landowner, she refuses to succumb to his charms. On a quest to save her family's land, Ruby knows she must put duty first, and silence the passionate stirrings of her heart. But Oliver doesn't make things easy for her. He's not taking no for an answer.

Risking everything to help the woman he loves to gain her freedom, Oliver entangles himself in an emotional net that alters his life forever. Sacrificing his own selfish pursuit to help Ruby, he realizes that you may be able to own something, but you can never own someone—especially the women you love.

Have you ever wanted to be with someone who sent your heart soaring but threatens your sense of security? Someone who lifts you clear out of the water, but you're not sure will be around to catch you when you fall head over heels in love? Flight of Passion is a rapturous tale of beauty, obsession and the transformational power of unconditional love.

PRAISE FOR FLIGHT OF PASSION

"This is a well written book that tantalizes your senses. Will Oliver be able to convince Ruby that she loves him enough to disobey her family? Can they find each other when all seems lost? An excellent book that I highly recommend. It will have you laughing with joy and crying with sadness."

~ Marie Fraser

"Mollie Mathews has written a beautifully scripted story of two people wildly attracted to each other, but too constrained by family expectations to allow themselves to commit. When they meet again after eight years can they move beyond old patterns of behavior or are they doomed to always want, but never have?"

~ Jane Whitmeyer

"This book is a carefully crafted, truly original story. Mollie's wonderfully descriptive narrative paints a picture in which it is easy to lose oneself—I really felt like I had been to Mexico by the time I had finished. Her butterfly theme echoes throughout the book both literally and figuratively. The main characters, Oliver and Ruby, are each conflicted in their own ways. Despite facing challenges, both ultimately find the strength to work through their difficulties to emerge better people, and most importantly, triumph over adversity together. A touching and heart-warming book, well worth a read."

~ **Cathy Rioran**

"Fast paced, heart wrenching, completely unexpected twists, excellent storyline, and a hell of a good read. You just gotta love Mollie's imagination and expertise in her writing."

~ **Rae Waterhouse**

"I fell in love with Ruby and Oliver, they are so good for each other, but both are so filled with garbage that their families filled them with, that they can't see what's in front of them. And when they finally realize that diamonds don't have a hold to what they had, they are about to lose it. The butter-flies remind me of how ethereal life is and it is up to us to not waste it, but live the fullest and best we can."

~ **Advance reviewer**

"I really enjoyed Flight of Passion! I loved the descriptions of the butterflies and of the setting of the farm in Mexico. Wonderfully descriptive writing that transports you to a golden orchard filled with butterflies. Perfect for a cold winter's evening curled up by the fire."

~ **Linda Buckhingham**

PROLOGUE

G ROWING UP OLIVER WAS LEFT WITH THE impression he wasn't worthy. First by his parents who at the age of four sent him to the bottom of the world. It was as if they didn't know what to do with their infinitely curious and energetic child. It was as if sending him to the most prestigious boarding school in New Zealand absolved them of their responsibility, the responsibility which was every parents—or should be, he thought bitterly—to love their child unconditionally.

After his run in with a box of matches they told him he would amount to nothing. He proved them wrong. At sixteen he left New Zealand and headed for New York. It was true. If he could make it there he could make it anywhere. With the ruthless determination he was both admired and feared for like King Kong on steroids he quickly climbed to the top of the property acquisition tree.

He was king of the beasts, the man everyone wanted at their dreary New York parties, full of checkbook philanthropists who would never stoop to get close to the people their showy donations benefitted. Parties, like the one where he'd first met Ruby Diaz

Ruby had fluttered into his life like a breath of fresh air. She had lit up the room with her illuminating presence and dazzlingly rare beauty, not just on the outside, but the inside too. Her authenticity had the scent of violets—too guileless for pretense.

His darling Ruby. Oliver swallowed hard, refusing to succumb to the wave of angry hurt that swum from his heart to his throat.

For three blissful years they were inseparable. But no matter how much success he acquired, how extraordinarily wealthy he became, he wasn't good enough for the Diaz's darling Ruby. He never knew why she flew from his life, disappearing as quickly as she'd arrived. She had said nothing, given him no explanation, not even the courtesy of a call.

The Diaz family and the way Ruby had callously abandoned him reminded Oliver he would never be worthy—he was unlovable. Perhaps he should thank them for sparing him further hurt. Thanks to them and his hopeless parents he swore never to love again.

And that suited him just fine.

OBSESSION

I would like to be the air that inhabits you

~ Margaret Atwood ~

1

WOULD SELLING *BUTTERFLY LOVERS* REALLY free him of painful memories he'd rather forget?

Common sense told Oliver Hart that *Butterfly Lovers* was just a painting. An inanimate object, incapable of controlling him. But that was the trouble—it did control him, seducing him with its beauty, twisting his heart with bittersweet memories.

He'd intended to keep it . . . her . . . forever. His heartbeat seemed to almost stop as he thought of Ruby Diaz, the woman who had inspired the painting's commission. He rubbed his powerful chest, trying to ease the painful tightness that constricted his lungs as he surveyed the crowd gathered for the charity art auction.

It was time to let them both go. But would he ever be free?

His gaze swept over the minimalist, exquisitely designed interior, lingering over the priceless abstract by Rothko adorning a charcoal-black wall, at Hillcrest, his newly acquired mansion, and New Jersey's most expensive country estate.

Tonight, though, it was *Butterfly Lovers* which held in its grip women dripping with diamonds, and men clad in Armani. Locked in shared awe, they clustered around the painting, studying every line, every pulsating color.

Oliver wondered if their eyes ached as his did with a heady mix of pleasure and pain just to stand in its spellbinding presence. Or were they trying to decode the painting's hidden secrets?

Like a moth to a seductive flame, his eyes drifted to the bottom of the painting. Nobody, but one other person, would ever be able to decipher the graffiti-styled line of poetry scrawled in throbbing orange along the bottom of the painting.

Painful memories bled into his consciousness. Why the hell couldn't he shake her?

Butterfly Lovers. The painting was aptly named, he mused forcing his mind from the woman who had inspired the purchase. The dancing kaleidoscope of color reminded Oliver of his collection of exotic butterflies—his hobbyhorse and quiet obsession.

Dazzling sapphire blues, glistening watermelon pinks, pulsating canary yellows with shimmering oranges—flew from the canvas, and ricocheted off the marble floor which had been polished to a mirror-like gleam.

He had commissioned the painting in a move of uncharacteristic impulsiveness eight years earlier when he was 22 and madly in lust with Ruby. A 20 year-old exotic beauty, she'd fluttered into his life, bringing with her eternal sunshine, and air so fresh it seeped through the iron fortress he'd built around his heart.

Butterfly Lovers encapsulated the vitality, optimism and

positivity she exuded. It was a rare piece which the serious art connoisseurs who gathered here this evening would die to possess. Oliver's brow furrowed, aware many were drawn here not by the desire to possess the contemporary art world's finest paintings, but insatiable voyeurs hungry to glimpse the inner world of one of America's wealthiest and most elusive bachelors.

Immensely private, he'd never opened any of his palatial homes to the public before. Not homes, *houses*, he corrected. He congratulated himself as he glanced around the clinical, museum-like surroundings. The dark walls and sophisticated lighting, spotlighting priceless works of art, created a sophisticated, yet austere, facade. If a building was truly a reflection of its owner, as many designers believed, the interior aptly reinforced the stereotypes perpetuated in the media—moody, dark, mysterious and strictly hands-off.

There was some truth to that, but it was not the whole truth.

Oliver's eyes drifted to the spiraling staircase and the heavy gold braided rope barricading the entrance to the upper level. He never let anyone get beyond the ground floor of his psyche. Some tried, but few persevered. No one, other than Ruby had ever penetrated his fortified armor. And that was a mistake.

He was complicated.

No doubt someone here tonight would go home and tweet that he was something of a social outcast, and arrogant to boot, Oliver thought as he hovered in the background. The fact was that he preferred his own company to engaging with his guests—predominantly wealthy financiers and bankers.

He knew his contempt was hypocritical, given he didn't care who reached into their pockets. But there was something decidedly unpalatable about bankers and the merciless way they preyed on the vulnerable. Tonight, he would gladly encourage them to part with their millions.

As he glanced at his reflection in the floor length window it struck him how far he had come from the days when just finding money to support himself and his little sister had been a struggle. Resplendent in an immaculately tailored Dolce & Gabbana tuxedo cut from the finest Italian wool, he looked like he belonged.

Oliver rubbed his hand over his pecs, powerfully aware of the Maori-inspired tattoo coiled over his shoulder that the crisp white linen of his shirt concealed. His hands pulsed with renewed conviction. It was his touchstone—a symbolic reminder that he was fierce and untouchable—a warrior businessman and an impenetrable lover.

On a good day, he even fooled himself.

But no matter how easy it was to make millions, no matter how many things he acquired, he'd never found a sense of contentment.

Except with—

Oliver bit down on his teeth, grinding them together in a futile attempt to crush memories he was determined not to revisit.

He glanced at his Rolex. 7:03:02. Irritability coursed through his veins. What the hell was the auctioneer waiting for? He fixed him with a piercing look, firing his unspoken annoyance through the crowd.

Tardiness was something he abhorred, and doubly-so tonight, he thought as he locked on the important call he had to make. In one hour it would be 8am in New Zealand and his sister, as punctual as he was, would be anxiously waiting.

As though feeling the pointed tip of Oliver's anger the

auctioneer looked up. His relaxed smile quickly shattered as he was forced to confront the aggressive glint in Oliver's eyes, the rigid set of his shoulders, the brutally hard line of his jaw.

The auctioneer banged his hardwood gavel on the sounding block with short urgent thuds, his florid face ballooning as the chatter continued.

"Ladies and gentlemen, can I have your attention?" More insistent hammering. "Attention! Attention!"

The chatter fell to an orderly whisper, extinguished finally by the auctioneer's solemn voice.

"As you know, tonight is a unique opportunity to savor the extraordinary passions of Oliver Hart. Renowned as an astute business man, Oliver Hart is also an obsessive collector," he said.

"He has one of the most significant collations of contemporary art in the world. Not only a man of significant wealth, Oliver Hart, founder of Hart Luxury Hotel Consortium, is a man of outstanding generosity. All the funds raised by tonight's art auction will provide relief for those affected by last month's devastating earthquake in New Zealand, where he spent much of his childhood."

Oliver studied his feet as a thunder of applause quaked through the room, amplifying as it echoed off the walls.

Childhood.

The word was like a vicious punch to his stomach. Oppressive memories pounded his brain, and this time there was no silencing them.

Suddenly he was four years old again. Four years old and frightened. Lonely. Abandoned. Trapped in a jungle of strangers. Abandoned by bickering parents into a boarding school, neither one willing to let the other have custody. Selfishly caring more about winning against each other than the needs of their own child. And then there was his father.

His jaw locked as he bit down hard, swallowing a toxic cocktail of grief and anger. The brutal beatings hadn't hurt nearly as much as the verbal abuse and discouragement he'd suffered when he told them he wanted to be like his grandfather and study butterflies. The abuse had only intensified when he turned his back on the legal career his father had wanted. *'You'll never achieve anything. I wish you'd never been born. How dare you defy me you worthless piece of shit,'* the pain of these beatings had long healed—but those words still hurt.

Freezing sweat clung to Oliver's body in a vice-like grip, as he recalled the scorn his father rained upon him during his few personal visits. He paced across to the open window, inhaling deeply as he struggled to rip himself free from the shards of the past. Jesus, what sort of father tries to have his son institutionalized?

To some, it might seem ironic that he should be so generous to a country where he spent such an unhappy childhood, but Oliver didn't like to think of others suffering.

He forced his mind back to the present.

"Tonight's opening painting *Butterfly Lovers* is a significant artwork," the auctioneer continued, glancing down at his notes.

Oliver didn't have to read his words to know that what he would reveal was a shallow rendition of the truth. Only two people in the world truly knew just what *Butterfly Lovers* meant.

He glanced around the room thinking Ruby might have come, hoping with all his willpower she hadn't.

2

H E FORCED HIMSELF NOT TO BETRAY THE turmoil of emotions jack-knifing through his body as the massive painting was carried to the makeshift podium.

The butterfly theme had held so much promise. He'd never really bought into Ruby's tales about the transformative power of art to heal. But back then privately he'd hoped her optimism might rub off. With her by his side, and by owning the painting, perhaps he could shed a skin, free himself of his deformed past, re-emerge in a new skin. Undamaged. Someone nearing perfection. A better man. The sort of man Ruby deserved.

He'd been a fool.

Oliver's spine stiffened. He'd intended to keep it . . .

her . . . forever. But even good intentions couldn't make up for a lifetime's inability to commit. He moved towards the terrace, widening the distance between him and the painting. He would no longer succumb to the painting's potent power to remind him of his failings.

"Created specifically for Oliver over seven years ago by

struggling contemporary artist CG Tombly—only Oliver could have foreseen its financial potential."

Oliver's brow furrowed. The suggestion he had acquired the painting for commercial gain, rankled him. If he wasn't such a private man he might have told the crowd the truth. He'd made the mistake of talking candidly once before—a mistake he wouldn't be making again.

In its place he'd created a new habit—a habit of keeping his emotional life to himself, one he wasn't about to break. Soon the painting, and the painful memories of the only woman capable of making him feel, would be shed and he could devote himself to less painful obsessions.

"As always, Oliver's timing is impeccable. The painting's value has rocketed in the same soaring capacity as the palatial hotel Oliver's company has recently constructed in Dubai–so high it almost touches the gods."

The auctioneer flung his hands into the air to accentuate his point. "Oliver Hart," he said, nodding in his direction and pointing to his towering 6-foot, 2-inch frame, "never does anything small."

Oliver thrust his hands in his pockets and glanced out the window refusing to look at the painting as the bidding began.

In a few fist-clenching minutes it would all be over and he could get on with his life.

His gaze drifted to the sculpture garden, lying beyond the pool, alighting on a solitary bronze sculpture by Brancusi. The modernist interpretation of Hercules holding the world on his shoulders, with its roughly hewn egg shaped sphere symbolizing earth had always appealed to him.

Balanced precariously on a towering sculpted wood base, the odd shape and the large crater severing the middle of the sphere challenged conventional notions of perfection and reminded him of humanity's rawness.

As his gaze lingered over the sculpture it occurred to him that repairing his scars, so deep that no relationship he started ever endured, required a Herculean effort.

No wonder the painting had failed.

But he still wanted to believe, as the ancient Greeks had, that art had a powerful ability to transform lives. He only hoped that selling the painting finally fulfilled this purpose. Perhaps then the painful memories that still haunted him could be turned to good.

He turned and fixed his gaze upon the audience. Who would be its new owner he wondered as the opening bid of one million was made. Would it go to Don Hermes, the impotent pharmaceutical giant, standing just ahead of him, or some other equally innocuous purchaser? Or would some anonymous bidder calling from China, Europe or the Middle East be the lucky buyer?

"$12 million? Do I have $12 million?" The bags under the auctioneer's eyes shifted as he tilted his head forward, and peered under his glasses.

"A small price to pay," he continued, his gaze briefly flickering to Oliver, "for a painting personally commissioned by a man who defies every category and transcends every cliché: a man with tremendous gusto and creative generosity."

The auctioneer's eyes flew to a scantily dressed blonde hovering hopefully next to Oliver. "A man who has yet to be pinned down."

Oliver caste her a dismissive look and moved further toward the back of the room.

"$12 million we have," cried the auctioneer's assistant,

nodding vigorously as he pressed his iPhone firmly to his ear.

Oliver's heart lurched as the bidding began.

"$13 million," the assistant taking telephone bids shouted, raising his hand.

"$13.2 million." The auctioneer's eyes darted between the phone bidder and two men determined to claim the painting as their own.

Explosive tension hovered as one of the two remaining bidders turned their attention away.

"$13.5 million! At $13.5 million the painting will be sold," the auctioneer warned. He suspended the gavel in the air, pausing as he scanned the room.

"$17.4 million," came a guttural, low growl from the front of the crowd.

A record price!

The room fell silent under the weight of the bid, then buzzed with irritatingly discordant voices, their murmurs of awe and envy a rising tide of white noise.

Oliver's eyes darted to the front row. Over $14 million? The price was ridiculous. Someone must want it desperately. But who and why?

He was acquainted with the deep pockets of unbridled obsession. He understood intimately the seductive power of the painting.

But this was crazy bidding.

There had to be a compelling reason surpassing the usual appreciation of an art-lover. At that price it could hardly be an investment buy.

So that left . . . what?

Oliver paced the back of the room in agitation unable to see the face of the man who had placed this latest bid. He caught a glimpse of the woman next to the anonymous bidder as she shook a sexy spill of sun-kissed curls down her back. The familiar gesture sent shockwaves to his heart.

It couldn't be.

Her head turned slightly.

Oliver stood still, as if immobile, as if turned to stone.

Ruby Diaz.

His Ruby.

3

A SYMPHONY OF EMOTIONS CRASHED through his veins as he saw a possessive arm snake around Ruby's waist and realized with horror the identity of the serpent she was with. Oliver threw back his shoulders, his muscular jaw tilted forward in defiance as he looked at the nauseatingly familiar figure.

Carlos Torres, the New York based, Mexican banking magnate and the-soon-to-be owner of *Butterfly Lovers.*

He could not let his painting—their painting—fall into her lover's clutches—a man as unscrupulous as he was deceptively charming.

Oliver's overactive mind raced with scenarios. He could draw from his own accounts the money for the earthquake fund—adding to the millions he had already donated.

But he knew with chilling certainty he was powerless to flout protocol, to bend the rules, to manipulate the outcome to suit his own desires. He knew only too well that once the auction had started, *Butterfly Lovers* could not be withdrawn.

"At this price, we'll sell," the auctioneer's eyes swept the room for any last bids.

The muscles in Oliver's chest tightened as he saw the auctioneer's gavel ascend into the air.

He watched helplessly as Carlos pulled Ruby toward him and folded her into his arms. The bitter taste of jealousy flooded his mouth.

The gavel sank toward the sounding block with freeze-frame inevitability. A splintering crack as wood met wood confirmed it was over with chilling clarity.

Oliver's hand tightened into a closed fist, crumpling the *Butterfly Lovers* catalogue into obscurity.

His heart rate pulsated making his chest feel as though it was about to implode, as Ruby turned and he watched with shock the way she wilted under Carlos' dominant presence, the light of passion missing from her eyes. She seemed sad and vulnerable—and the Ruby he knew was neither.

Something was wrong.

His rational mind thundered a warning. Don't get involved.

What business was it of his if she wanted to make a life with that snake? None. Not ordinarily. But Ruby wasn't ordinary. Accepting and accommodating maybe, but something told him there was more to their union than met the eye.

He clenched his fists and cursed softly fighting against the impulse to save her from a big mistake. Playing rescuer would invite complications he didn't need.

Especially now.

What he needed was a distraction. What he needed was uncomplicated sex—not to reignite an obsession. Ruby had already proven herself capable of breaking his heart mercilessly.

Not so with paintings and sculptures and his beloved butterflies, he mused, forcing his thoughts back to his collections. Once possessed they would never leave without his consent. And he could never make them cry. His jaw clenched as bitter memories of his parents' feuding pounded in his ears. His mother's heart-wrenching cries once heard, never forgotten.

He must not be distracted. He must not allow Ruby to get close. Obviously she had engineered Carlos to buy the painting, knowing full well how it would torture Oliver. She tortured him all those years ago and it was clear she intended to continue the onslaught. She could have that damned painting, he mused as unwelcome, undesired, uncontrollable passions, long forgotten but now unbridled, threatened to escape.

He rested one shoulder against the floor length window, his attention locked on Ruby as she freed herself from Carlos' clutches and fluttered through the swelling crowd toward the patio.

She possessed an innate and natural elegance that caused his glands to salivate, wetting his appetite in open defiance of his will. Her legs screamed danger—their long, slender length accented in scorchingly sharp stilettos that threatened to kill.

Kill his resolve. Kill his self-control. Kill him all over again.

He reached for a glass of whiskey from a passing waitress. He rocked the glass from side to side and studied the rough ice-chunks crashing through the amber liquid, then knocked the drink back, drowning his conflicting emotions.

Like a moth drawn to light he savored the way her floor length, silk dress clung to her lithe figure, her hibiscus red dress shimmering under the halogen lights like the wings of a newly emerged butterfly.

The way the vibrant color of her dress contrasted so deliciously with the flock of black cocktail dresses and designer dark suits everyone else favored brought a smile to his lips. Ruby had always stood out from the crowd.

Walk away, stay away. The voice in his head pitched high and shrill like an ambulance siren, as he fought an instinctive need to free her from a bad mistake.

The irregularly cut crystal pressed into his fingers as he gripped the glass. His life had rapidly become complicated.

He craned his neck as he momentarily lost sight of her, searching over the sea of heads and glittering diamonds.

Like the shards of ice in his glass, his hardened intention to stay detached was fracturing.

Plastering on a face of extreme nonchalance, he pushed determinedly towards her through the crowd as she stepped onto the patio and gazed forlornly up at the stars.

Why the hell was she with a dickhead like Carlos.

Glancing at his watch, Oliver wondered if he could find out what he needed to know in less than 20 minutes?

DID YOU ENJOY READING THIS
EXCERPT?. . .

Thank you for purchasing and reading my books. You are more than my livelihood—you let me live my passion. Without your love of romance and belief in the power of love, this book would never have been born. I really hope you loved this excerpt from my full-length novel *Flight of Passion* as much as I enjoyed writing it.

Purchase the full-length copy and discover what happens next.

Flight of Passion: Book One in the True Love series available now from all good bookstores

Flight of Passion: Book One in the True Love series available now from all good bookstores

Here's to an extra-ordinary level of love and happiness in all our lives.

With love,

that the child isn't their biological son. Salim is Tariq's son, with his former lover, a renowned architect.

Three years ago, after being banished by Tariq from his desert kingdom, Melanie Jones secretly gave her baby to Tariq's childless brother and his wife, in a swap the world was never supposed to know about.

The tragedy pulls her back to the world that rejected her and the man who abandoned her--the only man capable of turning her carefully controlled world upside down.

Tariq will do whatever it takes to protect his legacy, including claiming Melanie as his bride and his son as heir before scandals ensue.

But Melanie has other plans for her future—a western-ized life where she's free to operate her own business and control her own life.

If you love true romance and beautiful love stories, set against a sensuous backdrop of the desert, art, and architec-ture you'll love *Claimed by The Sheikh.*

Book two in the *True Love* series **available now, in audio, paperback and eBook**

www.ingramcontent.com/pod-product-compliance
Lightning Source LLC
Chambersburg PA
CBHW021811110726
47902CB00006B/1738